FORGIVE OUR SURVIVAL

THE FORGIVE ME FATHER SERIES

BOOK THREE

CAITLIN MAZUR

WPC PRESS

To all the girls who ever doubted themselves.
Go give them hell.

Those who can make you believe in absurdities can also make you commit atrocities.

—VOLTAIRE

AUTHOR'S NOTE

This story takes place across New Hampshire, upstate New York, and Vermont, with the Coutts commune established in what was once White Mountain National Forest and Coutts Peak established on what was once Mount Washington. For the sake of storytelling, some details of the landscape may have been altered.

1

MORGAN

Go ahead. I narrowed my eyes, daring the man who leered before me. *It's useless, anyway.*

He pulled his hand back, elbow at his side, nose and lips curled into a sneer. I braced for impact, teeth clenched. My cheek still throbbed from his last few hits, but I refused to give him the satisfaction of my tears.

Luke wore a green, long-sleeved shirt tucked into a pair of denim jeans. Not a wrinkle or stain in sight. A wife's doing, of course. The idea of a woman washing and ironing this man's garments sickened me. Was she forced to scrub blood stains from his sleeves? Did she ever question where it came from, or did she believe him when he undoubtedly told her he was fulfilling God's purpose?

His slicked-back blond hair made his widow's peak prominent, giving him a sharp look. He was so close, I saw the nose hairs in his nostrils and the broken blood vessels in his cheeks. Once, I was sure, he'd been handsome. Before becoming my father's right-hand man. But fill a person with enough hate and rage and any beauty that lived inside them will seep right out.

If I'd known where my older sister had run off to months ago, I'd have already chased after her. It was no business of his whether I thought her dead or alive, though, if I were being honest, the former seemed much more likely. Maura wasn't built for the world out there. There were no truths to divulge, no matter how badly he hurt us. She left without so much as a note, so much as a whispered goodbye. But I knew my sister better than anyone. She wouldn't have left that way if she had another choice.

His palm connected, the slap reverberating through the room, forcing my neck to strain. A sharp slice of pain suggested my lip had split in the same spot as the last three times I'd been here. My ears rang. I squinted through tears, blinking away the sign of weakness and swallowing my cry.

"You're a *wicked* girl," Luke spat.

I licked the side of my lip, tasting iron. "So I've heard."

His face reddened, nostrils flaring — men were so easy to anger.

All you had to do was not be afraid of them.

Luke's beefy hand stretched outward, his greedy fingers wrapping around my neck. My eyes bulged, but I forced a smile. Even I knew that was too much, too disobedient, yet delightfully satisfying in its own right. He tightened his hold, and I felt, for just a moment, the bliss of slipping away. My consciousness rippled at the edges. I might finally feel what it'd be like to be *free*.

He lifted me from my chair with his vice grip and my arms fell limply to my side. I grinned madly at his anger. Would he do it? Did he have the courage to release me from this wretched prison?

But, no. At the moment my lungs began to tighten, he changed his mind. I could only assume because he wasn't willing to find out how Father might react to the sight of his daughter lying dead on the floor. No. I was still Coutts blood. Explaining that one away was bound to be a bit too tedious, what with the bruising around my neck and the size of his hands. Couldn't chalk that up to a suicide.

And so he released me. I gasped a glorious breath as my rear found the chair, bothered by my disappointment. There comes a time you reach your threshold for bullshit, and I'd gotten there that afternoon. My fingers gripped the armrests as he lowered his head to mine.

"Get out of my sight," he spat, spittle clinging to his chapped bottom lip.

"Gladly."

He grasped the back of my shirt. Forced my body upward. I got to my feet, stumbling forward as he shoved me toward the door. Blood came away from my lip as I wiped my hand across my face, crossing the threshold into the hallway. A tight sting from the remnants of his grip pulsed in my neck. A bruise would form. Abigail would insist I cover it. Probably with some hideous scarf she'd find in her collection of clothes.

Mother sat on the bench outside Luke's door, the skin around her sunken eye still purple and green. Burst blood vessels swam like fireworks in the whites of her eye. They would not bring her to medical care for a broken eye socket. It hardly interfered with her duties.

I took a seat beside her, lowering my face level with hers. She studied me with the tips of her fingers, assessing my injuries without words, though I saw tears forming in her dark brown eyes.

"It's okay," I soothed, nuzzling my forehead against hers, eyes closed, wishing I could take her pain, too.

"Get in here, Mary." Luke's low voice traveled through the open door.

My stomach rolled with guilt. My defiance put Mother at risk. Old, frail woman or not, she was now past child-bearing age. Luke wouldn't hesitate dealing her greater damage. Abigail had warned me of that; not as a kindness, but as added shame for my disobedience.

I still did not know how Maura had tolerated her.

The pair disappeared as Luke closed the door, its paneling seamlessly blending in with the wall. A hidden room beside Father's office, perfect for Hunters to carry out punishments. Luke called it a penance room. But his words didn't disguise what it actually was. His own personal torture chamber.

I turned to go, eager to flee from the church and back to the place I now called home, as foreign as it was. I would not be permitted to wait for Mother.

But before I took another step, the door to my father's office creaked at the end of the hall. I froze, rooted to the spot. A sliver of light spilled across the red-carpeted floor. A tall, familiar shadow crossed it.

"Luke?"

Father's pleasant voice was melodic, like a lullaby drawing me near. My feet answered first, covering the distance slowly. My heart beat in my throat.

"No, Father," I said. "It's Morgan."

His footsteps faltered, weight shifting as he neared the door. I heard him inhale before he pulled the door open.

"Morgan."

Sun filtered through his large, circular office window, silhouetting his figure. I expected a grimace or a sneer, but was met instead with a smile painted on his sharp features. His wide pupils made his eyes dark as he studied me in uncomfortable silence. I looked at my feet, feeling small beneath his gaze.

"Come in."

I had done my best to curb my obedient tendencies, but when it came to Father, my efforts remained futile. His command prompted my legs to move, and I followed him into the room.

Father's office had never been a place of refuge — on the contrary, it was a reminder of my past disobedience. Of my failings and inadequacies. But I'd never seen the space in such a state of disarray.

Gaps in his normally neat bookshelves looked like missing teeth on the far wall. Papers, pens, and empty cups covered Father's desk, notes with hurried writing sprinkled between. Blueprints, both rolled and splayed, lay on the floor in the far corner. Even the circular window, usually a breathtaking, unobstructed view, was clouded with foggy handprints, as if he had been resting there, lost in thought, for quite some time.

"Sit," Father said, as if I'd been ridiculous for not thinking of the idea first.

I scurried to the seat in front of his desk and looked at him. He hung his head, revealing the bald spot forming on his crown. Was that from stress? Age? A mysterious fatal illness? One could only hope. His fingers tapped the papers upon the wood before he lifted his chin, meeting my eyes.

"Good news, Morgan," he said, his smile widening. "Would you like to know what God has informed me of today?"

No, I wouldn't.

"Of course, Father."

He frowned, apparently unconvinced by my conviction. "You should be so blessed to receive news of your sister."

My stomach dropped. I met his eyes as I gripped the armrests, nails digging into the wood, feeling my nostrils flare. It couldn't be. He was lying.

"What?" I asked.

His cheeks flushed pink as they raised into a wider, unnatural smile. I struggled to manage my breath as it got heavier.

"Your *sister*," Father continued, "has been out gallivanting beyond our borders since the summer. Last week we made contact with an Outside group who vaguely remembered seeing someone who might've looked like her. But we couldn't be sure."

So that explained Luke's excessive force over the past few days. The bruising around my neck and cheek. Mother's broken eye socket.

"Well." His eyes glittered with malice. "Those same men just so happened to stumble upon a scavenging group yesterday." He cast his eyes toward the window. "And wouldn't you know, someone in their party said Maura has been living in their community for the past few months. Living in *sin*."

I swallowed.

"Meaning she's still alive?" I hated the quaver in my tone.

"It would seem so."

A glimmer of hope blossomed in my chest. Just as quickly as it appeared, Father's sneer squashed it dead. If Maura was still alive out there, she was in grave danger. In the past few weeks, Father's demeanor had changed. He had gotten more erratic. More violent. There was no saying what he might do if she returned. Still, Father's revelation — his admission — was startling.

Over a year ago, I'd been on the outskirts of this very commune, willing to be exiled from the chains my Father had shackled us with. They'd found me and dragged me back. A show of compassion, so many said. What a kind and forgiving Prophet. But my brief trip showed me the Outside. I'd seen what Outsiders were capable of. There hadn't been a day since that I truly believed we were the only survivors.

I pressed my lips together, choosing my words carefully.

"So, you're admitting there are other survivors out there?" I whispered, my heartbeat thudding in my ears. "And Maura's with them?"

"Oh, Morgan." He narrowed his gaze before he lifted it to the doorway. I turned, my chest tightening as I watched Luke shove Mother into the room, her bloated face wet with tears, her left eye swollen shut.

I gasped at her appearance. My frail mother whimpered, barely catching her balance. Her tawny skin was darker than mine, but we shared our head of curls, though hers were thinning at the edges of her forehead. She smoothed her shaking fingers down the sides of the long blue dress she wore. Fingers that had wiped our tears, mended our clothes, and held our hands when we were scared. She was always so poignant, always ready with answers. But since Maura had disappeared, the men reduced her to nothing more than a shell of her former self.

I turned back to Father. "Now, we wouldn't want to be spreading lies through the commune now, would we? What might that mean for your family?"

Every nerve inside of me tensed. This would be the only time he'd admit this — to me, and only me, forcing me to carry the burden. He knew nobody would listen, let alone believe me. My escape had made me a heathen. And he used that to his advantage.

I wanted to scream, to lunge over the desk and push my thumbs into his glittering eyes, to claw at his throat with my fingernails. He'd revealed just enough to make me understand my options. Maura was still alive, but she was being hunted. My family and I were at his mercy.

"Send her to the island," Father said, waving Mother off as if she were nothing more than a nuisance.

"No!" I stood, pushing the heavy chair aside as I tried to climb around it, but caught myself as I looked at them in the doorway. Fear filled Mother's wide eyes as Luke's large hands gripped her shoulders. He'd crack her collarbone in one squeeze. I clung to the back of the chair to stop myself from going any further.

"Please." I turned my desperate gaze to my Father. "She's your *wife*. She's hurt — look at her!"

"She produced not one, but two defiant children." His eyes raked over Mother before he closed them and shook his head. "In order to ensure none of our other children are tainted by her poor parenting, she must serve penance and listen to God's guidance."

He nodded at Luke.

"Father, please." But even to my ears, my plea sounded weak. He'd made up his mind. There would be nothing to convince him otherwise.

I love you, Mother mouthed, before Luke pulled her from the room.

"Morgan." Father's voice was stern. Commanding. I grit my teeth, clenched my fists, and turned once more. He tilted his head. "You'd be wise to go into the church and ask for penance yourself."

It was a warning. If I didn't behave or do his bidding, the same fate awaited me. My body trembled with anger, but I heard my voice — a distant echo, as if being spoken by someone else.

"Yes, Father."

The obedience made me furious, but I was helpless to stop it.

2

—

MAURA

SOMETIMES I IMAGINED the noises stirring me from sleep as morning birds. A high-pitched giggle might be a robin. A sneaker squeak, a song thrush. The men chattering over coffee? They were the singing crows. If I tried hard enough, I could feel the morning sun on my face, even smell the fresh mountain air. I clung to those memories, desperate and guilt-ridden. Nature was the thing I missed most inside this rotting building.

I *was* grateful. We were safe and alive, with a roof over our heads. Though cold permeated the large space in continual rotation, we remained fed and healthy. The Centre gave us a reason to wake up in the morning. It tired us until we had a reason to go to bed at night. But sometimes in these early hours, I longed for familiarity.

I turned in my sleeping bag on the hard mattress in the dim light of the old store we'd transformed into our new home. Spare pegboards, wooden posts, and duct tape made up the flimsy walls of my room, while a curtain rod and fabric acted as a makeshift door. I reached for the water bottle next to my annotated Bible, which had become a permanent fixture on the bedside table. Below that lay a book titled *Freedom of Mind Control: Leaving the Coutts*, also annotated, but less so. A cluster of Mia's crayon drawings hung on the wall behind it — depictions of our group, one of her and me, and one of Holli's garden.

Water quenched my dry mouth. I pressed my palms into my face to warm my cheeks before I dressed — a pair of wool socks, old work boots held together by silver duct tape, stiff jeans, and a cotton waffle-weave shirt. On the other side of the curtain, I heard Eli clear his throat, pull aside his curtain, and settle in our common area.

My stomach fluttered in anticipation. I had grown fond of our unspoken morning ritual. Dare I say, I looked forward to it. Over the last few months, our friendship blossomed. We were two of the same from different worlds, never quite fitting where we were placed. Although we never discussed it directly, I had a feeling he felt a kinship for that reason too.

Attempting to soften my grin, I rubbed sleep from my eyes before grabbing my toiletries and a ration card. Morning sun spilled from the skylight in the hall, through the closed metal security gate that shuttered us inside our room. Eli's tall frame leaned against the jamb as he peered out. His dark eyes blinked away tiredness, brown hair tousled from his pillow. He wore a plain white shirt under a red and black flannel with a pair of patched jeans.

The new community agreed with him. In recent weeks, he'd taken to trimming his once overgrown beard, revealing his strong jawline and plump cupid's bow. There'd been a handsome face beneath all that facial hair, after all.

His lips curved upward as he watched me cross the common area.

"G'morning." Sleep tinted his gruff voice.

"Good morning," I answered, tucking my bag under my arm. "Sleep well?"

Eli shrugged. "Same as ever."

I nodded in agreement. There was safety within these walls, but sleep still came in bouts. My nightmares all involved Father, Andrew, Mother, or my sister Morgan. Sometimes the Coal Creek men. The others never mentioned hearing me, but I woke many nights with a scream hanging on my lips, heart beating like it might burst from my chest.

Eli lifted himself from the frame and opened the gate, allowing us access to the well-lit walkway that ran the length of the old shopping mall. There would be no pretending we were outside once the community came alive. Stale air ran through the building, every noise amplified against the high ceilings. Children ran across the vinyl flooring, playing together before school began. Adults sat in chairs outside of their rooms, chatting with each other, reading, or eating breakfast. Others bustled around inside their rooms, preparing for the day.

When we'd first arrived, there'd been too much to look at. Too many people, too many *things*. After being outside for so long, I thought nothing could feel too big, but this place felt like a different world. The colors were all wrong — too muted and monochrome. The noises were so loud — echoey and pronounced. But the scrutinizing looks were the worst of all. Narrowed gazes and judgmental sneers came with whispers, with the shake of a head, the pull of a child out of my walking path. My Coutts ancestry couldn't stay hidden forever.

"Any big plans for today?" Eli joked, closing the gate behind us with a clang. "Work?"

"Hardly." I tried not to roll my eyes. After we'd settled into the new community, Avi assessed our skills. Though I had knowledge of horses and scavenging, those teams were already full. The only other talent I brought to the table was housework. And so, they'd assigned me to Housekeeping. How fitting it was that I'd traded my life of homemaking in the commune, only to continue a life of service here.

Eli chuckled. "You know, it's okay to hate your job," he offered, nudging me with his shoulder. "Normal, really. And it's not like I'm gonna tell anyone."

I opened my mouth and shook my head, trying to find the right words. "I'm grateful. I enjoy Kendra's company."

"Maura." There was a warning in his tone that reminded me of Morgan. "You don't have to do that anymore. Remember?"

I glanced sideways at him, shrugging off his worried gaze. "I know."

"You're supposed to be working on that kind of stuff with Leo, aren't you?"

This time I rolled my eyes. While Leo had once been a part of the commune, he'd taken it upon himself to act as some sort of expert on Father and his actions, which I found to be flawed at best, insulting at worst. He hadn't spent his whole life beneath Father's thumb. He barely interacted with Father during his time there. I didn't understand why he thought he could help me heal. But when I'd come through the gates of this place, Avi made it mandatory that I sit with Leo to help encourage the deconstruction of my past life. They said I'd been a victim of a cult. It was a word I'd never heard before. At first, I'd been comforted by the idea that someone else from the commune was here. But as I'd gotten to know Leo, all he seemed to give me was grief.

"We *are* working on it," I insisted.

"Okay…" He shook his head, waiting for more.

"Fine." I sighed, throwing my head back. "It's just so gross." I lowered my voice. "People are disgusting."

"That's more like it—"

"I mean, the dirt is one thing, but the smell is another thing entirely. Do you know how long it takes to clean one cloth diaper?" I wrinkled my nose. "Oh, and don't get me started on what people leave in their pockets! I found *half* a mouse in someone's overalls the other day."

"A mouse?"

"Yes! Why, pray tell, would someone put a rodent in their pocket, let alone part of a dead one? It's maddening!"

"I mean, maybe they were saving it for a snack—"

I gagged.

Eli laughed hard at this, hand at his chest. "I'm sorry," he wheezed, struggling to calm his chortles as we reached the cross at the center of the building. "But it's *kind of* hilarious."

"Oh, ha ha," I retorted, eyes narrowed playfully. "See if you get any clean laundry back this week!"

He grinned at me. "You wouldn't."

"I might."

At the end of the walkway, the Mess Hall buzzed with conversations, laughter, and forks scraping plates. Some people sat at tables while others stood in line waiting on their breakfast, empty plates in hand. My stomach grumbled at the smell of fresh-cooked eggs.

We entered the bathroom space on our right, to an area with a network of mismatched plastic pipes, water pumps, and a door to portable toilets. We sourced our water from both a well and a rain catchment system, using it for everything from drinking to brushing our teeth. Once I freshened up and tamed my unruly curls into two low pigtails, we tucked our toiletries away and walked back toward the Mess Hall.

An assortment of mismatched tables and chairs cluttered the eating area. Food sat in large, silver trays on a long table to our left, served by three young teenagers. One collected ration cards, one served eggs, another served a small roll with pads of butter or a dollop of preserves. My stomach growled again.

"Hungry?" Eli asked as we got in line.

"Starved."

A short blonde woman standing ahead of us scoffed through the noise of conversation. My stomach dropped as I saw her shoot me a malicious sneer. I averted my eyes, heat rushing to my cheeks — the familiar feeling of being noticed in a bad way. The world pulsated. Though there was nothing in my stomach, it gurgled, hunger dissipating. I kept my hands in my pockets, fixing my gaze on Eli, who gave her a sideways glance. She raised her eyebrows and gave him a once-over before narrowing her eyes on me. She crossed her arms and turned away from us in a huff, not bothering to keep quiet as she said, "Imagine *actually* starving!"

"Oh, shut up," Eli said under his breath.

"What did you say?" The voice came from behind us. An older bald man stepped out of line and crossed his arms, giving us both a mutinous look. I reached for Eli, wanting to pull him back from what was about to happen. But anger flooded his dark eyes and his nostrils flared as he took a step toward the older man.

"I *said* she should shut up," he repeated himself, louder now so that the woman could hear him. "We were having a private conversation. There was no need for her to be rude."

The woman ahead of us scoffed. "Someone needs to say something."

"Something about *what?*" Eli pressed.

My face flushed. I sucked air through my tight chest, focusing my gaze on the food tables we approached.

"Listen, if you want to collude with the enemy—"

"What *enemy*?" Eli seethed. "What the hell has Maura ever done to you?"

"It's not about that—"

"Then what's this about?"

"She's right," interjected the man behind us. "That girl shouldn't be here. We barely have enough food to feed our own community—"

"Exactly," agreed the woman.

"We feed everyone," came a new voice, an older, silver-haired woman sitting at a nearby table. "Avi would be ashamed to hear you speak this way about a member of our community."

She flashed me a reassuring smile.

"It's *wrong*," said the mean woman ahead of us, throwing her ration card at the teenager collecting them. "This is a safe haven from the Coutts. Not a shelter to house them."

"Well then, it's a good thing you aren't in charge," Eli continued, "with a narrow-minded view like that."

"What's she even doing here?" the woman said, her gaze drilled into me. I kept my eyes on my shoes. "Where she comes from, she's probably never struggled for a meal. Or a doctor. Go home!" she yelled, her face red.

"That's *enough*!" Eli shook his head, his lip curling.

The woman gave Eli a smirk. "Thanks," she said to the teenager serving breakfast. "I'm just so *starved*."

I saw Eli's neck muscles tense, his hand curl into a fist at his side. "You know what—?"

"Eli…" I put my hand on his back and he looked at me, his brown eyes impossibly dark. "Card." I tilted my chin toward the teenager who held out her hand for Eli's ration card. He dug into his back pocket and produced the wrinkled thing, still glaring at the woman who had gone to find a seat.

My heart beat wildly as I handed over my own card. I wished Eli would avoid confrontation. He had no trouble fighting on my behalf, but I hated it. I'd taken worse blows. It was easier to let it be. But that was not how he saw things.

"Thank you," Eli said loudly, throwing his voice toward the woman who went to sit at a nearby table. "Manners are so important, you know—"

The teenager handed me my tray of food. I carried it in one hand, tugging Eli by the shirt with the other, to a table far away from the rude woman.

"C'mon," I said, settling into a seat. "Let's just eat and move on."

Eli came around the other side and sat across from me, stabbing his eggs with a fork, his eyes flicking upward toward the woman every few seconds. "You should fight back," he said with a mouthful of eggs, before swallowing. I met his fierce gaze.

"It's not worth it."

"Yes it is," he stressed, leaning towards me over the table. "This is our home. We pay our dues. You deserve to feel comfortable and respected, just like everyone else."

"I understand why they're angry."

Eli looked at the ceiling and shook his head. "Let them be angry at your father, then. You didn't *do* anything," he retorted, his voice loud enough to get a few stern glances thrown our way.

"Eli," I said, looking down at my lap. "Please, just let it go. I've heard worse, okay? You know this. It isn't worth causing a scene every morning over. If they want to hate me, that's their choice."

Eli's face pinked, and he looked back down at his eggs,

no doubt remembering his initial reaction to me. I could deal with the whispers and even the occasional rude comment if it meant keeping Eli out of trouble. The last thing I wanted to do was make waves. This place was safe. Holli, Sid, and Eli were happy here, and if I tried hard enough, I could be too.

I wasn't willing to do *anything* to jeopardize that.

3

ELI

MAURA DISAPPEARED around the corner and into Housekeeping, with a half-hearted wave in my direction. She was annoyed with me. No matter how hard I tried explaining the fierce need to fight against ignorance, Maura insisted we take the path of least resistance. But that was what got us here in the first place. Keeping quiet, staying the course, not disrupting the way things were done. Silence was acceptance and only made people think they were right.

As my adrenaline wore off, I walked toward Inventory. My job wasn't much to write home about. It certainly wasn't as prestigious as Sid's new job managing the Armory, or Holli's, who'd become Mick's head nurse.

We were lucky to be part of the Centre, aptly named for the shopping mall's original title: Champlain Centre. Dirty looks and comments aside, the community had been our refuge when we'd needed it most. I couldn't imagine what state we'd be in if we hadn't crossed paths with Neil that fateful night.

I shoved my hands in my pockets as I retreated through

the emptying Mess Hall. Breakfast stragglers scraped the last of their meals into their mouths while the three teenagers wiped down the serving tables to be used again for dinner. The area beyond the Mess Hall was once what they called a big-box store. And it was where I spent most of my time nowadays.

Initially, I had hoped for a position on the scavenging team. Hunting was something I knew how to do, something familiar. But when Avi assigned me to Inventory, I became surprisingly content with his decision. The monotony of the job appealed to me. I liked knowing what to expect every single day.

The well-traveled path to Medical split the area in half. Windows lined the far wall. Four dim overhead lights lit the rest of the space, made possible by our new solar electricity system. Shelving units stocked with goods were stacked in rows, extending into the dark belly of the store. Solar-charged lanterns hung on hooks at the ends of each unit, to be used if needed.

My daily work companion, Jae, stood hunched over at the edge of the shelving units closest to the windows, clipboard in hand, scribbling something on paper. He was a tall, lean man, with milk-white skin, a wide nose, and small eyes. Deep-set wrinkles lined his face, his graying hair receding from his forehead. Sunspots covered his scalp, likely from the decades he'd spent working on his father's potato farm. He and his wife Kendra had known Avi since he was a child.

He looked up as I approached. Dark circles beneath his eyes gave him a perpetually weary look, but for good reason. Jae was the hardest worker here. By the time I arrived for my shift in the mornings, he'd typically already eaten breakfast, had a cup of coffee, and been at work for an hour. He created material lists for the scavenging teams, managed food inventory for the cooks, medical supplies for Mick, and just about everything else for the community.

It often made my job obsolete.

This morning he looked more worried than usual, his lips pulled back into a tight grimace. He rose to his full height, tucking the clipboard beneath his arm.

"We've got an issue," he said, skimming over any pleasantries I might've had with someone else.

"What's that?"

"Nathan's scavenging crew that went south missed their check in three days ago. Usually we give a day or two of leeway in case they got off track or something else happened, but they should've been back by now."

"What's that mean?"

"We're going to have to cut expected inventory and Avi will want to send out a team. He'll probably pull from the group we have making candles from deer tallow." He shook his head. "It'll put us behind by at least a week, if not more, and we do not have that kind of time. I knew we should've started the candles back in August."

He led me around the corner of the shelves to a row of canned goods filled with preserves we'd made in the fall.

"So what do we do?" I asked.

"I have to talk to Avi. We can use some of the older kids — what the hell are they learning now, anyway? Geometry? Candles..." He let his fingers trail over the tops of the sealed cans. "...are much more important."

I considered reminding him that we were quickly becoming reliant on the new solar system the community had implemented at the end of the summer. But Jae was a traditionalist, and there was no use in having that argument now.

"What does it mean when the scavenging teams miss

their check ins? Does that happen often?" It was the first instance I'd heard since we'd gotten here.

"No."

"Could they be hurt?" Silence filled the space between us as he took a few seconds to count the cans of raspberry jam in one row. He marked the number down on his clipboard.

"It's not my responsibility to worry about those kinds of things. If Avi's worried, he'll take care of it."

I raised a brow, but didn't comment further. Over the past few months, I'd come to believe Avi was a good leader. He was calm and collected, level-headed during disagreements and debates. He garnered respect, making decisions that were best for the community, only after hearing everyone's opinions. He was fair, thoughtful, and easy to like.

But there were flaws I saw, deep beneath his facade. His personality felt political sometimes, like there was something hiding behind his smile. He was just a little *too* easygoing, a little *too* relaxed. It was hard to believe anyone genuinely felt that way, even behind large, sturdy walls and an arsenal of guns.

I spent the rest of the morning checking in new canned goods from Culinary while Jae continued his rounds. As I reached the last of my counts — one-hundred and six cans of snap-peas — I saw the cook enter to speak with Jae about lunch. Hot meals were only prepared mornings and evenings to conserve food, with a lighter meal served midday.

As they broke into the boxes of packaged chips and applesauce preserves, the radio at Jae's hip sounded, static blaring through the large space. I came around to the Mess Hall's entrance, wincing at the loud noise. But as I opened my mouth to ask what the hell was going on, I realized it wasn't just Jae's radio going off — every radio in the vicinity rang with the same static, and then the same booming voice.

"NEED MEDICAL ASSISTANCE. SIDE ENTRANCE. MICK'S TEAM, WE NEED A STRETCHER, IMMEDI-ATELY. REPEAT. MEDICAL ASSISTANCE NEEDED AT SIDE ENTRANCE—"

Time stilled. Everyone who'd assembled for a mid-morning break in the Mess Hall looked at each other with wide eyes. Then, the cook dropped the box. Jae's hands flew to his radio. Chairs skidded against the floor as people sitting at tables in the center of the room stood, conversations forgotten. Mick's office door slammed open somewhere in the distance, followed by pounding footsteps.

Across the Mess Hall, from the middle of the mall's walkway, a blur of figures ran toward us. I recognized Nadia, the tall, blonde woman who headed up the security team, as she lifted a radio to her mouth. Her voice rang through the wide space as she sprinted past the bathrooms, disappearing down a small corridor that led to the entrance only used in emergencies.

"Security incoming!" she shouted, her voice amplified by Jae's radio. Two more men followed, Avi on their heels at a slow jog.

Wheels screeched against laminate. The middle-aged doctor, Mick and his brown-haired nurse, Shelly, sprinted through Inventory into the Mess Hall, pushing a stretcher.

"Somebody call for Holli, please!" Shelly shouted as they ran through the tables and chairs, disappearing as they followed Nadia and Avi's path down the corridor.

"I'm here!" Holli's voice came from the far end of the walkway. I glimpsed her skidding out of the Armory, pulling her graying hair up high on her crown as she ran after the medical team.

Tension rippled through Inventory. I glanced at Jae, who had his arms crossed, head leaned in near the cook as they spoke in hushed whispers.

Could it be the missing scavenging team? Had they simply mismanaged their time and arrived back late? Were they injured? Followed? The voice on the radio had only mentioned a single stretcher. The thought made my blood run cold. Maybe the entire team didn't make it back.

The radios went off again. The voices on the other end were calmer now, but I couldn't make out what anyone was saying. More shouts came from within the mall, difficult to place because of the echoes. I remained frozen, hands clutched around my clipboard.

Silence settled. A door slammed. Wheels whined and urgent voices carried as the corridor filled back up with people. My muscles tensed. I backed up against one of the shelves, not wanting to be in the way when they came through.

Chaos turned the corner. The stretcher skidded around the side of the Mess Hall, pummeling past the bathrooms. Mick and his nurse were on either side, their blue gowns covered in blood. Both had masks pulled up over their nose, eyes darting over the figure as their hands worked, masks bubbling with heavy breath. The medical team, the stretcher, and their patient came barreling through the old box store.

The stretcher's occupant was wrapped clumsily in a white sheet. Blood stained through near his ribs and shoulder. His face was pale, a deep gash down his left cheek. He moaned in pain, his knuckles white as his hands gripped the side rails of the bed. I vaguely recognized his features and tried to remember his name.

I looked up, waiting for the others. But nobody followed the security team as they emerged from the side hallway. He was alone. The stretcher passed, and I heard the man struggling to say something between his pain as they veered off toward Medical.

"They're gonna kill them," he moaned, his quavering voice carrying to the room's ceiling. "All of them."

THE STRETCHER DISAPPEARED through the medical area's door, shouts muffled as the door swung closed behind the group. Jae's eyes were on me, but I couldn't meet his gaze. There was a lot of blood. No one else from his team was with him. And what had he said?

They're gonna kill them.

Did he mean the rest of his scavenging team? And who were *they*?

A chill settled in my bones, uneasiness twisting my shoulder muscles taut. We'd been lucky since we arrived to have no emergencies, no traumas, no intruders. Small accidents. A couple of colds. The issues we'd had to work through were minimal — laughable, even. An occasional lack of showers. Cloudy days that impacted solar power. Popped tops on canned goods rendering some food inedible. Child's play.

This type of panic disrupted the guise of safety this place held. It was a reminder that despite the walls, despite the weapons, and our distance from the Coutts commune, safety could never truly be realized in this world.

I tried swallowing the fear settled in my throat, but it stuck in my chest. Avi, Nadia, and Mick would know what to do, how to fix this situation. They would assess the threat, identify a solution, and do whatever they needed to do to make it right. I held onto that, trying to untangle myself from my anxiety.

"Eli," Jae crossed onto the walkway. "With me." He waved me in step with him and led the way toward Mick's office.

I trailed the older man. Iron scented the air, sharp in my nostrils, making my stomach churn. Was that blood or dirt in the corners of the walkway? How hurt was the man?

"Are you okay?" He kept his voice low, head turned in toward me.

"Yeah."

"We'll need to assess how many supplies they'll need for Dale." His voice seemed distorted, like smoke drifting. "Okay?"

"Right," I said, keeping pace with Jae. "Supplies."

An alcove beneath a low overhang led to a wooden door we pushed through into what had once been a pharmacy and medical office.

"They're gonna kill them!" the man screamed, his voice rising in panic, as if he'd only just realized what he was saying. "Are you listening? They've got them locked up and they're gonna kill them! All of them!" I recognized Holli's calm voice, attempting to soothe him with words I couldn't hear.

"Jesus," Jae hissed under his breath as we entered the small lobby preceding the hospital area. We crossed the room, approaching what was usually a locked door. It hung open, the key still hanging in the lock, a single bulb buzzing with electricity.

Wire shelves lined the walls, neatly packed with medical supplies and Holli's healing remedies. A large safe sat to our left, its door open, revealing the assortment of prescription pills the community had collected. Boxes of gauze, gowns, and clean cloths had been ripped from the shelves in a frenzy, the remnants in a pile on the floor.

Jae clucked his tongue at the mess, scooping the extra supplies into his arms.

"Jae, what the hell?" I asked, unable to steady the quaver in my voice. "Why's he saying that?" The question sounded childish coming out of my mouth.

"I'm not sure," Jae answered, his voice level. "He could be delirious from dehydration or exhaustion. He'll calm down once he's gotten some rest." He seemed certain, but I was doubtful. "Eli." He placed a hand on my shoulder and I met his gaze. "Why don't you take this and see what else they need? I'm going to clean up in here." He ripped a piece of paper from his clipboard and handed it to me.

"Yeah. Alright."

I gripped the paper and left the closet, head spinning. Dale's continued screaming chipped away at the calm I clung to. Fear hovered over my shoulders as I moved into the next room.

The smell of antiseptic blended with iron and sweat made my eyes water. I tucked my nose beneath my shirt collar as I pushed deeper into the room. Bright fluorescents lit the tiled area with six stationary beds. The stretcher lay discarded on the right side of the room, stained with Dale's drying blood and mud, though it was hard to distinguish between the two. Holli, Mick, and Shelly hovered over the injured man on the bed beside the stretcher, their movements slow and precise as they tended to a shoulder wound so deep I saw his muscle.

Blood stained almost everything on or around the bed — their gowns, gloves, the sheets, the man's white skin — an impossible stain that only seemed to grow larger. Dale's eyes rolled with pain, fingers gripping the sheets, heels pressed into the mattress. Mick injected a needle near the wound and the man screamed like the world was on fire. I winced and turned away, holding my breath beneath my shirt's fabric.

Holli hushed him as I steadied my breathing. "The local will take some of the pain away," she explained in a soft voice. "We have to cauterize, Dale. We've got to stop the bleeding."

"I need Avi," he moaned. I turned to glimpse him rolling his head against the flat bed, ear to ear. "He needs to know."

"Okay," Holli said. "We'll tell him what he needs to know."

"I can tell him," I piped up, eager for an excuse to get out of the room.

Holli and Shelly turned at my announcement. Mick remained focused on his task. But Dale lifted his head, meeting my gaze in a brief moment of focus.

"They took them," he said. "My entire team. They're gonna kill them."

"*Who* took them?"

His nostrils flared. "The Coutts."

4

MAURA

UNEASE COATED the halls like a thick layer of paint. The echoed distress calls from this morning still rang in my ears as I stood in the dinner line at the Mess Hall. I could usually count on seeing Holli, Sid, or Eli to sit with, but they hadn't arrived yet.

After collecting my food, I found a free seat at an empty table, trying to ignore the conversations around me. No sense in panicking until I knew more, though it seemed my anxiety had other plans.

Midway through my meal, I glimpsed a group of people emerge from Inventory's wide opening into the Mess Hall. Sid's tall frame hovered over the rest. Eli walked beside him, running his hand over his mouth. Their expressions were somewhere between somber and indifferent, but I was pleased to see Eli glance around the room, stopping once he met my eyes. I returned his wave as he got into line, both relieved I wouldn't have to eat alone and that they might have some answers about what had happened this morning.

After getting their plates, Eli and Sid weaved through

the crowded tables, taking a seat on either side of me. Tension rippled between the pair. They caught each other's gaze before picking at their food without eating it. I set my fork down and turned my chin between them before I leaned back in my chair and crossed my arms.

"What?" I asked.

Eli looked up first. "Huh?"

"What is it?"

Sid glanced at me, shaking his head. "I told you she'd know."

"Know what?" I swiveled my gaze between them.

Eli pointed his fork at his brother. "Shut up."

"Know *what?*" I repeated.

Sid hunched his shoulders, piling food into his mouth. Eli sighed before he peered around at the filled tables. "Not here," he whispered. I met his dark eyes. "Somewhere quieter. After dinner." There was no warm smile or reassurance accompanying his words. I stirred my gravy with rice as I studied his expression.

"Well, I assume this has to do with the radio call today?" I asked.

Eli clamped his lips around his fork and pulled it slowly out of his mouth.

"Yes," Sid said, beside me. Eli shot him a look I didn't miss. "What?" He raised his brows at his brother. "Everyone heard that call. She's not stupid."

"I never said she was," Eli growled.

Sid gave him a skeptical look. "You were insinuating it."

"Shut *up.*" Eli turned to me, his features softening. "I do not think you're stupid."

"How bad is it, then?" I pressed, keeping my voice low.

"We should wait for Holli." Eli's eyes shifted toward Inventory, as if expecting her to come rushing out. "She'll have more information for all of us."

"Sid?" I turned, but he had his gaze fixed on Eli. He glanced at me before looking down at his plate.

"No, Eli's right," he said.

"So it's a medical issue? Is someone hurt?"

Sid choked on his food. He slammed his fist into his chest, coughing, before he took a large gulp of water.

"You know you have to chew before you swallow?" Eli shot at his brother.

Sid stuck up his middle finger.

"Maura." Eli's tone was heavy with exhaustion. "Please? Holli should be done soon."

I sighed, knowing I was pushing my luck. "I *hate* being the last to know."

THE THREE OF us walked from the Mess Hall to our room in silence. The sun had nearly set, only a dim blue glow visible through the skylight. Others traveled in huddles like ours, back to their collective living spaces. I wondered if they were equally as curious about the circumstances of the radio call earlier that day. But it didn't seem it. Most people chatted lightly, laughing among themselves. I knew they weren't free from worries, but I still felt the separation between us.

Sid lifted the gate to our dark room. Eli lit the four lanterns sitting on a table beside the opening, illuminating the space with a warm glow. We each took one for ourselves, leaving the last for Holli when she arrived.

Our common area filled the front part of the store, complete with an assortment of lounge chairs and a red loveseat situated in a circle around a colorful rug. Sid and Eli had put together two bookshelves which hugged the left wall, now cluttered with things we'd collected over the last few months — books, Holli's personal herbal concoctions, and board games. An occasional trinket rested upon notebooks and art pads.

Large totes holding clean towels, bedding, and spare clothes were piled on the floor between the bookshelves. A bar Sid had crafted for himself from spare wood was the feature on the other side of the room. It was a small structure, covered in what looked like hay and tulle. Half-filled liquor bottles were displayed on top — rewards from his security team poker games. When nights were quiet, he said, they'd sit up on the roof, bet and play. Though, recently, most of his team vowed to never bet against him again. He kept wiping them clean.

Holli had left her reading glasses on the end table beside Sid's recliner, which he plopped himself into with the sigh of an exhausted man who wanted nothing more than to sleep. All in all, it was a comfortable space. It was familiar. A home, of sorts. Though there was something about it that never felt quite permanent.

Eli settled on the loveseat, placing his elbows on his thighs, chin in his hands. I remained standing by the gate, peering out for Holli. Soon, she walked down the walkway, looking weary and winded, her frazzled gray-red hair framing her face like a strange halo. Even from a distance, I could see the droop of her eyes, the way her head rolled heavily on her neck. She clutched a tin-foil wrapped dinner.

"Hi honey," she greeted me as she reached the gate. She rubbed my shoulder and gave me a small smile as she walked past. I wanted reassurance, but instead I felt her pity. My stomach dropped. There was something more at play here, something they were keeping from me.

But why?

"Hey Hol," Sid said, watching as she placed her dinner down on the end table with her glasses. "You okay?"

Holli grunted her indifference, making her way to the bar. She poured a small amount of brown liquid into a plastic cup and carried it with her as she settled on the lounger beside Sid.

A knowing look passed between Eli, Sid, and Holli before they brought their gazes to me. I felt my cheeks flush. This was an all too familiar feeling. I was always the last to know. Too delicate to burden with bad news. My muscles tensed in anger. I turned to close the gate, taking a deep breath to suppress my emotion as it closed with a clang.

"Well?" I couldn't help the shake in my voice as I faced my friends.

Holli looked up, and I met her gaze. "It was a rough day."

"No kidding," said Sid.

"The alert that came through the radio — is that what this is about?" I asked impatiently.

Holli nodded. "Yes." She met my eyes. "A scavenging team went missing. They missed their check-in, and Avi was preparing to send out a team after them. This morning, Dale arrived with severe chest and shoulder wounds." She looked down at the drink she held in her hands and tipped it back into her mouth. It took her a moment to swallow, and she hissed as it coated her throat. "He said some…things."

"Some things," I repeated. Nobody would look at me. My heart fell into my stomach. "Some things about the Coutts?"

Holli sighed, deflating in her seat as she placed the plastic cup down on the table. "I guess he and his team were intending to get near the Coutts' waste center to scavenge medical supplies. According to him, they got maybe two hours south of here when they were greeted by a group of men. They weren't Hunters," she clarified. "At least they weren't dressed like them. Dale said they had regular clothing on and looked malnourished. All signs of survivors outside of the commune. So they stopped, tried to talk to them and see if they'd be a good fit for us.

"Apparently, the men attacked them. More came out of the forest, like an ambush. They easily subdued our group, tied them up, scanned them for disease, then blindfolded and put them in a truck. He wasn't sure what direction they went, only that they ended up in a place that had cells. Like a jail, he thinks. Avi's doing some research on ones that were still standing as of the last few years. After a day or two, a Hunter came to see them. Masked. No distinguishing details. He interrogated them for days, one by one. Starved them. Tortured them. Kept them separated in cells.

"And then, a few days ago, one of them took Dale out of his cell. Put him in the back of the truck. He thought maybe they'd go back to the commune, but..." Her voice cracked, and silence filled the room.

"They hurt him, then dumped him out of the truck in the middle of the woods," Eli finished. "Nearby, within at least ten miles. Told him to deliver a message. Probably waited for him to start walking back to the community. Avi suspects they were trying to figure out where we are."

"They must have an idea," Sid mused. "To get that close."

"How'd he get back here?" I asked.

"One of the other scavenging groups found him on their way back. He was totally off course. Trying to throw off the Hunter's scents. Before coming back here, our team went looking for the men following him. Found them and…took care of them," Eli said, his face darkening.

The room spun. I braced myself against the gate, palms flat against the metal, head involuntarily shaking. This information violated everything Father had told us since the start of the Great Plague. If he was working with other groups outside the commune, he must have known they existed. He must have spoken with them and made deals. Given them resources. People like the Coal Creek men. Men who wouldn't hesitate to kill, maim, rape, or steal. The idea that those types of men were doing the Hunters' bidding made my blood run cold. How far did Father's reach extend?

"It was necessary," said Holli. "If they got back to Peter with any information about our whereabouts, we'd need to abandon this place."

Sid nodded in agreement, then met my gaze. "It also means Peter is working with other Outside groups. He knows our community is out here. And he may suspect we have you."

It was like he'd read my thoughts. I wandered over to the loveseat and sat beside Eli, leaning against his shoulder. If men like that got access to Coutts resources, *none* of us were safe. Not even behind Avi's walls. They would take until there was nothing more to give.

"What are we going to do?" My voice sounded small and far away. I looked up at the three gazes fixed on me, swiveling between them.

"I'm glad you see the concern," Sid grumbled.

I raised my eyebrows.

Eli sighed, turning in his seat to look at his brother. "Avi's not going to take this lying down."

"I dunno…"

"He *can't*," Eli said. "I know you think he's too soft in

most of his strategies, but this isn't something he can just sweep under the rug. If the Coutts or any other group out there know where we are, or even that we exist, it puts us in danger. We have Maura and four other members from the community. If anyone from the commune or otherwise gets a whiff of that—"

"We're screwed," finished Sid. "What else is new?"

"So *what do we do?*" I asked again, desperate for an answer that made sense as panic rose in my throat.

Sid frowned. "Avi and Nadia are discussing that now. But don't worry," he said, his voice softening. "For now, we're safe. We have the walls, the watch team, plenty of security. Roof cover. There's no reason to think they have any idea where we are." He sighed. "We should all be kissing the ground Dale and the others walk on for that. We'll know if there's something to be concerned about. The entire city perimeter outside our walls are equipped with triggers and traps. If a Hunter sets foot within a mile of here, we'll know about it."

I nodded, unable to stop bouncing my leg as I tried to see reason in his words. He wasn't wrong. Avi had readily shared all of his security measures when we'd first arrived. Part reassurance and part, what I assumed was deterrence, against me, should I have chosen to turn against them. I also knew Father would need to be absolutely certain to deploy a large group of Hunters this way. That many men gone for that many days would raise a lot of questions he wouldn't want to answer.

"We should get some rest," Holli said, eyeing the dinner plate she hadn't touched. "Whatever comes of this, I'm sure we'll all have a part to play."

We mumbled goodnights to each other. Sid and Holli retreated to their respective rooms, but sleep was the last thing on my mind. I reeled from this new information, terrified that Father might know I was out here. The anxiety made me squirm in the chair, shifting my weight back and forth as I fought to get comfortable despite the knot in my stomach.

After Morgan's escape, he'd found and dragged her back to the commune. Back then, there'd been a lot more people out here. One wrong move — one slip up, and Father and his men could find us. What might that mean for our community? For the children and families living here? For Eli, Holli, and Sid? Plus, the idea of having to return to the commune, potentially having to return to Andrew? I wouldn't survive that.

Absentmindedly, I picked at my fingernails, glancing at Eli, whose forearms were still draped over his legs. He raised his concerned gaze to me, dark eyes studying my face. I felt a flush creep up my neck and looked away.

"You okay?" he whispered. I glared up at him through my lashes, and a ghost of a smile spread on his lips. "Okay, dumb question."

"I'm *fine*," I said.

"Are you?"

I forced a breath through my nose. "I can't help feeling like I'm putting this entire community in danger. If I wasn't here—"

"Stop that."

"Am I wrong?"

"Yes," he said, sternly. "You are. You have to stop assuming you're the catalyst for all of Peter's decisions. Not that you're not important. But even if you weren't here, he'd hate the idea that a place like this existed." He tilted his head. "Either way, he'd want to threaten us. Peter doesn't seem like the kind of man okay with the existence of another leader in a world he's built to suit himself."

"I suppose." I looked at the floor. "I just wish I could

escape it. Pretend to be someone else. I hate the way people look at me. What they think of me. And all of this will just make it so much worse." I couldn't help the ball of emotion welling in my throat. Tears stung the edges of my eyes.

"Hey." I looked up. Eli's features had softened, eyes scanning my face. "You've got us, okay? Don't worry about the rest of them. What do they know, hm?" Warmth spread through me at the shadow of a smile on his lips.

Once, I had felt scrutinized beneath his gaze, but now, his concern made me feel seen. It was something I'd never gotten from Andrew, and certainly never from Father — the men who had promised to protect me. Instead, this man, whose existence they had denied, who they had warned was filled with sin, protected me more than any Coutts man ever had.

I nodded. "Okay." I offered a small smile in return.

He shifted his weight, as if he meant to embrace me, but instead extended his hand, which grasped my shoulder.

"Peter's actions and threats aren't your responsibility to carry, Maura. Know that." His brown eyes reflected the lantern light in the room, pupils shifting as he kept his gaze on me. "Now, get some sleep." His hand squeezed my shoulder and instinctively, I let my ear rest on his hand for only a moment before I pulled away.

We stood, and I followed him to our sleeping quarters. As I passed Holli's curtain, I paused, watching her pull on wool socks.

"I left you some tincture," she whispered, pointing at the pegboard that separated our rooms. "To help you sleep."

My heart swelled with gratitude. For so long I'd felt alone, struggling to wrestle with the emotions and feelings I'd been taught were sinful. But this group — Sid, Holli, and Eli — they understood me better than anyone ever had, maybe except for Morgan. They offered the support I needed because they themselves understood how these things felt. Stress. Fear. Uncertainty. They didn't force me to pray it away. They didn't laugh in my face when I told them how I was feeling. They simply accepted it.

I downed the tincture in a single swallow before climbing into my bed and extinguishing the lantern. Darkness washed over the room and I closed my eyes, waiting for Holli's gift to weigh me down to sleep.

5

MAURA

THE COMMUNITY'S atmosphere changed overnight. By the time we left breakfast, the details of what happened the day prior had made its rounds. Complete with heavy embellishments, of course. Apparently, Dale had outrun sixteen Hunters, and they were parked on the outskirts of the city. We were going to war. We were under attack.

Even though I knew none of this was true, the spiteful glances in my direction were hard not to take personally. They were more pointed than the usual ones. Angrier and more aggressive. I might as well have been the person who kidnapped the group of scavengers.

"They're looking for someone to blame," Eli said as we walked toward Housekeeping. "But it's not right. I think we need to go to Avi."

"We are *not* going to Avi." I crossed my arms. "I can take it. It'll die down, eventually." Eli shot me a sharp look. "It has to. Right?"

"I don't know if it will. Clearly we live among a bunch of absolute ignorant ass—"

"Eli."

"—clowns."

I laughed, which seemed to soften Eli up. By the time we arrived at Housekeeping his face returned to its normal color.

"I'll see you for dinner," he promised, shoving his hands in his pockets. "Don't go without me."

"I'm *fine*." He tilted his head, giving me a knowing look. "Okay, okay." I lifted my hands. "I'll wait for you."

Satisfied, he smiled and left.

Housekeeping operated out of a small store wedged between the schoolhouse and library. The schoolhouse had once been an eating and indoor play place, while the library filled half of an old department store. Square metal tubs equipped with washboards covered a quarter of my work area. Two dozen laundry hampers sat beside them, mostly full. It smelled like sweat, dirt, and mildew, scents I constantly tried scrubbing from my skin when I could get in for a full shower.

Bottles of both scavenged and homemade cleaners lined large, bulky shelves on the other side of the store. Dustpans, brooms, mops, dusters, and rags filled the rest of the free space. Clotheslines split the room in half, hung with laundry we would sort, fold, and leave on the table outside the front door to be picked up or delivered when time allowed.

Kendra moved through the clothes, her gnarled knuckles the only visible part of her as she unhooked a large sheet at the front of the store from its pins and gathered it in her arms.

"There you are," she said. She handed me one side of the sheet and we worked together to fold it. Kendra had short, gray curls, a crooked nose, and a rosy face full of wrinkles — symbols of a life well-lived. If I could guess, I'd say she was in her late seventies, but I'd never dared to ask. Not that it mattered. She was strong as a mule.

When I'd first arrived, I expected Kendra to be hostile, or at least a little wary of my presence. But we were more alike than I thought. She was childless and believed in God. She was the eldest of her nine siblings and enjoyed hard work. And she never brought up the fact that I was a Coutts. She treated me like every other person. Today was no different, and she made no mention of yesterday's commotion.

The morning passed as we pulled down the clean laundry and folded it. Then we went to work on sorting the large bins outside the storefront where people threw soiled clothes and linens. As I gathered up a large load of whites to carry inside to the basin, I glimpsed Eli coming down the hall. I frowned. What was he doing back here so soon?

I nodded at him, so he knew I saw him before carrying the load to Kendra. Eli hovered at the doorway, running his fingers over his bearded chin.

"Hey," I greeted him, raising my eyebrows. "What's up?

He took a deep breath. "Avi wants to see us."

"About what?"

He shrugged. Fear prickled at the base of my spine. I wasn't afraid of Avi, at least not in the way I was fearful of Father or Andrew. But the request worried me. The community leader had never asked to see me since we'd arrived.

"Do you think it has to do with Dale?" I whispered.

Eli's eyes darkened. "I can only guess," he said, expressionless. "But that was my thought, too."

"Okay." I turned to my work mate, running my fingers up and down my jeans. "Kendra." She looked up. "Avi wants to see me. Will you be okay here for a little bit?"

She smiled. "Sure. Any idea when he'll be done with y'all?"

Eli shook his head. "Not sure what it's about."

"I'll come right back when I can," I promised.

Kendra nodded and waved us off. I wrapped my arms around myself as I followed Eli out of the store and into the bright walkway. I could understand Avi wanting something with Eli, Sid, or Holli. But me? What could he want with me? Had Dale said something that led them to believe I was part of the attack? Perhaps Andrew had been the kidnapper? Or, maybe it was something worse. Maybe they decided it was too dangerous to have me here. Maybe they were going to kick me out or send me back to the commune. The thought made my chest tight. I clenched my fists.

"Hey," Eli said beside me. I looked up, meeting his pained gaze. "It's going to be fine." His gaze flickered to my fists, which I released. I appreciated the reassurance, but still knew Eli had no idea what Avi wanted from the pair of us.

We walked around the corner as if walking toward the Mess Hall, but instead took a turn into the Armory. It had once been something called a sporting goods store and was situated just before the small walkway where the stretcher had retrieved Dale. The high, wooden ceilings were mostly empty and dark, spare the sunlight shining through windows on the far wall. The weapons were stored out of sight, only accessible by the security team.

We followed the laminate path past carpeted areas I assumed once held various merchandise for purchase. The path veered to the left, leading to a sales desk with empty glass cases. Mounted animal heads hung from the wall behind them. Eli led us around the counter to a half-open door with a STAFF ONLY sign. Eli knocked twice before nudging his way in.

Chatter filled the room. Avi's office had enough space to fit the dozen people inside comfortably. Mismatched rugs covered most of the tiled floor. Shelves lined all four walls, filled with collections of books and knick-knacks from woodworking statues to framed photos to small plastic figures, paintings, and everyday items.

A handsome U-shaped desk sat at the far end of the room, the front of it covered with colorful graffiti and magazine cutouts. More unorganized books, files, and paperwork lay scattered on top of the desk, as well as a rectangular tank that held a large lizard-like creature I'd never seen before.

I searched through the crowd of people for those I knew. Sid stood in the far left corner of the room, leaning up against the wall, his head lowered as he spoke with Nadia, who sat in a chair across from him. I recognized a few others, too. The head of each scavenging team stood in a huddle— Gloria, a petite woman with a bad eye, who had been part of the team that brought us back here. A red-haired woman named Genevieve. A man with dark skin named Francis. Nathan, the leader of Dale's scavenging team, was notably missing.

Eli's boss, Jae, spoke with Avi at his desk. And a dark-skinned man named Darius stood near the door, looking like he'd rather be elsewhere. A soft chortle alerted me to Leo. The older man ran a hand through his mostly gray curls that hung over his ears as he spoke with a dark-haired woman who oversaw our perimeter on Nadia's team. As we moved to close the door behind us, Avi looked up from his conversation, waving us toward him. I clung to Eli's side like glue, so close I could grab the back of his shirt.

I didn't want to be here. If there was anywhere I *knew* I didn't belong, it was here. I wanted to fade into the shadows, keep to my work, and worry only about the simple tasks I was responsible for. Getting here had been hard enough. I hoped Avi understood I had no intention of making waves and that there was only so much I could do about Father's actions. If he was preparing to kick me out of here, perhaps I could plead my case. Offer what little information I knew about Father, Andrew, and the Hunters.

Before we could greet him, Avi cleared his throat loudly and stood from his chair, letting his eyes sweep across us. Avi was a broad-shouldered man with a thick mustache and dark skin. He was more round than he was tall, but his compelling presence made up for it. A natural silence fell, and we turned our attention to him as he placed his hands down on his desk.

"Thank you for coming on such short notice," he said pleasantly. "I know we all have important work to do, and I assure you, this is no less important." He paused. "I'm sure you've all heard by now what's happened to our scavenging team on the south end, but here are the facts. Spencer, Jin, Violet, and Nathan are missing. Dale is the only member of his team to return with concerning information about their whereabouts. He claims the Coutts' Hunters kidnapped their team, kept them in locked cells for a little over a week, and tortured them to give up key information about our community.

"Now, if you know anything about our scavenging teams," he said with pride, glancing at the group of remaining scavenging leads, "you'll know their number one priority, besides finding supplies, is to keep our location secure and safe. I have every reason to believe Nathan and his team will hold the information and not break.

However." He looked down at his cluttered desk. "They are only human. It would be foolish to wait and see what happens next." He frowned, raising his gaze. "We must act."

His words hung in the air. Surely he didn't mean going out after the Hunters. That was bound to end badly, whether or not they had our people in their grip.

"Based on Dale's estimations, we're uncertain if the group made it into the Coutts commune. We've identified three possibilities where they may be held. I'm proposing we send two scavenging teams out to check out two separate prisons over the next week, and one to evaluate an area inside the commune's borders.

"Since we're already down a scavenging team, we'll need to create a fourth so we can keep Genevieve's team here to continue that important work, especially if we're looking at more injuries to treat." His eyes shifted to the group of scavengers. "Darius," he said, and the dark-skinned man looked up, his jaw set. "You'll lead the extra team." Darius gave him a curt nod.

"Jae and Eli," Avi said. Eli straightened beside me. "We're already low on inventory and this incident won't help. We'll need to ration medical supplies. Discuss what Mick needs and figure out what we can spare. Whatever medical supplies we're low on, give that list to Genevieve."

"Nadia." The blonde woman looked up. "Security will need to be tightened around the perimeter. We'll post more guards overnight, so tackle that list of volunteers. Anyone over the age of fifteen. And Sid." He turned to face the tall man. "You'll vet the volunteers for the new scavenging team. Once you have a solid list, run it past Darius."

"Now." Avi looked back at the desk, and I followed his eyes. Two maps lay spread across the surface, marked with thick highlighter. "Leo," Avi said, scanning the room. His gaze fell on me. I froze. "And Maura," he said. "I'd like you two to help me with our maps. Despite our best efforts, we currently have an extremely outdated version of our Coutts commune and I'm hoping if you two can work together, we can create something that's more up-to-date to aid the team going in. I'm mostly interested in borders, Hunter outposts, traveling routes, and scavenging zones."

I felt my face pale, my lips press together, and every muscle in my neck tense. A map? They wanted me to help them with a map? I nearly laughed in relief. I forced a nod at Avi as I processed my new obligation. A map of the Coutts commune. I scanned my memory for the intricate details of my life before all of this. Confined to Coutts Peak. My scavenging duty had been contained to a small area. I'd done most of my exploring on my own after the Island of Repentance, but I wasn't sure I could remember everything clearly.

My momentary relief slipped away. Avi assumed I had more intel than just a couple of routes. He was expecting more from me. Important knowledge that aided our teams. Didn't he understand I was only a woman in the commune? That they kept us under lock and key, only allowing us to venture as far as they could keep an eye on us? My intel was laughable. Here was my moment to be of some use to this community and help them navigate something important.

And I couldn't even do that.

BY THE TIME Leo and I left Avi's office carrying a large, rolled-up piece of canvas, it was late afternoon. I stopped in to let Kendra know I'd be gone for the rest of the day before accompanying Leo back to his room.

The older man shared his living space — once a

greeting card store, whatever that meant — with the others from the commune. There were five adults in the Centre from the Coutts commune — Leo, me, Fiona, Sonja, and Hank. Fiona and Sonja were sisters with lithe limbs and sharp features. They'd followed Father after the SARS pandemic when Sonja had fallen ill. They left together, after Fiona's husband left her with a broken collarbone and refused her medical care. Fiona had three children, and Sonja had two. I could only imagine how angry Father had been when he'd heard his commune had lost *children*. They were his most precious commodity.

Hank had freckled skin and thin red hair. I estimated him to be in his late thirties. He had joined for religious reasons, lasting eight years in the commune. He'd left after refusing to take a wife thirteen years his junior. But none of them were here now, all likely at their respective jobs. I was glad not to have an audience.

Leo opened the rolling gate to their room. It was clear they'd been here a long while — longer, at least, than the crew I'd arrived with. Rather than our makeshift walls, someone had used drywall to cut the space in half. On our right was a kitchen, the large glass window allowing plenty of natural light to shower the array of green plants sitting atop a counter. Shelves lined the walls, filled with jars, snacks, and plates and utensils for children. On the left was a lounge similar to ours, with two immaculate high chairs, a fenced-in play area, and an assortment of children's toys organized in bins. Leo settled on a long leather couch that had been patched with duct-tape.

"Okay," he said, unrolling the canvas and laying it on the coffee table in the middle of the seating area. He used a few toys to weigh each corner flat. "This is the old map I helped Avi with when I first arrived, with some input from the others. I'm sure we can update a few things based on your knowledge."

I nodded despite my wariness. Avi's instructions had been clear, but I was certain I had nothing of substance to offer. What I knew of the commune was insignificant, aside from my own scavenging zone and Coutts Peak. None of that would be helpful when looking for the hostages.

I glanced at the canvas he'd unrolled. The square was so large it hung over the edges of his coffee table. Some writing was more faded than others, but it was immediately clear the map had been separated into four different sections.

North, they had labeled a wide expanse of blank area as FOREST. The waste center was clearly marked on the edge of the commune border, a large black blemish. I followed the border east to a lake that had question marks surrounding it. Land ended at the ocean to the east of that, and lower, south, they had marked OCEANS near the coast. Even farther south was a large star labeled CITIES, the border situated just beneath it. Directly north was a label that read MOUNTAINS, with a clear circle labeled Coutts Peak. West of the peak were dots with arrows that read Coutts Valley. In this space, they'd identified HEALTH CENTERS, TELEVISION AND COMMUNI-CATIONS, and ENERGY.

Some roads had been drawn in thick, bold lines. I could still see remnants of faded lines that must have been long forgotten — roads that were unusable, perhaps — or ones that had been demolished and reformed.

My stomach turned over. It was strange to know Outsiders knew anything about the commune. This was once the only place I knew — it was the entirety of a world I had once lived in. It was where I'd come from, where I'd grown and learned, lost and loved. A sudden sadness washed over me. It was merely a drawing of the commune, but it was where my siblings and my Mother still lived. It was a place I may never return to.

"We at least know the borders have expanded west," Leo said, his finger tapping near the waste center.

"They've expanded out to that creek," I said, pointing toward a long blue line to the west labeled CONNECTICUT RIVER. "This was my scavenging area for the past year or so. We had *firm* instructions to never cross the water. That was the creek I must've fallen into." The land west was labeled VERMONT. That must've been where Eli's camp had been. It felt strange to put a name to the place.

"Good," Leo said, standing to grab a pencil from the kitchen area. When he came back, he adjusted the line outward, extending it farther west.

"And this…" I let my finger hover over the island with question marks. The wide lake sat east of the waste center. "The Island of Repentance," I breathed, looking up at Leo. We locked eyes. I saw his hesitation, the sadness that swam in his irises. But he only nodded, using his pencil to label it. If that was right, then it meant I'd crossed nearly thirty miles into Coal Creek.

I closed my eyes, trying to remember, letting my finger trail from the Islands to the waste center, to where I thought the ranch might be, where I'd first encountered Chance, the horse I'd ridden leaving the commune. The first scavenging zone I'd come across — 256 — and the numbers I'd passed as we'd ridden to the waste center. From there, we could label and guess many of the other zones, filling in nearly all the scavenging zones on the northern border. I tracked my journey to my scavenging zone from the JC Family Ranch, which Leo labeled, too.

We labeled the main church, Coutts Estate, then the lower three tiers of houses, where Mother and Morgan still lived. I located the schoolhouses and where we young girls took some of our purpose training with Abigail. Coutts Valley, with its different labels, became the Sciences and Innovation area. And finally, we labeled the nuclear energy cooling towers I had only seen from a distance.

I sat back on his couch, my heart pounding. I'd had more knowledge than I'd realized. Leo's eyes sparkled with accomplishment.

"Avi will be pleased," he said. "We had an idea of the northern borders, but this will help significantly. I'm sorry we didn't come to you sooner."

I wasn't, but forced a smile anyway. It had been months since I was under Father's influence, but there was still a deep sense of betrayal in my belly. I had gone against the Prophet before, but only for my own gain and survival. This was different. This was a cardinal sin against Father. I was committing treason. I was disloyal. And I knew, if Father had any idea I was here, sharing secrets of his commune, he would kill me the next time he had the chance.

6

ELI

I SAT down to eat as the last dinner stragglers left the Mess Hall. The beans were cold, but I scarfed them down, anyway.

Jae had been in rare form tonight, barking orders and demanding recounts before he collapsed in a metal chair and mumbled it was time for him to go back to his room. I knew something was off. So I pressed him on it, and he told me what he'd done.

The elderly man had volunteered for the new scavenging team.

It was a reckless move, possibly a death wish. But Jae insisted his decision was right. There were *kids* on Avi's list, he'd said, and they were too young to volunteer. If Jae took their spot, he could keep them out of danger.

He was afraid. We all were. It was one thing to think the Coutts might be looking for us. It was another thing to know they knew we existed. We had a lot of protections, but we all understood the reality. The Coutts could decimate us. Not to mention we'd lost an entire team of healthy adults. Our community couldn't afford to lose anyone else. We needed all the manpower we could get.

Footsteps approached. I scooped up the last of my beans with a piece of bread and shoved it into my mouth. Sid's figure was visible in the distance. He walked with his head low, hands tucked in his back pockets. I crumpled up my paper plate and stood from the table, meeting him as I threw it in the trash.

"We were looking for you at dinner," he said in greeting.

"Yeah. Sorry. Jae needed some extra support tonight."

Sid nodded.

"You heading back to the room?"

"I was actually looking for you." His gaze shifted away.

"Because I'm the most fun person you've ever met?"

"Because you're the biggest pain in the ass, I've ever met."

"It's okay to admit it," I said.

"I did admit it. You're a real pain in the ass."

I gave him the finger. "What do you really want? I'm not up for a security poker game, I already told you. I have nothing I want to trade, anyway."

"I wanted to let you know I joined Darius's scavenging team." He said it so casually, I thought I might've misheard him at first.

"You *what?*"

"I volunteered for Darius's—"

"God damn it, Sid, I heard you. Just wanted to make sure it was as crazy as it sounds."

"It's not crazy."

I shot him a look. "You just recovered from a major injury."

Sid rolled his eyes. "Oh, come on. That was months ago."

"You're deaf in one ear!" I shouted. "You haven't even taken the time to get used to that and you're already jumping into a scavenging mission? Your balance still isn't even near what it used to be."

"You know I've been wanting to get out there and help." He glanced down the empty walkway. "It's great here and all, but I want to get out and do something else beyond the walls. Being inside is driving me nuts. I miss hunting," he said. "And out of all the people eligible for this trip, I think I'm the best asset."

"Oh now, don't be modest." My voice came out with an edge. Sid looked away.

"I'll be fine."

I scoffed. "How can you say that?"

"Listen," he said, irritation spotting his tone, "I know what happened in Coal Creek freaked you out. But I want to do this. I want to help Avi. I want to find those people. If Maura hadn't found me at that lodge, I don't know what would've happened to me. The idea that they're out there somewhere, having to deal with the Hunters … it isn't right." He turned to look at me and I caught his gaze. "I want to help get them out of there. I feel like I owe it back to the universe or something."

"You don't," I said, shortly. "You belong here." *With me*, I wanted to say. I had almost lost him once and the thought of having to do it again made my throat fill with bile.

"Well…" The muscles in his neck tensed. He turned away from me. "I just thought I'd tell you before you heard it from someone else."

"You already told Avi?"

He looked back at me. "I'm about to."

"And there's nothing I can do to convince you otherwise?"

"Eli…"

It was juvenile, I knew. Selfish, even. But Sid was the last person I had from home. The last person who had known me before things went to shit. Losing him was not an option.

"Fine." I kept my face as neutral as I could. "I'll come with you to Avi's."

"Well, alright," he said, tilting his head toward the Armory.

"And you really thought this all the way through?" I asked as we walked, searching his features for flickers of doubt.

"I did." He sighed. "I know you think I'm crazy. But you gotta remember, most of the people in this place survived by chance. Jae signed up and his argument was that a lot of the young kids volunteering for this kind of thing are incredibly inexperienced. They aren't soldiers. They're not fighters. This community has shielded them from the worst of what's out there. Most of them would be dead before they could even raise their gun." He shrugged. "I know how to handle myself. I can save a life this way, E. I can save a lot of lives."

He wasn't wrong, but it didn't make me like the prospect any better.

"And what about Jae?" I continued arguing as we reached the cross in the walkway. "He's old. What if he can't keep up? What if—"

"Jesus, Eli," Sid interrupted. "There are always risks. I know that. You know that. I'm not saying there's not."

"And you're okay with that?"

"Yes! Because I'd rather it be me, okay?" He paused, spinning on his heel to round on me. "I can take a bullet. I've done it before. I know what to expect out there. I've lived and breathed it for over a year now. I can do this. And I need you to let me."

His tone was final, and I knew it.

We reached the Armory, which served a number of purposes — Avi's office and apartment, weapon and ammo storage, security headquarters, and a small jail. If you were looking for the leader of the Centre, this was where you'd often find him.

Lantern light spilled from the door to his office. Sid knocked before nudging the door open with his shoulder. Inside, Darius and Nadia sat in two chairs facing Avi's graffiti-covered desk. They looked up as we entered.

"Sid," Avi greeted in his booming voice. He caught my eye. "Eli. How are you gentlemen doing this evening?"

"Very good, sir," Sid said. "I wanted to let you know I'll be volunteering for Darius's scavenging team."

"Excellent!" Avi's face brightened. "I expected as much. I know Darius and Jae will value your expertise."

My heart pounded in my chest. I heard the words before I formed them, but they still came out forced and muddied, because, really, I wasn't sure my decision was right. I *did* know Sid's safety was one of the most important things to me, though. I couldn't lose him again.

I wouldn't.

"Sir," I said, clearing my throat. "I'd also like to volunteer."

Tension rippled in the air between me and my brother. He turned his head, narrowing his dark eyes at me. I raised my brows, challenging him, before I looked back at Avi. If this was what Sid wanted to do, he'd have to live with me being by his side.

"Well, gentlemen," Avi said, standing from his chair. "That's the best news I've gotten all day. Adding you both completes the fourth scavenging team. Darius?" The dark-skinned man raised his head as Avi gestured toward us. "Your new recruits."

Darius looked unimpressed, but I wasn't sure I'd ever seen him have an actual expression besides anger. So there were four of us. Darius, Sid, and I were strong and capable. Jae was a bit of a concern. His age could slow us down, but it wasn't a worry I'd voice out loud. Jae was a hard worker. He was smart, motivated, and calm under pressure. If Avi thought he was up to the task, then who was I to argue?

But I couldn't slow my heart down. Adrenaline pumped through my veins so forcefully I felt dizzy. I'd made an impulsive decision. I knew it was rooted in fear, and I knew that was wrong. But I was in it now, whether or not I liked it. Letting Sid go out on this mission alone wasn't something I was willing to do. Some of the worst days of my life were losing Sid to the Coal Creek men, then watching as infection nearly killed him. I was so desperate to save him, I'd put myself and Maura in danger.

Maura.

I froze as I thought of her — her warm smile, the way her eyes twinkled every morning when I greeted her at her door, the way she went about her days without complaint despite how difficult it must've been for her. She wouldn't take this news well. And as much as I tried to convince myself she could find her own way without me, I still knew she wouldn't be pleased. Familiar guilt edged its way into my body. Maura had given a lot of herself to me and Sid — more than we'd ever asked. Had we betrayed her?

"We were just talking about the three routes," Darius explained, wasting no time getting down to business. He pointed to Avi's desk at a few crudely drawn maps. "We're taking this one." He tapped the topmost paper, labeled Sorona Penitentiary. "It's a little over fifty miles southeast of here. It used to be a high-security prison, and it's situated in the middle of a town that'll be guarded. It'll be..." he clucked his tongue, "tricky to get into."

"That's close to the commune," Sid observed.

Nadia tilted her head. "Based on the map Maura and Leo put together, it's about twenty miles north of the nearest scavenging zone. It has potential, but we won't be sure until we get in there. The initial job will be to scope, to retrieve if possible. If not, once we identify where they're being held, we can come back in with reinforcements."

"That'll take weeks," I said.

"Not if we leave the morning after tomorrow," Darius said.

"That soon?" I asked.

He looked up at me with dark eyes. "There's no time to waste. All we're waiting on is gas. Once we're fueled and packed, we can head out."

"Sounds good," Sid said, crossing his arms. "Do we have any idea what kind of state the missing people are in? If there are four people in there, we'd want four able bodies to help transport them to safety."

"In an ideal world, yes," Darius said, giving Sid a look of warning. I got the feeling he didn't want to be overshadowed by my brother. "But Jae was adamant about being on this team. You may not know this, but he and Kendra arrived with Jin. He feels like he owes it to him to get it out. We're low on volunteers and border security takes priority right now. Sparing twelve people for this is enough as it is."

Sid grunted in understanding. Guilt made my stomach heavy. It wasn't common to ask each other about *the before*. What happened before we all got here. Because the answers were usually painful or traumatic to relieve. Sometimes we'd get glimpses of those details, but I'd never asked Jae how he'd gotten here or what his life was like before. I knew the basics. His wife was here. He had no children. And he really liked spearmint gum and dancing.

"Did Dale give any more information about what this prison looked like?" I asked.

"Just that it was big," Darius answered, looking at Nadia.

"Big and cold," she added. "That makes me think they're on the outskirts of the commune. I suspect the place doesn't have power, but…" She shrugged. "We could also be wrong."

"We'll know more once we get out there," Darius repeated, glancing back at Sid. "I'd like us to meet tomorrow evening to solidify the travel plan, divvy up our resources. The winter solstice celebration is tomorrow. We'll meet here afterwards before we go to sleep. It'll be an early night." He narrowed his eyes at my brother and me. "We'll leave a few hours before the sun comes up."

"Noted," Sid said, looking over his shoulder at me. "We'll see you tomorrow, then."

After bidding Avi, Nadia, and Darius a good evening, we left the office and walked back down the walkway.

"Just couldn't help yourself, could you?" Sid said, slipping his hands into his pockets.

"Meaning?"

"You didn't have to volunteer just because I did."

"I know that." I looked at my shoes. "But this way, I can make sure you come back alive."

"You don't have control over that, Eli," Sid said with a sigh. "But selfishly, I'm glad you're coming."

It was a loaded statement, and I was too tired to dissect it too deeply. But the fact that Sid felt comforted by the idea of my presence justified my decision a little more.

We walked to our room, sliding the gate up and down as quietly as possible. My stomach dropped as we tiptoed past Maura and Holli's rooms, and I thought of what had transpired over the past hour. Emotions would be high tomorrow.

I could only hope Holli and Maura would see our reasoning.

7

ELI

I CHEWED MY LIP, pacing back and forth in front of the open gate in the common area. A crisp draft ran through the mall on this cloudy morning, matching my mood. Plastic rings slid against a tension rod, and I turned, watching Maura emerge from her room, dressed in a fitted hoodie, jeans, and boots.

Our routine had been like this for the past few months, but still, my heart pounded in my chest. I'd practiced my speech the night prior as I struggled to find sleep, rolling silent words over my tongue.

I volunteered to go rescue the missing people from Dale's team.

I'd imagined all the scenarios — Maura agreeing it was the right thing to do, Maura screaming at me and never speaking to me again, Maura bursting into tears and begging me not to go, and even Maura so proud of my bravery that she'd jumped into my arms.

She lifted her gaze to meet mine, but as soon as our eyes met, her smile faltered. She crossed her arms and frowned.

"What's wrong?" she asked.

"What?" Heat rose up my neck. "Nothing," I lied, as my carefully planned explanation evaporated from my tongue. Her eyes raked over me with suspicion. "Sleep okay?" My voice sounded higher than usual.

"Fine. You get everything straightened out with Jae?" she asked. "You must've been there late to miss dinner."

That, among other things.

"Yeah," I said, leading her out into the walkway. "His counts are driving me nuts, though. I'm convinced over-counting is a thing." I closed the gate behind us. "How did the map drawing go?"

"Really well, actually," Maura said as we began to walk toward the bathrooms and Mess Hall. The knot in my stomach eased slightly. "I wasn't sure how much information I would be able to provide, but we ended up getting a good amount of the northern borders drawn. Leo and the others had already started a pretty good shell when they did this last time, so that helped. When I left the Island of Repentance, I passed a number of scavenging zones, so we were able to fill them all in. It's weird seeing the commune from this perspective, though."

"I bet."

"It's *huge,*" she said, tucking her hands into the front pocket of her sweatshirt. "The Island of Repentance is on the edge of the borders, way past the scavenging zones. They'd drawn it but didn't know what it was. From there, I was able to trace my way back." There was a sense of pride I caught, a bit of a bounce in her step. Rarely did she exude that kind of confidence. But if there was anything she knew well, it was that commune. And that was the knowledge Sid, Jae, Darius, and I needed to stay alive.

Of course, Maura didn't know that yet.

"Avi's going to be psyched," I said.

She tilted her chin up to me, brows knotted in confusion. This happened on occasion, the reminder that Maura was from a different world. Certain words didn't have meaning for her.

"Psyched?"

I tipped my head from side to side. "Excited?" I suggested.

"Psyched." She tested the word on her tongue. "I'm *psyched.*"

I laughed at the strangeness of the word coming out of her mouth. "It's valuable information Avi wouldn't have without you."

Maura nodded as we rounded the corner to the Mess Hall. "It's nice to be able to provide something helpful," she said, and before I could comment further, she turned her head sharply and held up her hand. "And do *not* say laundry is helpful."

"I don't know...without you and Kendra, this place would smell like ass."

We walked the rest of the way to the bathroom, joking about the cleanliness of our fellow community members. I waited for an opportunity to tell her my plans — that I was about to venture off for a week, if not more, to do something extremely dangerous. But she radiated so much joy from her map-making session that I didn't want to disturb it. Not yet.

But when?

I would tell her after we had breakfast. Bad news was always easier to swallow on a full stomach. With our plates loaded with oatmeal, berries, and buttered bread, we settled at an empty table. I kept an eye out for Sid, expecting him to plop down in the seat beside Maura to blurt out what had been bursting inside of me since last night, but he didn't appear. Probably off cleaning our weapons, making sure they were ready for the journey ahead of us. I felt shame at that thought — that Sid was doing something worthwhile and I was here, sitting in the middle of the community center, hiding a secret behind my oatmeal.

"Eli!"

I looked up. The voice belonged to Shelly, Mick's nurse, who waved at me from the breakfast line. Her brown hair was tied back in a neat braid. I let my fingers splay into a wave before I looked back at Maura, who was intently focused on her bowl of oatmeal.

"Shelly," I said.

Her face tightened. "Oh," she said, shoveling three more spoonfuls into her mouth and yanking the bowl away with her. "I've got to run — just remembered…something that Kendra…" She trailed off, avoiding my gaze.

My heart sank as she stood from her chair, giving me a small smile, before she went to put her dishes away in the washing station. I wanted to tell her to wait. That I had something else to say, but the words wouldn't form on my tongue. Just as she rounded the corner to Housekeeping, Shelly sat down in the chair beside me, her grin wide and eager.

"You're here early!" she exclaimed.

"Oh, yeah," I said, scraping the bottom of my bowl with my spoon. "Didn't sleep well."

"Oh no," she said, looking at me with concern. "Everything alright? You know, Holli said she makes tinctures for that kind of stuff. I bet she'd hook you up with something."

Hook you up made me think of *psyched*.

"Oh yeah," I said. "Thanks."

Shelly was a nice enough girl. She was pretty, smart, and, strangely enough, interested in me. I still couldn't figure out why.

"Are you going to the event tonight?" she asked.

I raised a brow. "What event?"

"The winter solstice celebration, silly," she exclaimed. "I'm on the committee. We've been working really hard on it. We've got a ton of really good food, music, and decorations." She looked off, dreamily.

"Oh."

"Avi's hoping it'll raise morale."

"That makes sense."

"There'll be lots of dancing." Her face flushed at this announcement.

"I'm more of a wallflower myself."

"Oh," she said, disappointment crossing her features. "You heard about Dale?" She had a polite spoonful of her oatmeal.

"I was there."

Her brows rose. "Were you?"

I nodded. "Me and Jae were doing counts of inventory at Mick's right after."

"Nathan's missing," she said, eyes darting around the community space.

"A few others too," I said. "I'm going out with a team to try to find them."

The words tumbled from my mouth and as I'd said them, I wished I could've taken them back. Why now? Why was it so easy for me to tell Shelly the thing I'd struggled to tell Maura all morning? Why couldn't I have casually thrown it into the conversation and be done with it?

Shelly placed her hand on my arm, her chewed fingernails caressing the thick fabric of my shirt. I met her eyes, and they brimmed with tears.

"Eli, that's so brave of you."

"Sid's going too," I said, unsure of why I was spilling out

these details to Shelly and not Maura. Irritation rose in my chest. I wanted to kick myself. Stupid, stupid, stupid.

"Sid's going where?"

My brother came around my chair and sat down in the seat across from me, not bothering to hide his smile as his gaze flickered between me and Shelly. I gave him an exasperated look.

"On the rescue mission," Shelly said, and Sid nearly choked on the coffee he'd just thrown back.

"I didn't realize that was common knowledge." My brother eyed me. "Do Holli and Maura know?"

I grit my teeth. "I didn't get a chance—"

"E." He narrowed his eyes at me.

"I gotta go to work," I said, annoyed. I rose from the table, gathering my utensils and plate, before I dumped them in the washing area, heart pounding wildly. I wasn't a person who liked to lie or skim the truth. I considered myself a fairly straightforward guy. This world had hardened me in ways I didn't completely understand. Thinking about feelings — particularly other people's feelings, was not my strong suit.

And yet, for some reason, I had been overly cautious when it came to telling Maura something I knew would hurt her. I wanted to avoid that, for her sake, instead of my own.

I wouldn't admit it to anyone, but it frightened me.

I SPENT the remainder of the day hoping to see Maura again. Eventually, I became desperate for the chance to explain, fearful she'd heard the news before I got to her. But she was nowhere to be found during lunch or even when I hovered beside Housekeeping, waiting for her to emerge. Kendra finally shooed me away, saying Maura had left with Leo almost an hour ago.

Defeated, I walked back to our room. About a dozen people milled around the halls, working on the party setup for the winter solstice celebration. Draped fabric hung across the walkway's cross-section from all four corners, held up by spare lumber. The effect created a low canopy through which sparkly streamers and paper snowflakes hung. Wreathes were attached to the lumber, complete with bright ornaments, painted pinecones, and ribbons. Taped cardboard with crayon-colored snowflakes — the makeshift dance floor — was the finishing touch beneath the canopy.

Two speakers for live music were set up on the outskirts among a variety of different furniture. Folding tables wrapped in blue and white tulle boasted even more decor between empty serving dishes, which would be filled soon. There was even an improvised bar that would serve water, diluted lemonade, and, if you tipped the bartender enough, a very weak vodka drink.

We'd had a few events take place since we'd arrived. Avi insisted on them. Said they acted as a reminder that we were still human, and that we could still have fun. At first, I'd found them horribly cheesy — a waste of labor and resources. But after attending one, I'd reluctantly enjoyed myself, even if I wasn't an active participant.

I found Sid grooming himself in front of the mirror as I entered through our room's open gate, scanning the space for Maura. This had gone on too long. I needed to tell her and Holli what was happening tomorrow. We were less than twelve hours away from leaving.

"Where've you been?" my brother asked without looking up.

"Working."

He rolled his eyes. "Did you manage to tell Holli and Maura what your plans are early tomorrow morning?"

"No. Did you?"

Sid sighed. "I told them," he said, and I could've sworn my heart stopped. "But I didn't tell them you were going. Just me. It's your business to tell them yourself."

I released a breath as gratitude bloomed in my chest. "I appreciate that," I said, though the cowardly part of me wished he would've done the hard work for me.

He glanced out the gate where the sky was beginning to darken. "Night's almost here, Eli. You can't wait until you're gone for them to find out. I'm not sure they'd forgive you for that. Holli, maybe. But not Maura."

A wave of frustration washed over me at his words. "I know."

Sid stood up from the chair, leaving his tweezers on the coffee table. "Just get it over with before the party gets into its full swing. We've gotta leave early to meet with Darius, anyway. At least let yourself enjoy a little bit of the party."

I got changed and ran a comb through my hair. I packed, unpacked, and then repacked the backpack I would take on our journey, leaving room for anything else I'd carry. We were each allowed a few personal items, mostly clothes. Jae and I had put aside the rest of the supplies for each scavenger — food based on body weight, water, sleeping rolls, and a few medical supplies. Sid and Nadia would assign us each a weapon and ammo we'd carry with us.

Voices outside our room grew louder. A microphone crackled in the distance. The party was about to start. Holli was still working her shift with Mick, but Maura still hadn't returned. Had she heard what I intended to do tomorrow? Was she angry with me? I decided to hope for the best as Sid and I walked down to the celebration.

The walkway buzzed as people packed in toward the center of the mall. Though the sky had darkened, the space was well lit with solar lanterns that cast light across the floor like diamonds. The smell of hot dinner wafted across the corridor and I glimpsed a few familiar teenagers carrying heavy dishes to the folding tables.

We walked toward the food, falling into line as the servers tied their hair up and put on their gloves to serve our plates. Two ration cards felt hot in my pocket — proof of tomorrow's journey. There was a simple solution for all of this, I knew. I searched the crowd for a curly head of black hair — but Maura wasn't here.

Dinner was corn, rice, and chicken. Sid and I received a heartier helping, and I tried not to cringe at it as we found our seats. The ration cards were easy to hide, but an extra helping made my upcoming mission obvious. I scarfed down my meal, savoring the flavors and meaty protein. We'd miss this while we were out in the elements, choking down beef jerky or cold cans of beans. We might be lucky enough to find game, but slaughtering, butchering, and cooking it would take up time we did not have. And knowing Darius, he was the last person I'd peg to take a detour for a more savory meal. The guy looked like he ate tree bark for fun.

I kept my eyes on the crowd, which moved in and out of the area in a steady wave as people found friends. Some settled into chairs, while others ate their meals, holding the plates in their hands. Then, I saw her. Her mop of curly hair was just visible between a crowd of people. My heart leapt at the sight of her, though my intestines felt like they were unraveling. Telling her wasn't hard, I tried reminding myself. But then why the hell did I feel like this?

It had been quite some time since I'd watched Maura from a distance. She stood beside Leo, her features drawn up in a smile as she chatted with him about something. They were a strange-looking pair, the older man with his pale skin, deep-set wrinkles, and green eyes beside the petite, dark-featured woman. As she turned, I noticed she'd chosen her favorite t-shirt for the event, a purple-bleached shirt that hung loosely over her figure.

The microphone whined, followed by a sheepish laugh. All heads turned to the people at the edge of the canopy — Marcia and Davon, a brother-sister duo who worked security.

"Evening y'all," the young, muscular woman said into the microphone. "Thanks for letting us play for you again. Hope you enjoy." Her voice reverberated through the space and with one glance over her shoulder at her brother with the guitar, he began to play an upbeat tune.

Live music was a rarity — something I'd only ever heard a few times. In another life, before Sid and I were born, Mom said she'd played piano. But like most other families, we were too poor to afford an instrument.

Music filled the space, bringing the hairs on my arms to attention. The melody, no matter the tune, always sparked something fierce in me, making me feel invincible. Like nothing could ever be wrong again. If only that were true. It took only seconds for me to remember the bomb I needed to drop on Maura.

My gaze drifted away from the musicians as I studied her. She'd stopped talking. Her plump lips were parted, eyes shining beneath the sparkling lights, joy spreading delicately across her features as she drank in the music. She dipped her chin, her focus catching someone else, and I felt my stomach clench with — fear? No. Jealousy?

But it was Neil who offered his hand. Her face broke into a dazzling grin, dimples deepening as she slid her hand into his. I watched as he pulled her gently onto the dance floor, their hands intertwined, eyes focused on their feet as they began to shimmy and shake to the music.

Time slowed, I could've sworn it. There was something about the way she looked, the way the light filled her face, reflecting off her features. Perhaps it was the music, imbibing me with the possibilities of what could be before I entered dangerous territory tomorrow. I saw her clearly in that moment, as if someone had brushed away the hate and fear and damage we'd endured.

Had the safety of these walls revealed something I'd tried keeping closed behind the curtain? Had this been brewing within me without my knowledge? I knew it had. It was the reason I couldn't approach the subject I'd needed to today.

This feeling was something I thought I'd quieted long ago. Desire, lust, love, whatever it was, had always seemed too dangerous. Too frivolous. Painfully beyond my reach. Yet here it was, erupting from my cold, dark heart without prodding. A spark. Something new. Something terrifying and wonderful all at once. It put Maura in a light I hadn't considered before.

A hand on my shoulder broke me from my trance and I nearly tipped my chair as I looked up to see Holli's shadowed face peer down at me. The lantern light made her look weary and aged. She sat down beside me.

"Enjoying the show?" Her eyes twinkled knowingly as she lifted her gaze to Maura and Neil. Grateful for the dim light, I flushed.

"Holli—" I lost the words and deflated in my seat.

She placed her hand on my arm and pressed her lips together. "I know," she said. "I knew the minute Sid told me he was going." She shook her head, squeezed my forearm, and sighed. "I know I can't change your decision, but it would please me greatly if you stayed."

Her pleading eyes searched mine for an answer. Guilt filled my belly. Holli had lost so much. If Sid and I didn't make it back, the grief might be unbearable. And yet…

"I can't," I said.

She nodded. "Then I won't ask you again. But please look out for each other. Be smart. Go slow. Stay vigilant. Come back to us, alive."

"I will."

She patted my arm in a way that told me it wasn't something I could promise her, but she appreciated the gesture, anyway. Then she cupped my chin in her hands and kissed my cheek.

I didn't think I could feel any worse about my decision, but I did.

8

______

MAURA

I FELT Eli's gaze as he slipped through the crowd, moving toward where I sat. My cheeks were still hot from dancing and energy pulsed through my limbs. The combination of lights, music, food, and people made me feel lightheaded and wonderful. I watched Neil and the group of others I'd left twirl Mia as she giggled, stumbling from hand to hand. It wasn't lost on me that even in the commune, children didn't smile or dance like this.

We had music in the commune, but it was very different. Music was a way to show respect for God, slow, monotonous, and proper. In other words, boring. But here, when I heard Marcia's voice accompanied by Davon's guitar for the first time, I felt like I once had during Father's sermons. Holy. Truly closer to God. Music was meant to be played this way. And when given permission to dance freely, it was like a whole new part of the universe had opened up.

Eli's shadow hovered over me. I looked up, meeting his dark eyes, which glimmered with a smile. His brows knitted together in a slight furrow, the line on his forehead deepening as he studied me. I knew that look. It was the same as this morning. He felt conflicted. Worried. Something was up.

"Enjoying yourself out there?" he asked, jutting his chin forward to where Neil had scooped Mia up in his arms. She threw her head back and giggled as they jostled to the melody.

I smiled. "I bet Neil would take you for a spin if you asked nicely."

He laughed. "Not sure I'm limber enough for that." He took an awkward step toward me before sitting down on the loveseat I occupied.

"Oh now," I joked, "you're not *that* old."

"Not old. Just uncoordinated. I'd be the laughingstock of the Centre!"

"Wait, wait, I thought we weren't supposed to care what people thought about us." I cocked an eyebrow playfully.

He laughed. "Using my own words against me?"

"Me?" I placed a hand against my chest in mock astonishment. "Never."

I glanced out at the crowd of dancers, relishing in their delight. There was nothing quite like watching others dance. Jae spun Kendra beneath his arm, the two a joyous pair. They kicked up their feet as if they were in the clouds, weightless and carefree. On the dance floor, they might've been half their age. Full of life and happiness we rarely saw day-to-day. Jae dipped his wife over his arm, and Kendra laughed, joy radiating through her wrinkled features as she stared up at her husband. He pulled her up and brought her in for a kiss.

"They're a beautiful pair," I said.

"Hm?"

"Jae and Kendra."

Eli lifted his eyes to find them and I watched as his cheeks rose in delight before he brought his gaze back to me. "I'm glad. Especially because he's leaving tomorrow."

I straightened. "On the scavenging team?"

Eli nodded. "He volunteered. Actually, I—"

"Picture?"

I looked up. Nadia held up a small plastic box.

"Whoa, is that a Polaroid camera?" Eli asked, breaking into a grin. "I'm not sure I've ever seen one."

Nadia nodded before lifting it to her eye. "Smile!" She tapped on the circular area. "Right here."

Eli slipped his arm around me and I leaned into him, my cheeks rising into a grin as I stared into Nadia's contraption. It had been a long time since we'd been this close. He felt familiar. Safe. A bright light flashed, and I blinked away stars.

Eli squeezed me with his arm, grip tight on my shoulder, before he released me and shifted away without meeting my gaze. Which was probably a good thing. I felt a flush creep up my neck. Nadia pulled something from the Polaroid, shook it out, then handed it to Eli. "Give it a few minutes," she said. "And don't touch it!"

She drifted away, weaving through the crowd with the strap of the camera around her neck. She raised it to Neil and Mia and they froze, mid-dance, to smile. I looked down at the cloudy square in Eli's grip, squinting. "There's nothing there," I said.

"There will be. Give it a minute or two." He handed it to me. "You should keep it."

"Yeah?" The blue began to fade, revealing two shadowy figures. I liked the idea of having a photograph of us. It was another thing to hang on my wall beside Mia's drawings.

To personalize my space. Proof there was more to me than my surname.

"So about Jae. And the volunteering."

Eli's tone changed so suddenly I thought I'd missed something. I narrowed my eyes, trying to study his gaze, but he shifted it away, focused instead on the dancers in the distance. Lantern light reflected in his irises. His jaw tightened. A shadow grew on his chin and cheeks and for a moment, I glimpsed the man who had rescued me from the creek. "I'm leaving," he said, his voice almost inaudible over the music. "Tomorrow."

"What?"

"I'm leaving tomorrow," he repeated.

"Tomorrow?" My heart dropped into my stomach. I ran my thumb across the corner of the photograph, letting the sharp edge dig into my skin. "To look for the scavenging team," I whispered, putting the pieces together. "With Sid and Jae." I held him in my gaze. "Aren't you?"

"Maura—"

"Tomorrow?" I asked again. Disbelief muffled the music, dampening the exhilaration I'd gathered since I'd arrived. Dinner turned in my stomach and I felt my nostrils flare. Eli was leaving to go after the Hunters. The men who had hurt Dale and kidnapped the others. Just when we'd found safety, he wanted to run out into danger again.

"Tomorrow," he confirmed. "Darius is leading the team. Sid volunteered last night, and I didn't know what to do. The thought of losing him again…I don't know, it terrified me. I don't trust anyone to protect him like I can."

And who's going to protect you?

"And Avi's okay with Sid going?" It was like speaking on auto-pilot. My gaze shifted as I dissociated from Eli. "With his ear?"

"He is."

"And you're leaving tomorrow?" I asked again. "What time?"

"In the morning." He hung his head and ran a hand through his messy hair, before pressing both palms against his face. "I'm sorry I'm just telling you now. I just—" He opened his mouth as if he had more to say, then closed it again.

"For how long?" My voice pitched higher, and I shook my head in disbelief. "Do you know? I mean, what's your plan?" A bubble of hysteria seemed to push its way up my throat. "Are you sure you're ready for this?

He turned his head and met my eyes. His hand crept up my forearm, gripping it firmly. My stomach jumped a mile. I wanted to cling to him, to hold him near, to tell him not to go. But there were unspoken rules between us. He was the savior, and I was the saved. I had no right to tell him not to leave, not to use his skills and strength for good. It was selfish to want him to stay here — for what? Me? To walk me to the bathrooms in the morning?

"I'm ready. I know how to do this. We've been doing it for a long time now. Sid and I are a good team. We'll be safe and take our time, but I'm not sure how long it'll take," he said. "I'd say at most, a week. It'll depend on what we find."

I nodded. "Into the commune?" I kept my voice as low as I could over the music's hum, but it dripped with desperation. Eli and Sid crossing commune borders was suicide. The Hunters might know what they looked like. If they caught them there, they wouldn't return.

"No," he said, meeting my eyes. "Darius said we're going to one of the prisons on the outskirts. Less dangerous, much closer. We'll scope things out, see what kind of guards they have, reassess our plan, and try a rescue. *If* the prisoners are even there." His lips curved into a gentle smile. "Chances are they're not."

The knot in my chest loosened slightly. I looked down at my knees, though I could feel his gaze still on me, trailing over my cheeks, trying to read my expression.

"Why *didn't* you tell me earlier?" I asked, annoyed by my frustration. But I couldn't help its presence. It latched onto the fear I already held, the annoyance I'd encountered the other day when everyone knew what had happened to Dale and waited to tell me. Poor, sensitive, Maura. And now again, I was surely the last to know. I knew something was off this morning and he brushed me off. Why?

"I didn't want to…upset you."

"Upset me?" My voice grew louder and I could see the conflict in his features. But the ball had started rolling, and I wasn't sure I could stop it. "Everyone always hides things from me. I'm always the last to know everything. Here, in the commune, it doesn't matter." Tears welled in my eyes. "I'm not weak, you know. After everything I've been through, you of all people should know I can handle things." But shame unfurled in my stomach as I spoke, because my emotional outburst was proving otherwise.

The music changed, something a little slower and softer. Marcia invited people out to a slow dance.

"Maura." Eli's voice was soft. He tilted his head toward me. "I'm sorry. Please don't be angry." I turned to face him, drinking in his wide brown eyes, pleading with understanding. He pressed his lips together. "I didn't mean to upset you. It's not that I didn't think you could handle it—"

"Then what is it?

"I—" He shook his head. Words did not come. "I didn't want to hurt you," he finally said.

But he had. Tears leaked down my cheeks and I hastily wiped them from my skin. "I know," I said, inhaling a shaky breath. "But you did." I tightened my hands into fists and stood from the seat.

"Maura, come on." He got to his feet. I felt his presence behind me, but I didn't want his comfort. He'd made a choice. He decided, yet again, what was best for me. After everything we'd been through. After telling me I should demand respect for myself. He was still treating me like a child, unable to handle reality.

I turned away and weaved through the crowd, bumping shoulders with someone before I took off down the walkway toward our room at a hurried pace. The noise from the party faded, but I still heard his footsteps behind me.

"Maura!" he called.

I stopped, crossing my arms, squeezing my eyes closed as I forced the rest of the tears away. I felt him behind me. His shadow drifted across the wall, then paused. I saw him reach his arm out, then pull it back.

"Maura, I'm sorry." I listened to him breathe beside me, waiting for me to respond. But what was there to say?

"Please come back," I finally said, looking at him over my shoulder. "I will never, ever, forgive you if you don't come back."

I left without hearing his response, barreling beneath the gate and into my room with its flimsy walls. Part of me wished he would follow, but the reasonable part of me knew it was better he didn't. There was nothing left to say.

I settled on my bed, still holding the photograph Nadia had taken of us. The blue film had disappeared, revealing the two of us sitting beside each other in perfect clarity, a white canopy in the background. A moment captured in time. Eli's forehead tilted toward me, his handsome face drawn up with a wide smile that rivaled mine. We looked so happy, so complementary. It prompted a fresh wave of tears.

I held onto that picture as I fell into an exhausted sleep that night. If I had known what was coming, I would've done anything to live in that moment forever.

9

———

ELI

We left the Centre in the early morning hours when the only other people awake were the security team's skeleton crew. Winter was an ideal time for this kind of venture. More hours of darkness meant we had a longer travel window. Once we made it to the safe house, we'd store our vehicle, rest, and get ready to move forward on foot when the sun went down again.

I had barely slept. Between arguing with Maura and the looming anxiety of the trip, I had only caught a few hours at most before Sid shook me awake. Now, I sat in the backseat of a black Jeep beside Jae, who snored lightly against the window, his breath fogging up the glass.

In the dark, everything looked eerie. I was no stranger to deserted settings, but the tightly packed buildings surrounding the mall filled me with dread. Anyone could hide in those shadows, crouching behind broken windows, waiting for us. It seemed even more likely after the scavenging team's kidnapping. The Hunters had some idea of where we might be.

I tried not to think how they could take us down. Pop

our tires with a spike strip. Land mines. Grenades. Shooting out our windows. But as the trip continued on and the city fell away, making room for large stretches of empty land, there seemed to be no immediate threat.

Dawn came more quickly than any of us liked, brightening the edges of the sky as the sun began its ascension. The appearing light made me sit straighter in my seat, hand absentmindedly brushing against the Glock's textured handle that sat in the holster on my hip.

We emerged from a tree-lined road, entering a stretch of unobscured land with side streets that led to clusters of looted, detached homes. Coutts Peak rose in the distance, a deadly but majestic backdrop. We were far from it, and under the cover of darkness, but I still hated how close it felt.

When I was a child, I remember remarking how beautiful the landscape was — how large and magnificent that mountain looked. Mom had glanced down at me, her face dark, struggling to explain to a young child that not everything was what it seemed. Now, of course, I understood. But as a young boy, I could not understand how something so bad, so evil and terrible, could also be so breathtakingly beautiful.

Darius drove the weathered Jeep down the road, turning right onto a new street. Dead, empty cars lined the trash-cluttered pavement, with a wide crack nearly splitting it in half. These weren't homes of my time. They were homes built before the Coutts claimed their power, neglected and left to rot in the elements. These kinds of multi-level structures had dotted the entire United States, left as carcasses when the economy tanked and no one could afford them anymore. The government had opted for people to remain homeless and to keep homes like these on the market for corporations to gobble up. For what, I was never sure. They'd sat here, empty, since the early part of the millennia.

Tall grass in the front yards had withered, slumped in defeat as the cold air sucked away their life. Vines, mildew, and moss crept up old, cracked siding, like spindly webs. Most of the homes had broken windows, no doubt looted over the years. The neighborhood was picked clean; a perfect place for a safe house. Still, my anxiety loomed.

"It's definitely safe here?" I asked, knowing the question was stupid. Darius wouldn't have set foot here if he thought we were in danger.

"Yes. We've used this place for scavenging for the past few months now. We change streets every few weeks."

"There are extra supplies in some of the basements in case we need them for an emergency," Sid said. Jae straightened in the seat beside me and I studied his aging face. The bags beneath his eyes drooped, puffy from lack of sleep. He seemed even thinner with his heavy coat. I wondered if we should've taken someone younger. But I had thought that of Holli once, and she'd proved me wrong time and time again.

"How far are we walking?" I asked, peeling my gaze away from my co-worker.

"Just about ten miles," Darius answered. "If all goes well, we should be able to make it there in under four hours."

Ten miles. My back ached just thinking about it. I tried not to glance over at Jae, but I couldn't help but wonder how well he would fare. It would be twenty miles when all was said and done. I wasn't convinced he was up for the trip, and we certainly didn't need anyone slowing us down. But again, Avi, Darius, and Sid knew better than I. If they'd had concerns, they would've voiced them by now.

"What if the team is injured?" I asked. "We can't carry them back."

Darius sighed. "Don't get ahead of yourself. We first need to make sure they're there. We'll assess the situation and figure out our plan from there. But we can't take the truck that far into Coutts' territory. They'll see us. So, we'll do our best. Sometimes not everyone makes it."

It was a heavy statement, but a truthful one. I appreciated that about Darius. To the untrained eye, he seemed like a heartless monster. But really, he was a soldier. When it came down to it, he'd make the tough decisions. Whether or not I liked him as a person, he was someone I wanted on my team.

He guided the Jeep into an empty driveway and parked before turning to the three of us. "On alert, gentlemen," he said, pulling his Glock into his grip. Jae, Sid, and I mimicked his movements.

Cold air bit into me as we opened the doors and left the car's warmth. I peered at our surroundings, inspecting the grass, the windows, and the road. Orange washed the edges of the sky, bringing daylight along with it. My heart thudded loudly in my chest.

"On me," said Sid, pressing his back up to mine. We circled the Jeep on alert for any movement or anything out of place while Darius and Jae worked on the garage. With a loud squeal, the two men lifted the door on broken hinges, revealing a dark, empty space. Sid and I stayed on watch at the end of the driveway while Jae held the door up and Darius pulled the car inside the garage. Once he cut the engine, we retreated inside to a set of wooden stairs and an open door that led to the rest of the house. Jae pulled the garage door shut and joined us.

We entered the house together, our muffled footsteps the only sound against the dusty hardwood floor. A narrow hallway led to what was once, I was sure, a beautiful kitchen. But the place had been heavily looted. The rear glass sliding door laid on the dilapidated back porch, allowing cold air to drift through the space. The cabinets were ripped from their hinges, all the unused contents pulled out and discarded across the floor. Tiles had been pulled up in areas. A broken light dangled from the ceiling at the far end of the room. Wallpaper hung in tattered pieces.

"What the hell happened here?" I asked.

Darius threw his backpack on the center island before walking toward the back door, boots crunching over shattered glass. "We scavenged it," he said, without elaborating.

"It looks like looters did this."

"That was purposeful," Darius answered. "Leaving it in good condition would compromise the whole idea of a safe house. Plus, we took a lot of the hardware back for the community. We could use pretty much everything in here. Tile for Mick's practice. Cabinets for storage. Wood for furniture." He glanced around at the light, which he pushed so it swung back and forth. "Pretty sure we even got a table and chairs outta here for someone." He shrugged. "It's not doing any good sitting out here. Might as well put it to use."

I nodded, hating the idea. I knew it was practical. But it made me think of the fate of Mom's house — of *my* house. What if someone did this to our little trailer? Our home? I clenched my fists at the thought.

"There's a rug on the floor in the other room," Darius said, pointing to an archway at the far wall. "It's mostly eaten up by moths, but better than nothing. If you can sleep, I'd suggest it. I'll take first watch."

After a quick meal of canned green beans, we packed up in the sunset's pink glow, dividing ammo evenly among ourselves. Rest had done me good. I saw the path ahead of us. I was ready. Alert. Energized to finish what we'd come out here to do. Darius spread the map out on the center island and went over the plan again.

"Eight miles through trees," he said, dragging his long finger across the map through a green patch. He paused at a gray line. "This is where the town begins," he said. "We pause here, before the road, scope out what we can." He moved his finger around a cluster of streets until he hit a thick line of red Sharpie he'd drawn before we left. "We'll move along the outskirts. Red line is the border Maura and Leo identified. The prison," — he tapped three times on a block sitting between the red line and the trees — "is here."

My heartbeat sped up. We wouldn't be officially in Coutts territory, but we'd be close enough. We needed to move carefully. Take in every detail. We'd be no good to the prisoners if we were shot dead first. My anxiety was making me feel sick.

"We'll assess the situation. Security, prisoner sightings, the amount of Hunters we're dealing with," Darius continued. "If we see the prisoners, the mission is a go-ahead. If we don't, we return here. If it's a go-ahead and we're safe in the trees, we'll decide if our distraction is enough," — he patted his backpack where he kept three grenades — "for a rescue. That's our simplest path forward. If we need reinforcements, we'll come back here, and get back to the Centre with a new plan." He scooped up the map and rolled it up, tucking it into his back pocket.

"If we get separated, we come back here," he said, meeting each of our gazes. "We give the rest of the team twelve hours to return. If they haven't returned by then, whoever is here returns to the Centre for reinforcements, if necessary."

If we're not all dead.

"Everyone got it?"

The three of us nodded, but I saw Jae's jaw tighten and Sid roll his neck. Nerves were normal. Essential to survival, really. The plan was simple. Pulling it off would be trickier.

With one last check we had left nothing behind, we pulled on our bulletproof vests and set out through the broken back door, across a rotting deck, past a graffitied in-ground pool, and into the woods.

The setting sun cast a reddish glow through the thick, tall pines. Orange-yellow rays lit the pine-needled ground, illuminating our shadows against nature's backdrop. Adrenaline masked the cold, though the tip of my nose went numb. I focused only on the sounds of our feet, the crunch of dead leaves beneath our boots. This felt good. Familiar.

Eventually, the sun sunk below the horizon, drenching us in darkness. Darius used a dark fabric to cover his flashlight, allowing us enough illumination to avoid any obstructions in our path. Hours passed. My calves and feet began to burn. We took a water break, then continued on again.

As the trees thinned, I saw the sliver of a crescent moon in the dark sky. The night was cloudless. But that wasn't all. Lights glimmered in the distance. Jae put out an arm to stop us in our tracks. My breath caught in my throat.

"There it is." Darius's whisper fogged in the cold air. He clicked off the flashlight. "On me," he said. "Stay quiet."

"Following you, boss," Sid whispered.

Darius crouched, and we all followed — Jae, Sid, then

me. We reached the tree line quickly, pausing as the town came into view.

It was larger than I thought it would be, larger than it looked on the map at least. We stood on an elevation overlooking the area, dotted with multi-level buildings made from brick and stone. But even in the dark I saw missing windows and boarded up doors — the telltale signs of decay. Behind, the lights we had seen through the trees shone brightly.

We moved sideways, following the trail Darius had traced with his finger on the map. Around the west side, small homes came into view, clustered together in narrow rows. The building with lights became clearer as we walked. High, barbed wire fences ran at least a mile through the center of town. A stone building was situated in the middle. The prison.

Lights shone across the property, making the grounds visible without binoculars. Tall, dead grass covered most of the area, with a few gravel walking paths and small structures dotted throughout. Something moved. A shadow appeared in the light.

"Come on," Darius whispered, pausing. I watched his breath dissipate in the dark air as he waved us past him. The terrain dipped. My calves strained as we began moving downhill, closer to the town.

Halfway down the new hill, the prison lights shifted. I looked up, chest tight. Jae, still crouched, continued to move forward.

And then he exploded.

10

ELI

THE WORLD ERUPTED in a cloud of smoke, the blast muffling my hearing. I stumbled, struggling to find my footing against the broken earth, blind in the dark. Guttural screams carried in the cold air, and I squinted, trying to make sense of what was in front of me. Sid remained beside me, the whites of his wide eyes the only thing visible in the dark. Darius rose to full height, taking slow steps backward until he crashed into Sid.

Ahead of us, Jae lay on the ground, bellowing anguished, pained cries. His bald head tilted toward us, reflecting the light sweeping across the terrain as it looked for the source of the blast. His legs were gone, flesh, muscle, and bone scattered in the grass and trees. Blood spilled from his wounds, pooling around what was left of his jeans. He wouldn't stop screaming. Darius looked at me and Sid, then back at Jae.

"Get him up!" I yelled, voice muted by the ringing in my ears. "Hurry up!"

I darted forward, caught by the hand gripping my

bicep. Sid clung to me with one outstretched arm, solemn-faced.

"Do it," Sid said, his gaze focused on Darius behind me.

I turned. Time slowed. The light moved again. Darius pulled the Glock from his holster, aimed it at the back of Jae's head, and shot.

The man's head split into a sea of red, splattering my forearm with warm brain matter. I wanted to scream, but every single muscle in my body felt frozen. Light splashed across us. I squinted, struggling to see in the brightness. Darius yelled something, his lips moving in slow motion. I might've been underwater.

"What did you do?" I heard myself ask.

But Darius was preoccupied with something else.

"RUN!"

I glanced at Jae lying in the dirt.

He's dead.

Sid's nails dug into my forearm. My limbs woke up. With my brain sparked, I ran after Sid and Darius into the trees. A loud crack in the distance and a *swoosh* beside me fully brought me out of the fog and into the present moment.

Shit.

Bullets littered the air, ricocheting off tree trunks and the dirt around our feet. The sudden shift from bright to dark made it impossible to see.

"Zig-zag!" Darius roared from somewhere up ahead.

I ran blindly, turning every so often, trying to feel for obstacles with the tips of my boots. It was useless. I crashed into the trunk of a thick tree that came out of nowhere, sending a searing pain up my right shoulder. The bullets had stopped, but that didn't mean we were out of harm's way. They'd seen us. Hunters would be on our heels in a matter of minutes. And they had night vision.

Darkness blinked out the shapes of my companions and I tripped over a large root, sending my sore body sprawling in the dirt. I coughed, unable to catch my breath. Adrenaline allowed me to push up on my palms and scramble to my feet. I kept running. Shadows disoriented me. The landscape shifted. I couldn't get a good grip on the pine-needled floor. Fear pummeled every part of me. I had no idea how to get back to the safe house if I lost Darius or Sid.

Where were they?

Nothing but darkness lay ahead of me. Shouts rang in the distance. I continued running forward. Or at least what I thought was forward. Had I gotten turned around? Was I running back to the prison? Directly toward the shooting men? Panic engulfed me. Footsteps pounded the ground somewhere to my right. Dim moonlight came through the trees and I glimpsed a tall shadow.

"Sid?" I croaked.

"E!" He reached his hand out to me. "This way!"

Fire filled my lungs. I couldn't steady my heart, but I ran after my brother, anyway. We raced up and over a small hill where I was forced to slow and suck in deep breaths. My chest was going to burst. No matter how high my adrenaline was, my body was giving out. I was in shock. I was exhausted. Distraught. Terrified.

There was no sign of Darius. More shouts echoed behind us. We took off again. The ground remained level and the tree cover thinned, giving us more moonlight to see. Another yell, closer this time. Had they caught Darius? And Jae. Oh my god, Jae. His screams rang in my ears.

We approached an embankment. Below, a shallow brook split the raised earth across from us. The drop was only a few feet down, but were we even on the right track?

Sid got to the ground, sliding his body down the side of

the embankment. I followed him down the moss-covered slope, slipping over rocks and extruding tree roots. We landed in the shallow water. Sid pressed a finger to his lips and moved to the side, away from the water, before waving me along.

The silence was eerie. Stark. Unsettling. At the bottom of the embankment, my senses were muted. There was no moonlight. We kept moving forward, hands up against the dirt that rose on our right side. I tried not to think about what easy targets we would be here.

Like shooting fish in a barrel.

Shouts rang out above our heads. Sid looked at me over his shoulder and though I couldn't see his features, I knew he was panicked. We needed to hide. And fast.

The carved sides of the earth were alarmingly flat and as we ran, I found no divots, enclaves, or debris to hide behind. We would need to get up and over the other side of the cliff in order to get to safety.

Sid seemed to realize this too and raised his hands to feel for a way out. Minutes passed. Finally, we crossed an area where tree roots emerged from the embankment's edge, weaving in and out of black dirt. Sid and I grabbed hold of them and began to climb. My brother scaled the side quickly, but I slipped, catching my breath in my chest. I regained my composure, watching as Sid's feet disappeared over the edge of the cliff. I had one more pull — the last branch — and I could heave myself up and after him.

The root was loose. It pulled free from the side and me along with it, sending me plummeting down to the hard earth below. I landed painfully on my back in the shallow water, frigid on my neck. White spots appeared in my vision and I tried desperately to blink them away. I lay still for a moment, assessing my body. Everything felt okay. My limbs worked. My head hurt, but it wasn't swimming. Slowly, I got to my knees.

"Sid?" I whispered into the night.

Pain registered before the shadow in front of me. Something solid connected with my cheekbone, the power sending me sprawling backward again. I felt a tooth crack and my cheek burn, the pain searing up the nerves in my mouth into my head, so agonizing I was sure it would split. Someone moaned. It took me a moment to realize it was me.

"Got you," said a bitter voice.

In the moonlight, I barely made out the green-helmeted figure who leaned over me, his assault rifle clutched in one gloved hand. He poked my chest with it. "Thought you could run," he taunted. He lifted his foot and pressed it to my neck. I smelled rubber and blood, tasted it in my mouth. The heel of his shoe dug into my airway, choking me, crushing my windpipe. I felt my eyes bulge.

My gun.

Desperate, I flexed my fingers, twisting my shoulder to try to reach the holster on my hip. Hunter suits were bulletproof, but I could damage his hands so he couldn't shoot. Pop him in the foot so he couldn't run. I could get him in the neck so he would bleed out. But those were slim chances. I tried to gasp. Couldn't. My lungs strained for air.

Couldn't breathe. Couldn't swallow. Blood dripped down the back of my throat. I choked. Fluid bubbled in my nose. My fingertips brushed the gun's rear sight. I strained. Grasped the frame. Pulled it into my hands. Fumbled. The world spun.

"Oh no you don't." The Hunter cackled as he used his free foot to kick the gun out of my loose grip. It made a *thwack* noise as it landed nearby in the mud.

Darkness crept into the edges of my vision, dimming the green suit, blinking away the stars in the sky. I clawed at the man's shoe, at the tight fabric cinched around his ankle, at his sock. But my body tingled and finally grew numb. My consciousness swam. My tongue felt at least four times its size. The man's cruel laughter lifted in the wind. Would that be the last sound I heard? My last moments, doomed to a vicious, nameless Hunter?

A thud came. The pressure on my neck released. I sucked in a hoarse breath through my bruised airway. Someone yelled. The rifle went off, successive hot blasts too close to my ear. A deep, hot pain seared up my leg, into my hip, side, and belly. I screamed, spittle and blood covering my face. Nausea rolled in my stomach.

I turned. The automatic lay forgotten in the mud. I should get to it. Pick it up, keep it in my hands so no one else could. But I could barely get a good breath between the pain. In the distance, two shadows wrestled for something glinting in the moonlight. Sid. And the Hunter.

I gritted my teeth against the unbearable pain in my leg, wincing with every movement as I struggled to lift myself on my elbows. I couldn't do it. I fell back onto the wet earth, panting. The embankment's side rose up like a mountain. A peak. It would be impossible to scale.

My heart raced. There was a terrible heat beneath my leg. Warmth pooled there, my jeans soaking it up like a sponge. Every movement was excruciating, threatening a loss of consciousness. The pain came in waves, like a heartbeat that wouldn't quit, radiating white-hot agony through every nerve ending in my body. But that warmth was worrying. A wound. Holli would tell me I needed a tourniquet.

Before I could attempt to sit up again, I heard a gasp and a gurgle, the unmistakable sound of someone choking.

Sid sat on top of the green uniformed man's chest, one hand yanking up his helmet, the other pin straight, gripped tight around the handle of his knife. The helmet came off, landing beside the gun. The man inside the uniform sported a receding hairline, and an aged, sun-spotted face. His mouth hung open, gloved hands clutching at his neck. With a guttural moan, my brother drove the knife deeper into the man's thin flesh, chopping away at his bloody, exposed trachea and drenching the man in his own blood.

Sid growled, a deep rumble from his belly as fury flashed in his eyes. He pulled the weapon from the man's neck. The dying man spluttered, reaching an arm out in one last-ditch attempt to swipe at the knife before his body went limp and fell to the ground.

Sid's chest heaved. Tears flooded his eyes as he met my gaze, relief softening his shoulders. He got to his feet, wiping the bloody pocketknife on his pants before he tucked it away. He fell to his knees in front of me and I smelled his sweat and the blood on his hands. His gaze traveled down my leg.

"*Eli*," he breathed.

I twisted my shoulders toward him. Pain blinded me. I released an anguished moan.

"Here." Sid shrugged off his backpack and coat, then removed his shirt. He ripped the seams, then pulled it taut before he reached out to touch my leg.

"DON'T."

"I've gotta tie it, E." He locked eyes with me. "I've gotta."

I knew he did, but I didn't want him to. At his touch, I fell back against the mud in sheer agony, my teeth biting through my lower lip as I tried not to scream. My head was going to split open. I rolled my head in the mud, fingers digging into the wet earth as Sid tied the fabric tourniquet around my injured limb. Every single nerve in my body was on fire. I would welcome death if it put an end to this pain.

"Almost done," he soothed.

"Go," I cried. "Please. They'll find us. I can't move. I'll slow you down, and then they'll find us and kill us both. Please, Sid."

"Like hell. Get up," he said, tugging the shirt tight around my leg. Everything went numb.

"Sid!" I sobbed.

"GET UP." Sid's voice broke, his panic palpable. He was desperate, and I knew it. Because I had been desperate before, too. Desperate to be out here with him. To save him.

My brother took his backpack off, then wrapped his arms around me and lifted me out of the mud, propping me up against the embankment's side. The pain was exquisite, pops of color appearing in my vision. "Stand on your good leg," he ordered. "And take off your backpack."

I handed over my pack and watched as he took my supplies and dumped them into his bag, which he put on across his chest.

"Sid," I said, trying to catch his gaze. "It's ten miles back to the car. I can't walk." I grit my teeth through the searing pain. "I can barely stand up."

"Shut up," he said. "We're going to get out of the embankment and find a place for you to hide. I'll find Darius, and then we'll come back for you."

"Sid."

"Shut the fuck up, Eli, and work with me!"

Sid turned his back to me and squatted, instructing me to wrap my arms around his neck and lay my belly flat against his back. Then, he lifted me and began to walk. Debilitating pain came with every bump, every slight movement. My consciousness was barely hanging on.

We moved slowly. The embankment had no end in sight and so Sid walked onward, grunting beneath my weight. Every movement, each branch crack, made me panic. My leg ached with excruciating pain. There was no way Sid could keep this pace for too long. And where were the other Hunters?

"There," he whispered as he carried me forward. "There's a dip."

A few more strides forward, and he paused, straightening so that I could put pressure on my good leg. I leaned up against the side of the embankment, lower here, but not quite low enough. The earth came up to my chest.

"Lean against the dirt," he told me before scaling the side. I pressed my back up against the embankment's lip. Sid leaned forward, his chin on my shoulder, then wrapped his arms beneath mine. And then he pulled.

My bad leg trailed against the earth. The world spun. I screamed. And everything went black.

11

ELI

WET EARTH HUNG in my nostrils. I blinked back the dark, eyes adjusting to a dim light and sharp pain that radiated from my thigh into my lower back. My swollen throat throbbed. My muscles were tight. I ran my tongue over my dry lips, wincing at the sudden pain. Upon closer inspection with my fingers, I felt teeth marks on the skin below my bottom lip.

My surroundings came to me in pieces. It was cold. My whole body shivered unwillingly. Everything smelled like old sewage and sawdust. I laid on some kind of bench, my upper body propped up. My jacket lay across my belly. I groaned as I reached my hand up to touch the wall, made from soft wood. Turning my neck hurt. I expected a little bit of space, but the other wall greeted my hand surprisingly fast. Was I in a closet? I couldn't even stretch one arm fully out.

My foot rested on a small wooden box, illuminated by small sun rays shining through the broken ceiling slats. My pant leg had been cut open, a makeshift fabric bandage wrapped around where I knew a bullet was still lodged in my thigh. Even looking at it hurt. More light came through cracks in the wood, drawing my eye to a door with an unlocked latch.

My heart began to pound.

Sid.

I reached for the door handle, but even that slight movement threatened to knock me out cold again. I hissed through my teeth. I'd have given anything for one of Holli's pain remedies. A local anesthetic. Hell, even an expired Advil.

I took a few deep breaths as nausea toyed with bringing up whatever remained in my stomach. By the way hunger pains rolled around in my belly, it wasn't much. I could yell for Sid, but I didn't know where I was. For all I knew, I was still in Hunter territory. Which led me to an even more troubling thought. What if they'd captured him? What if days had passed, and I'd been sitting in this closet none the wiser? My adrenaline came back to life.

I looked around the enclosure, hands skimming the walls for some sign that Sid was okay. A note? Some of his belongings? Nothing but splinters met my skin, a slight annoyance compared to the horrendous pain in my leg.

The bandage was a good sign. It meant Sid had enough time to bandage my wound and set it properly. Somehow, he'd moved me from where I'd blacked out. Found shelter. Stuck me in here. He *must've* found Darius. But the silence still troubled me.

I leaned forward again, gritting my teeth against the pain, fingers fumbling for the crack in the door. With a groan, I pushed against it and the door creaked open on a pair of ancient hinges.

Sunlight blinded me momentarily, and I raised my arm to shield my eyes, allowing them to water before adjusting. The light gave me a better look at where I currently sat.

The rotting wooden structure was succumbing to the harsh forest elements around it. Rusty nails stuck out where the boards had come apart. Moss grew between cracks and a few moldy spots sagged where the ceiling met the wall. Beneath me, a wooden plank covered a crude hole.

So that's where I was. An outhouse. If I wasn't in so much pain, I might've laughed.

As I adjusted to the new light, the world came into sharper focus. Leaves lay scattered across patchy grass, charred trees visible in the distance. Between the trees stood a brick chimney, the only remaining feature of an otherwise blackened structure. Greenery had grown and then died up its sides, Mother Nature slowly claiming it as her own. A breeze lifted the leaves, swirling them in a delicate dance until they settled somewhere new.

"Sid?" My hoarse voice came out in a whisper.

Tears leaked from my eyes at the unbearable pain down my neck. I reached up to touch my skin, wincing as my fingers made contact. Bruised to all hell. I tried clearing my throat, but regretted it instantly. My windpipe was on fire. I needed water — something to ease the ache and dryness.

Restless panic settled in my legs and I felt the urge to try to stand, despite my injury. Being disoriented in a new place was one thing, but not knowing where my brother was or how long I'd been out terrified me. My stomach was sick with hunger, but I was more worried about water.

I braced myself against the walls, using what little strength I had left in my shoulders to lift myself from the bench. The wood disappeared beneath me and, emboldened by that success, I turned. Sharp, excruciating pain slapped me back to reality and with a grunt, I released myself, my tailbone hitting the wood at a weird angle. I grunted, frustrated, slamming my fist into the wall.

"Fuck."

C'mon. Try again.

I gritted my teeth and lifted myself from the bench again. But I was weak. I knew I'd lost blood and my body was injured in several places. As I tried holding my weight on the walls, my biceps shook from exertion. Unable to hold myself, I fell back onto the bench with a pathetic, pained cry.

What the hell was I going to do? Blood trickled out from one of my fingers. I leaned back against the wall, tears stinging the edges of my eyes, wondering if I'd die in a fucking outhouse. I had felt so foolishly heroic at the start of this journey. So confident. And now, not only was I possibly on a fast track to an early death, but I'd lost my brother and Jae was dead.

Leaves shuffled in the distance. The silence made the disturbance clear. A set of footsteps approaching. The open door was too far to reach while sitting. At this point, was it even worth it to try to close it? I was a sitting duck without a weapon.

Was it a Hunter? Sid? Someone else? No matter how I looked at it, if they were a threat, I was done for. Something bumped up against the wood. I braced myself against the wall, ready to fight. A hand rested on the door frame, followed by heavy breathing. Dark skin beneath a long-sleeved shirt. Long fingers, trimmed fingernails.

"Eli?" I saw my brother's telltale dreads and my arms fell slack. Sid's face came into view, his smile brightening his features. "You're up."

"Sid," I breathed, my voice so gruff it was almost intelligible. "What the—"

"Sorry, sorry. Didn't mean to scare you. Wasn't sure how long you'd be out. How're you feeling?"

"Like shit."

"I can imagine."

I lifted my hand, gesturing to my surroundings as if to say *what the hell is this?*

Sid sighed before lowering himself to the ground, sitting awkwardly in the doorway. "Sorry about the shitter," he said, not sounding sorry at all. "It was the only thing that still had a roof." He inhaled. "Doesn't smell too bad, except for your sorry ass."

"Please don't make me kill you."

"Me?" He flashed me a look of humored shock. "Save your life and this is the thanks I get?"

I gave him the finger, but his humor reassured me. We must be out of harm's way. Whatever that meant.

"I found Darius," he confirmed. "I got your heavy ass up and over the embankment, hid you in some dead brush, and then came back for you. We managed to carry you maybe a quarter of a mile before it became impossible with his dislocated shoulder. We used one of the sleeping mats and..." He gave me a guilty smile. "...dragged you through the woods."

I rolled my eyes.

"Things went quick after that. We're sitting about a mile out from the safe house. Darius is getting the Jeep."

"And the Hunters?"

Sid brought his knees to his chest and hugged them as he looked away. "We took care of them. There were only three more and one of them was drunk. Darius thinks it was a setup. They knew we'd be looking for prisons. He thinks that if the scavenging team was here, the place would be crawling with Hunters. But I don't know." He shook his head. "Either way, someone'll be looking for them *and us* soon."

"You should've gone with Darius!" My raspy voice did a

poor job of displaying my urgency. "What the hell are you doing sitting out here like this?"

Sid met my gaze. "I'm protecting my brother."

"No." I shook my head. "No way."

"Well, there's nothing we can do about it now. Darius will be back soon, and we'll get back to Mick so he can get that bullet out of your leg."

My limb ached at the thought of it. I rested my head against the wall. "I came out here to protect *you*. Not the other way around."

"Nope. You know that's not the deal. We protect each other. I know what I signed up for. Besides, Mom would rise from the dead and kill me if I left you."

I tilted my head. "Yeah. You're not wrong."

"Hey, about…Jae." Sid ran his hand over his mouth. "I'm sorry. I know you were…somewhat close."

My heart dropped into my stomach. For a moment, I'd forgotten what had happened to my work companion. I'd buried my shock beneath the pain in my leg. Poor, unsuspecting Jae. Who had single-handedly built our inventory system. Who had taught me how to can and preserve things, to dry meat, to create tallow candles. Could he be curmudgeonly sometimes? Sure. Endearingly so. Grief hovered, but I wasn't ready to sit in it yet.

"Land mines are new," I said.

"Concerning, to say the least," Sid agreed. "That's why Darius thought it was a setup. They can't put land mines all around their perimeter since it's so big and they're constantly moving outward. So they suspected something. Which I guess isn't a surprise. We probably did exactly what they wanted us to do. And we can't even warn the other groups until we return to the Centre."

"Isn't that something we should've thought of? At least Avi? Or Darius?"

"It was discussed," Sid answered. "But we also thought the border was farther in. We were miles out from where the commune was. I think Darius thought we'd have time to inspect further in the daylight."

"Yeah," I said, trying not to think of the way Jae screamed in the aftermath.

"It's no one's fault," Sid said. "Jae knew what he was signing up for."

I knew he had. He'd said as much. He'd rather take the place of a younger kid, someone with the rest of their lives in front of them, someone who had more to offer the future. But Jae had so much to offer himself. His dedication and work ethic, the way he loved his wife. I couldn't even think about Kendra.

"How long do you think Darius will be?"

Sid glanced up at the sky. "Should be back soon. Hopefully within the hour. He'll get the truck as close as he can and I'll carry you the rest of the way. The deal was I'd give him until dark before I went looking." He studied my face. "Don't worry. We're going to be alright."

I let my shoulders sag. He meant to soothe me, but his words did the opposite. He couldn't predict whether we'd be okay. There was so much that could go wrong with this plan. Darius could get captured before he got back. Or worse, he could reveal our existence. The Hunters could find us. Darius could lose our location. Get hurt. The possibilities made my head spin.

But I nodded. Things could always be worse. We were still alive to see another day. And the last thing either of us needed was more doubt cast over our journey to get back to the Centre.

12

MAURA

WITHOUT ELI AND SID, the Centre felt empty. It didn't help that Holli worked a twelve-hour shift and then went straight to sleep. I soaked in the aftermath of my fight with Eli. The wound was still fresh, even though I knew my anger was misplaced. He could've told me a few hours earlier, sure. And what would I have done then? He didn't owe me anything. We were friends. Weren't we? Or was it more than that? Not inappropriate, per se. But familial. Still, I snuck a glance at the photograph I kept in my pocket every chance I got, wrestling with my conflicting feelings.

Worry clung to me like a dark cloud. Despite keeping busy at work, I wondered where the men were and if they were safe. What if Avi came to us with bad news? What if they died or were badly injured? I grappled with the idea of surviving without Sid and Eli. What did that mean? What did that even look like? For the first time in my life, I belonged somewhere and now it could all disappear? I couldn't stand it.

It made me feel unbelievably selfish.

It was Saturday. The third and last day of laundry that week. I sat beside a pile of clean linens, sorting them into bags their owners would pick up the next morning. Dark clouds cloaked the sky and moved with the wind that battered the Centre's sides. Down here there would be no snow, but I couldn't help wondering what Coutts Peak looked like this evening. A thin blanket of white would cover the grass, flakes falling like sparkles from the sky.

Guilt came heavy with those thoughts. Longing for the commune or the remnants of good in my old life continued to be strange and complicated. I had no desire to return to what my life had once been, but there were things I still missed. Glimmers of nostalgia. Worry set aside for my siblings. My mother. Even, at times, Andrew.

A blonde figure flew past the front window, lifting me from my thoughts. I stopped mid-fold on a pair of pillow-cases, dropping them on the table as I stood from my metal chair. I approached the store's entrance, peering down the long hall. My heart dropped. At the end of the emergency side entrance hallway, Nadia clutched her radio, speaking something into the receiver I couldn't make out. But her wide blue eyes held fear so palpable it stopped me dead in my tracks.

Squinting, I tried making out the words on her lips. It was no use. Whatever it was, I was sure it had to do with Eli, Sid, Jae, and Darius. I glanced at Kendra, who was bent over the tub, wringing out socks from dirty water.

"Be right back," I said.

I gathered the bag with clean linens for the medical center as an excuse to pass by Nadia. Not suspicious at all. Something I did often.

My heart pounded as I stepped out of Housekeeping and into the walkway, ears on alert. No matter how quiet

Nadia tried to be, the ceilings and long halls made everything echo.

"...to get prepped," Nadia said. "They'll be here in a few hours. We don't have anyone on inventory, so you'll need to document that yourself. Have Mick radio once he's set."

The tall woman turned, eyed me, and gave me a small smile before darting off. I watched her disappear into the Armory. Probably going to speak with Avi. Had her smile been sad? Filled with pity? Or was it just a pleasantry?

I was so distracted I walked into one of the tables in the middle of the Mess Hall. As I righted myself, I caught the red and gray wisps of Holli's hair emerging from Inventory, her face pallid and pulled into a worried frown. She faltered as I approached.

"Hi," I said, holding out the bag. "Sheets."

"Oh." She blinked away her surprise.

"And also—" I pressed my lips together and shook my head, unable to control the question on my tongue. "Are they okay?" Desperation dripped from my tone. "I just heard Nadia saying someone should get prepped and to get Mick ready...I couldn't help but think—"

Uncertainty crossed her features, and she looked around at the empty Mess Hall before she closed the space between us, putting her head beside mine. She grabbed the bag in my hands.

"Sid and Darius are fine."

"But Eli?" I met her gaze, frantically searching her eyes. "Jae?"

"Eli is hurt." She took a breath.

"Badly?" My heart raced. My throat felt like it was swelling to twice its size.

"Shot," she answered. "Don't know how bad, but he's conscious. And Jae..." She bit her lip and shook her head.

"He's—?"

"Please don't say anything to Kendra. Avi will want to tell her himself."

"Okay." I couldn't breathe. I released the bag. Holli frowned, then nodded at me.

"We'll know more, soon." She studied me for a moment, then said, "You should stick around. He'll want to see you."

Warmth grew in my chest at her words. I hadn't missed that distinction. *He* not *they*. But we didn't know what kind of state he'd be in when he returned. She left with the clean bag of sheets, turning back into Inventory. A place where Jae would never step foot again.

How could I go back to Housekeeping now? I couldn't face Kendra. She would know. My face would give it all away, and she would figure out that something was wrong.

Rage filled me, blooming in my chest like a wound. I was never sure I could be capable of something as vicious as hatred, but I hated Father today. I hated that he was still in the commune, hiding up in his church behind his deadly Hunters. Delivering kill orders from the comfort of his desk.

He had taken so many things from me. My freedom. My family. My choices. My self-worth. How could he still hold so much power over me even after I'd left? I always thought adjusting to this new world would be the hardest part, but I was wrong. He still had the ability to hurt me and the people I loved. The people I cared about. People who had become family.

Would it ever stop? Would it ever be enough for him? I didn't think it would be.

I walked back to Housekeeping slowly. My chest felt heavy. Delivering the news of Jae's death to Kendra was unthinkable. Devastating. She and Jae had made it through so many things together, so much pain and chaos and heartbreak. Years of uncertainty, of horrible injustice, only for it to end in an instant.

My worry of facing Kendra disappeared as soon as I approached Housekeeping. In the store's dim light, I recognized Nadia and Avi sitting in two chairs beside her at the sink where she'd been washing the socks. She gripped the side of the basin, head turned into her shoulder as she heaved with sobs.

<hr>

After dinner, I waited in the Mess Hall. Neil and Mia played Go Fish to keep my mind busy until the six-year-old yawned and Neil declared it bedtime. He scooped her up from her chair, wrapped one arm around my shoulder, and pressed his cheek to my head.

"It'll be okay," he promised.

I was left alone with my thoughts, watching the occasional passerby and listening to the sounds of the Centre — coughs, laughter, babies crying, splashes of water from the bathroom, or footsteps down the corridor. The sky was pitch black beyond the skylight. Dim lanterns lit the main walkway.

Eventually, Holli came out from Inventory. Her lips rose in a faint smile as she approached.

"They're almost here," she said, her voice airy with relief. "They made it back safely. Eli is stable."

I took a shuddered breath, the tightness in my chest easing as I stood from my chair. "That's good," I said. "That's really, really good."

Still, I imagined the worst. Eli with half a leg, with no arm, blinded by the terrible thing that had killed Jae. But he was stable. No matter his condition, he was still alive. Shelly and Mick emerged, rolling the stretcher, its wheels squealing against the linoleum. The radio crackled at Shelly's hip. She met my eyes and gave me a small smile, which I returned. For the first time since she'd shown an interest in Eli, I was glad for her presence.

Holli rubbed my back. "We'll bring him in to evaluate him. I'll let you know when you can come in."

I nodded, watching as she followed Shelly and Mick down the side corridor. Minutes ticked by. I sat down, then stood back up again, pacing the length of the Mess Hall. I prayed, uncertain if God was still listening to me. Nadia arrived, her pretty features pulled tight. Even from a distance, she looked exhausted. A metal door creaked open. Frantic voices. Mick calling orders. Nadia looked down the small hallway, watching. I moved, trying to get a better vantage point.

The stretcher rolled down the hallway. Shelly led the charge, Mick and Holli at the rear, with Sid behind them. Eli sat propped up against the adjustable headrest. They turned the corner toward the Mess Hall.

Dried mud caked almost his entire body, lightening his dark hair, staining his face and beard. Someone had cut his pant leg so it lay open on either side, revealing the white hairy flesh of his muscular calf and thigh. A beige shirt, tied around his limb, was soaked in deep red and brown. The tension in my shoulders loosened. A leg wound was fixable.

He turned his head, and I held my breath. He seemed disoriented, his brown eyes struggling to adjust to the flurry of attention around him. Beads of sweat covered his brow up into his matted hair. His bottom lip was raw red, some of the skin chewed away. But his neck was the worst-looking part of him. Angry, purpled skin bulged beneath his chin.

As he passed, his eyes found mine. The cloud of pain

lifted, if only for a moment. He raised his hand, and I matched him with a small wave, wishing I could do more. That I had said more. That we'd shared more in that moment before he'd left. But it was gone. A fleeting wish. And just like that, they whisked the stretcher past me, into Inventory, and toward Medical.

Sid walked into the Mess Hall, his hands intertwined, resting on top of his head. His jeans hung from his hips loosely, secured by a braided belt. He wore no shirt, only an unbuttoned jacket over his shoulders. Dried blood covered the bottom of his face, neck, and throat.

He walked over to me, head tilted. "Never been so happy to be back inside this place," he said.

I vaulted forward and pulled him into a hug. He smelled of earth, sweat, and blood, but still like Sid. Once he released me, he kicked out a chair with his foot, then settled himself into it with an air of relief.

"Can you guys stop trying to get yourselves killed?" I asked as I sat in the chair beside him.

"I *tried*," Sid sighed. "But Eli said it was out of the question."

I pressed my hand to my forehead and shook my head before I could look at him again. "Thank God you two are okay. What happened out there?"

"You really want to know?"

I thought of Kendra. Of Eli's leg. Of Father and the fury I carried in my chest for him.

"Yeah," I said. "I do."

Sid sighed, his shoulders sagging. "Well," he said. "We did fine until we got close to the prison. We were maybe a mile out from town, trying to assess the area. A land mine got Jae." He looked away. "There was nothing we could do."

"A land mine? Like an explosive?"

He nodded, his eyes distant. "Darius thinks it was a

trap. They knew we'd come for the prisoners, and they planned for it, so they set them a ways out. Jae had no chance of coming back from his injuries."

I winced, wishing I could forget the image that appeared in my mind. I hoped anyone who spoke with Kendra would spare her the details.

"After that we ran. But it was dark. We got stuck in an embankment and a Hunter found Eli. By the time I got back to him, he'd nearly choked him out with his foot. I was able to take care of the Hunter. And Darius helped with three others." He turned his hands over. They, too, were covered in dried blood.

With his words, I saw tension slip from his shoulders. As if the admission of murder relieved him of the burden. More murder. More blood. Father would be furious, but what right did he have to be? He was the one doing these things. Father had the power to stop this madness. To stop the killing of his own men. He chose not to. He chose to keep his power, to force this oppression, to continue chasing and kidnapping and driving fear into people's hearts. It was a *choice*. Not a calling from God.

This blood wasn't on Sid's hands. It was life or death for anyone who went out there who wasn't serving Father. For the people trying to protect us and save the others. No, this blood was on Father's hands. He was a puppeteer, forcing us to kill to survive.

Any good man would choose to stop that suffering. Instead, he hid behind the guise of God's word. For that, I would never forgive him.

13

——————

MAURA

WE WANDERED into Inventory and found Sid some dinner, marking down what we took on Jae's clipboard that hung at the end of one of the shelves. Then we settled on the floor near the windows so we would be the first to know when Mick finished with Eli.

"Jae's going to haunt us," Sid said, his mouth full of preserved pears. "He's going to straight up possess us for this. We'll have to ask Leo to perform an exorcism."

"Sid!"

He grinned. "You know it's worth it."

I licked syrup from my fingers and narrowed my eyes at him. He could be so crass. I blessed myself with the sign of the cross. "God forgive us," I whispered under my breath.

He tipped the jar and drank the rest.

It was late. The Centre was so quiet we heard Darius coming from the center of the mall's walkway. He walked toward Inventory, his hands shoved in his front pockets, head hung low.

"Oh, no."

I glanced at Sid, who put the lid back on the empty jar. "What?"

"Darius." Sid shook his head. "I wondered where the hell he was. I think he feels guilty about Jae."

Sid got to his feet and met Darius at Inventory's entrance. I strained my ears, not wanting to eavesdrop, but unable to curb my curiosity. Darius's voice was too low to make out words, but I heard the anguish beneath his tone. Sid slipped his arm around the younger man's shoulders and led him toward Medical.

The pair disappeared inside. I sat in silence for a few minutes until the door opened again, but instead of Sid emerging, it was Holli. She scanned the area, found me, and smiled. I stood up, brushed my jeans off, and ran my fingers through my curls.

"He's all mended up," she said as I approached. "Mick performed a minor surgery to remove the bullet. It was a clean shot, easy to get out. He'll need to use crutches for some time, but he'll be just fine. He's got a damaged larynx, so it's difficult for him to talk for too long, plus a few other bumps and bruises. But nothing that'll affect him long term."

"Thank God."

She led me inside and through a dark lobby area where the stretcher had been discarded. I squinted in the bright overhead lights as we entered the tiled medical room with six beds. It smelled of antiseptic and iron.

Shelly and Mick tended to Sid and Darius at the far end of the room, getting them settled for what I assumed was a quick assessment of any injuries. But Eli lay on the bed closest to the door, the curtain separating him from the others. A sling hung from the ceiling elevated his bandaged leg. Someone had wiped the dirt from his face, but he still had long streaks in his hair and sideburns. I had been thinking about this moment since Holli told me he'd been shot. I'd wanted to hug him. Tell him how much he meant to me.

Instead, I burst into tears.

Everything flooded out: relief that he was okay, confusion about my conflicting feelings, embarrassment at my anger before he'd left. In that brief moment, I understood what I could've lost and how painful it would've been. Though thrown together by chance, Eli was an important part of me. He had changed me for the better. He had saved me. The idea of no longer having him in my life was unthinkable.

I hiccuped and gasped, unable to get words out through my sobs. Then Holli was behind me, wrapping her arms around my shoulders and pulling me close.

"I'm sorry," I gasped, my chest shuddering.

"Don't be sorry," she soothed as she ran her hand up and down my hair. It took me a minute to calm, but once I did, I wiped my remaining tears from my cheeks and spun to face Eli. He had a sheepish and slightly smug grin on his face.

"Does this mean you forgive me?" His voice was so raspy it was almost difficult to make the words out. He cocked a brow.

I nodded, wiping my tears as I moved forward and gently wrapped my arms around him. He smelled familiar, like home — earth and pine mixed with body odor and antiseptic — and felt warm, a little sticky with sweat. He dragged his hand up my back, over my shoulders, squeezing them.

I pulled away, letting my hands rest on the bed's edge as I inspected his injuries. "Your throat. Your face." I dug the rest of the tears out of my eyes.

"Hey now."

"Oh, Eli." The tears started again. He looked so battered. His face was drained of color from his blood loss, and his cheek was split just below his eye socket, making the skin swell. He brought his hands up to the angry, bruised flesh on his neck.

"What do they make those Hunter boots from, anyway?"

"Eli, I'm so sorry." Tears blurred my vision. I gripped the blanket. "I should've known the Hunters would extend the borders. I should've accounted for that when I drafted the map. And Jae? I—"

"Maura." Eli slid one hand over mine, squeezing. I wiped at my face. "This isn't anyone's fault except the Hunters."

"That's right," Holli agreed.

I pressed my lips together and nodded. I did know, but it didn't ease the guilt. It didn't stop the way my insides curdled every time I looked at Eli and his injuries. I gave Avi the information about the borders, which is what our teams based their plans around.

"Avi told Kendra?" Eli directed the question to Holli.

She nodded. "Him and Nadia."

"I'd like to do something for her," he continued. "And a memorial for Jae, something to remember him by."

"She'd appreciate that," I said, sliding my fingers up through his to grip him tighter. My heart felt heavy as I thought of how deep Kendra's grief would wound her. I hadn't lost someone like Kendra had, but I'd sure experienced loss before. The loss of my community and family, the loss of what I once knew to be true. It was an agonizing ache that never ceased, and just when you think you'd forgotten it, something else would inevitably remind you.

"When will you get out of here?" I asked, looking between Eli and Holli.

"Stitches come out in a few days," answered Holli. "Crutches for a few weeks. We'll keep him overnight tonight for observation, but I can't see a reason why he won't be able to come back to the room tomorrow."

"Yeah, to lie in bed." He looked skeptical.

"That's what you *need*," I stressed.

He rolled his eyes, but tightened his fingers around mine. Warmth spread in my chest at his touch, at the reminder that he was here, safe, and alive.

"Any word on the other scavenging teams?" He directed the question to Holli.

"Avi mentioned Gloria's team checked in yesterday. They came up empty-handed, but no land mines." Eli twitched at the mention. "Hopefully, Francis and his team are closing in on something. I hope they have the sense to come back for reinforcements."

"That, or they encountered something worse."

Holli's face darkened. "Stay positive," she said softly. "We have to assume their mission goes as planned."

Eli shook his head and looked at his lap. "It's just not Coutts style," he said. "They've never been worried about people coming *in* before, only people going out."

"Things change," Holli said. "Peter's desperate to keep our existence hidden from his followers and that means new defenses in keeping people out. People have always been desperate, he's made sure of that. He kept the population poor, tired, and sick, so people didn't rush his borders. Now he's dealing with the people who are left. The people who fought hard to stay alive. There's not as many of us, but we *are* dangerous."

Holli's words gave me some reassurance. She was right. Our numbers hardly mirrored the commune, but we were still strong. Father wouldn't worry his Hunters with our existence, otherwise. The idea that he might be threatened by us made me swell with pride.

"What are you birds clucking about?" Sid came around the curtain, both hands heavily bandaged. He glanced at the sling holding Eli's leg. "My god, could you be any more dramatic?"

Eli chuckled, slipping his hand out of my grip as he adjusted himself on the bed. "You're just jealous I get painkillers."

"He gets *painkillers?*" He gave Holli a mock look of disbelief.

"I'm going to need them soon with all this grief you two give me."

Sid laughed, a genuine, hearty sound that came from his chest, before he slipped his arm around Holli and hugged her to his side. "You love us," he said.

"Too much," she agreed. "Anyway." She patted the bed with her hands. "It's late and we should let Eli rest." She met my gaze before she turned on Eli. "No more talking. Shelly's taking the night shift, so she'll be here if you need anything. But I expect you to sleep, please." She dug into her pocket and produced a vial, similar to the one she'd given me the night Dale had returned home. "Take a little of this and you'll be out in no time."

"He gets all the good stuff," Sid complained.

"That's because she loves me most," Eli quipped before he popped the top, took a long gulp, and swallowed. He handed the rest to Sid.

"Best brother." He took the bottle, pocketed it, then gave me a wink. "I'll share."

"See you in the morning?" Eli asked, swiveling his gaze across us.

"Of course," said Holli.

"I'll be by." He matched the smile I gave him.

"Me too," Sid said.

"C'mon." Holli pressed herself into Sid, who moved toward the door. We waved to Eli, said a goodbye to Mick, Shelly, and Darius, and left the medical room. Adjusting to the dark in Inventory took a moment, but before long, we were through the Mess Hall and walking back to our room. There was an air of relief that followed us, knowing Eli would be okay. But it disappeared the minute we turned the corner at the walkway cross.

Kendra sat on the floor, propped up against the wall. Her head rested on her shoulder as she snored lightly. A large, empty glass bottle lay beside her. Holli approached, squatting down to get to her level. As I got closer, I saw the sick down her front and her wrinkled face swollen from tears.

"Kendra?" Holli's gentle voice traveled the length of the walkway. She gave her a little shake. Kendra opened one bleary eye. "Honey, how'd you get down here?"

Kendra's eyes rolled before she brought one hand to her face, wiping at her skin, smearing vomit across her chin.

"C'mon, now." Holli looked up at Sid, who went to Kendra's other side. Together, they hoisted her to her unsteady feet.

"I've got her," Sid said, scooping her into his arms like a rag doll. "Where should I take her?"

"With us," Holli said, jutting her chin toward our room. "I don't want her to be ill again while she's sleeping. Let's get her cleaned up." She turned to me. "Maura? Can you run to the laundry and get her something clean?"

I nodded, swallowing stomach acid, trying to curb my horror. Kendra was always so put together. She was always smiling, always busy, always consistent. She was wise and kind and gentle. It was jarring to see her in this state of grief and turmoil. And I knew nothing anyone did could fix it for her.

That evening, after we'd cleaned Kendra up, collected her a sick bucket and draped a blanket over her on the loveseat, I covered my cries by biting my fist, so hard I woke with teeth imprints the next day. Anger settled into my very bones. None of this was fair. I prayed that God would make Father pay for his many sins.

That night, I'm certain, God finally heard me.

14

ELI

SLEEP CAME IN BOUTS. The hospital bed was too narrow, too rickety. The room was too quiet, too warm, then too cold. Shelly woke me every few hours for a dose of pain medicine, startling me from dreams of Jae without legs and Hunters without throats. My leg hurt, but unexpectedly the worst pain came from using my voice.

Darius still occupied the bed at the far end of the room, but Shelly had pulled the curtain all the way around so I couldn't see him. The few times I did wake, I could've sworn I heard him crying. I thought of calling out to him, to reassure him he wasn't responsible. That this was just as much my fault as it was his. And that Jae wouldn't want him to be sad. But my throat and exhaustion had other plans.

It was morning the next time I startled awake, this time by the pain in my leg. Had I missed a pain medication dose? I turned my sore neck, looking for someone. My tongue ran over my chapped lips. My throat was dry as the desert. Water. I needed water. The empty cup at my bedside taunted me.

The sun splashing in through the windows meant it was morning, but the room was oddly quiet. Typically Mick stayed in the vicinity and by now, Holli would've been here for her shift. Where was everyone?

I sat in silence for a few minutes, wishing I had something to read, before I heard the familiar swish of the medical center door open and close. Holli's footsteps were distinctive, and I knew it was her before she entered the room.

"Well, where the heck were you?" I asked jovially, my throat burning from use. I flashed her a smile, but it fell away as soon as her face came into view.

Her eyes were wide, lower lip trembling, hand at her chin. She shook her head, looking at her feet, before she acknowledged my existence. She looked surprised to see me. Uneasiness settled in my chest, letting me forget my pain for a moment.

"What is it?" The question hung in the air between us and she seemed to consider it, shake her head, then met my gaze. Holli, who had been calm, cool, and collected after Mom died. When I brought Maura back to camp. After Sid got sick. That same woman now looked panicked and unsettled. Like she'd seen a ghost. She approached the edge of my bed, clutching at the blanket with white knuckles.

"Holli?" Panic soaked my voice.

"There's something going on at the outskirts of the city," she said, her eyes flashing. She glanced at the curtain that separated Darius from the rest of the room. "I need to get Darius up."

I touched the back of her weathered hands slowly and she looked down, unclenching her fingers, letting the blanket go slack.

"What's going on? Hol?" Her distant gaze unnerved me. I moved like I was going to get up, pain shooting down my elevated leg, through my hip, and up my back. I winced, falling back against the bed.

"Oh!" She blinked at me, finally seeing me.

"Holli?"

"I'm so sorry." Distracted, she left the room momentarily, then came back with a closed fist and a jug of clean water. She filled my cup and handed me two pills. "Here."

I took them, savoring the liquid as it coated my throat. My heart pounded. I followed Holli's gaze as she looked toward Darius.

"What the hell's going on?" I asked, but she ignored me as she left my bedside and moved toward Darius. I had never been so frustrated in my life. I glared at the stupid sling my leg hung in, cursing the dead Hunter who'd put me in this predicament in the first place. I was absolutely *useless*.

"Darius?" I heard him grunt in return. "How are you feeling?"

Anger edged his gravelly voice, but I couldn't make out what he answered.

"Listen, there's something going on at our border. Avi wants everyone to report to him immediately. Are you up for it? They could really use you."

Silence, then a shuffle of the plastic mattress.

"I'll get your clothes."

Holli darted past, out the doors, then back in again, with a pile of clean laundry in her hands. I tried to catch her eye, to no avail. Something at the borders. Something at the borders wasn't necessarily bad, but the way Holli was behaving suggested otherwise. Something was deeply wrong, and she didn't want to worry me. Oh, the karmic retribution.

After a few moments, Holli walked Darius to the door, where he disappeared. She stood there, watching him for a moment, before she turned back to me with a sigh.

"Are you going to tell me what's going on?"

She looked at the ceiling and pressed her fingers to her forehead. "Are you going to let it go if I don't?"

"You know I won't."

She laughed. "I do know that."

"Is it the prisoners? Coal Creek? Coutts?"

She looked up at the name, crossed her arms, then squeezed her eyes closed. "It's the Coutts," she said. "They've found our borders."

No.

The combination of shock and fear tunneled my vision. The room swayed. Holli faded. Where was Maura? Avi? Or Sid, for that matter?

I knew this had always been a possibility, no matter where we were. But we'd been here months with nothing on our radar, slowly acclimating back to some semblance of normalcy. And all of that was going to be taken away.

"How?" was the first question out of my mouth.

Holli sat down at the end of my bed. "I don't know much, only that Avi asked to see a few people. Word on the street is that one of the prisoners talked. That, or…"

"They followed us."

I didn't think it was possible to feel as guilty as I did at that moment. We had a community of around 400 people. Even if we'd had the time, how would we move them all? Where would we go? It was an impossible feat.

"What do they want?" I asked.

"I don't know. So far, we haven't communicated with them, but Avi called in all security reinforcements. No shots have been fired. Yet. But…"

"It doesn't look good." I paused. "Where's Sid? Maura?"

Holli looked up. "Sid's with the rest of his team, but

may go out to patrol the border. I haven't seen Maura yet. I was eating breakfast and Nadia came out to tell me to get Darius, and I came straight here."

"We have to tell her." I reached forward to the sling holding my leg, tugging at the fabric, desperate to loosen the knot from the hook in the ceiling. "What if they're here for her?"

She turned sharply at my comment, as if she'd just considered it, her eyes landing on my hands.

"Stop that," she hissed, swatting at me.

"No." I pulled harder. One of the ceiling slats slipped out of place.

"Eli." Holli's voice was stern as she placed her hands over mine, squeezing her small hand over my knuckles. "Stop."

I cringed with frustration, releasing my hold on the fabric. Even if I got out of the sling, I wouldn't be able to do much.

"You need to take her somewhere, Hol," I said. "Go get Sid and run." Urgency grew with each word. "You have to keep them safe."

Because I can't.

If I knew anything, it was that if the Hunters were here, Maura was in danger and Sid would stop at nothing to take them down. They'd gun him down, stomp over his body, and take her away again. They'd lock her away and throw away the key, or worse, dispose of her completely. Throw her body in the river, forgotten by all except us.

I refused to let that happen.

"Eli." Holli's eyes widened. "It's not that simple. Sid's already in place. And Maura—"

"What's not simple?" I sounded hysterical.

"There's no way in hell Maura leaves without you. Or

Sid. Or me, for that matter." Her face reddened. "Think about what you're asking us to do."

"This is life or death."

"And so we abandon everyone here?"

I let out an exasperated breath. "These people aren't *Coutts*. You know the risks with Maura!"

"Everyone knows the risks, Eli!" She threw her hands up. "Avi isn't going to parade her in front of the mall. He's a smart man."

"And what if he uses her as a bargaining chip? What if he sacrifices her for the people here?"

Holli sighed. "That would be a choice for Maura. Not Avi. He wouldn't do that to her and you know it." She ran a hand through her unruly hair. Did I detect a tone of doubt?

"Avi wouldn't do what to me?" Maura's voice rang out clear as day through the empty medical room. Both Holli and I straightened, sharpening our attention. Maura stood at the doorway with two plates of hot food in her hands. Her hair was slicked back into a low ponytail, her face still flushed from the shower she must have taken earlier.

"Hi," Holli said, but her pleasantry didn't do much to cover up our panic. Maura frowned, uncertainty crossing her features. She inspected me, then Holli, before she came to the side of my bed and plopped the plate in my lap. My stomach gurgled with hunger, but there was no way I could eat. Not now.

"Breakfast." Her usual upbeat tone was gone, replaced by monotonous disappointment. I had made this mistake once. I wouldn't do it again.

"The Coutts are at our borders," I said, skipping over pleasantries, eyes flashing to Holli, then back to Maura. "You need to leave. Go with Holli and Sid and find some-where to hide out. If they find you here—" I shook my head. "Please."

"What?" Her eyes widened. She looked at Holli, who stood from the bed, hands out in front of her, as though she could shoo the truth away. "Holli?"

"I don't know much," she said, her gaze focused on the floor. "Just that Nadia said there are Hunters at the border and she needed the security and scavenging teams assembled. I came to get Darius."

"What do they want?"

"I don't know," Holli answered.

"And we're sure it's Hunters?"

"That's what Nadia said."

"Maura!" The yell sent a fresh wave of agony down my throat. I winced, fighting through the pain. "Hunters. Here. You *need* to leave." Forcefully, I shot my arm out, pointing at the door.

She looked down at her breakfast plate and took a bite of her French toast. Why the hell wasn't she moving? Or crying? Or freaking out? Why was I the only one who seemed to understand the urgency of the situation?

"Maura!"

She met my gaze. "If there are Hunters at the border, the worst thing I could do right now is run. That gives them proof I was here, proof that Avi and the community harbored me. It'll make things significantly worse for everyone inside these walls."

"So what? You just want to sit here and wait it out?" Frustration bubbled in my chest. I had the sudden urge to throw my breakfast plate at the wall.

Maura took another bite of her food and raised her eyebrows. "Yes, I do. Avi will have a plan."

"Who knows how long that'll take!" The painkillers had begun to kick in. I felt the ceiling move and the sweet bliss of cloudiness settle over my limbs. *Shit.* Now was not the time to be high.

The door to the medical center opened and closed again. Heavier footsteps announced Mick's arrival. His full head of silver hair shone as he turned on the overhead lights, eyes behind his circular specs scanning the room. I assumed he'd be looking for me, his patient, but instead, his gaze fell upon Maura.

"You're the Coutts girl," he said, in a tone that suggested indifference.

She nodded.

"Good." He pulled his clipboard, which hung on the wall, off its perch. "Avi's looking for you."

"Well." She had a few more bites of her breakfast before she offered the rest to Holli, who took the plate from her. "I guess it won't take as long as we thought."

"Maura."

She looked at me, her lips in a thin line. "Avi will know what to do. Have a little faith, will you?"

15

____

MAURA

THEY'D FOUND ME. Some part of me always knew this day
would come, and I supposed that was why I felt so calm
about it. There was no world where I didn't live beneath
Father's iron fist. There was no world where I could truly
be free. Father would always make sure of that. He'd chase
me until my dying day.

I trusted Avi. The minute we arrived at his gates and he
met us, dirty and disheveled, in the garage, he knew what
he was getting into. Inviting me, Leo, and the other
members of the commune into his community was a
choice, and he knew it could have consequences. Plus, the
Hunters could have found this place without suspecting I
lived behind these walls.

After shutting down one last plea from Eli, I left the
medical center, holding myself tall as I walked through
Inventory and the Mess Hall toward the Armory. Breakfast
was in full swing, almost every seat and table filled, the air
noisy with chatter and laughter. So nobody else knew,
then. Avi was keeping this under wraps for now. That was
good.

But who was at our gates? Did I know them? Had Andrew led them here? Would I recognize their faces as ones I'd seen in church? I thought of how Andrew might react to meeting Eli, Holli, and Sid before shaking the thought away. It was unimaginable. These were two separate lives. And never the two shall meet.

The Armory was cold and dark. A few security team members hovered near weapon storage, cleaning and reassembling long hunting rifles. Avi stood at his office door, leaning against the wall as he spoke into the black radio he held in his hands. His eyes flicked upward, noticing my presence. He wore black clothing, a sweatshirt hood covering his silvering brown hair. As he lowered the radio, I saw he'd begun to let his beard grow in. I supposed there were higher priorities than a good shave.

"Maura," he said, his voice gentle. The knot in my chest loosened.

"Avi," I greeted him. "You wanted to see me?"

He nodded, waving me in step with him as he took off back the way I'd come. I fell in line with him, trying to keep up with his long strides, and waited for him to say something. We exited the Armory and took the hallway past the apartments toward the garage. My heart was pounding, icy fear settling at the base of my spine.

It's going to be fine.

I took a deep breath.

Avi isn't Father.

I clenched, then unclenched my fists.

He's not going to betray you.

I ran my fingers across my denim jeans. We reached the end of the walkway, turning down a dark hallway that led to the garage. He paused at the entrance.

"There's two men who we believe to be Hunters at the border," Avi said in a low voice.

I unraveled his words. Two Hunters. Not an army?

"Only two?"

He nodded. "They willingly surrendered their weapons to us. We have them guarded on the outskirts of the Centre. Two young men, blond hair." He raised his brows. "Any idea who they could be?"

Half the boys in the commune were blond and young. "That could be anyone," I said. "Did they give you their names?"

"No." His face darkened. "They only want to speak with you."

I took a step back, surprised. "What? *Why*?" And more importantly, how did they know I was here?

"I don't know," he said. "We can't get any information out of them except that they don't want to bring us any harm, and want to speak with Maura Coutts. No matter what we ask them, that's their answer."

"How long have they been out there?"

"Since last night." He sighed. "I know this is a lot to ask of you, but the longer we keep them out there, the more attention we draw to ourselves. We've confirmed there is no one else in the vicinity, so to the best of our knowledge, they are here alone." He frowned. "You'll have protection from all angles. We'll give you a bulletproof vest. And Sid will go out with you. What do you think?"

"You want me to go talk to them?" So much for Eli's suggestion of hiding.

Avi nodded again. "Think of it as a peace offering. We're giving them something they want — to talk to you. And in return, you can figure out how the hell they managed to find us."

"And Sid will be with me?"

"Yes."

I took a deep breath, settling my gaze at the end of the

dark hallway, where the garage began. What if they asked me to come back with them? What if they threatened me with the safety of Mother? Or Morgan? Or the rest of my family? I tried to settle myself. I didn't know what they would ask without going out there first. I looked up at Avi and said, "Okay."

He nodded, and we moved through the hallway into the well-lit garage. At the far end, sunlight fell through an open door large enough to fit the trucks parked on the garage floor. I glimpsed Sid leaning against one of the vehicles. It was the first time I'd ever seen him fully armored. He wore a black helmet and dark clothing, similar to Avi. A bulky vest was attached to his chest, an automatic rifle slung across his back.

"Nadia, come in?" Avi said into his radio. He stopped walking, but I continued on, eager to be near someone familiar. Sid smiled as I approached. A cut he must have sustained swelled near his left eye, making his eyes look lopsided.

"Doing okay?" He considered me for a minute. "Still in shock?"

"I'd say."

"These are young, unarmed men. We have dozens of patrols on the borders, and more who will watch us closely. You have nothing to worry about." His tone was even and reassuring. But he didn't know the commune like I did. He didn't know how Father spoke to his men, how his men had the ability to manipulate and lie just like the Prophet. The Hunters were highly trained, highly skilled men. Weapons or not, they were dangerous.

"Here." Sid turned to the truck's hood, grabbing a vest similar to his, and a dark jacket. "Let's put these on." He ripped apart a few Velcro straps, then slipped the vest over my head. It was heavy, stiff, and a little too big. Sid took me by the shoulders, positioning me in front of him, then adjusted the straps to fit it tighter to my body. I pulled the jacket over the vest, feeling strange in my own skin.

"They're ready for you," Avi said, pocketing his radio. "Nadia knows to expect you in five minutes. Remember to get the key things." He looked at me.

"How they found us?"

"Yes."

"And what they want."

Avi nodded, then glanced at Sid. "And you know the rest." Sid gave a curt nod before moving toward the truck.

"Hop in," he said, jutting his chin toward the passenger seat.

I climbed into the truck, squinting in the sunlight. Sid started the vehicle, saluted Avi, and drove us out of the garage.

It took a moment to adjust to the punishing brightness the morning offered. It was the first time I'd been outside on this side of the building since we arrived.

"What did Avi mean, *and you know the rest*?" I asked.

Sid kept his gaze forward as he drove us around the back of the building into the parking lot at the front of the mall. "What we'll do with the Hunters after you're done talking."

I turned to him. "And what's that?"

"It'll depend on what they say."

"You're not going to kill them." I surprised even myself. Sid gave me a skeptical glance.

"Not unless they give us a reason to, Maura, but...come on. The Hunters have given us plenty of reasons to kill them."

He wasn't wrong. But two men alone at our borders, who gave up their weapons and freedom at a chance to talk to me, didn't seem like a threat. But I had been naïve before. I could be naïve now.

We drove through the parking lot at the front of the mall. Dust-covered cars sat in parking spots, some with their doors hung open, others sealed tight. Long light poles scattered the lot, with numbers and stickers peeling from their edges. Dead bulbs remained screwed in at the top, never to be used again.

From this angle, the mall looked like any other rotting building I'd seen on the Outside, which I supposed was the point. Blend into your surroundings to lessen the chance of being found. Boards covered most of the doors and windows, graffiti covering much of the outer walls. Weather had done a number on the exterior, greening every hard edge I could see. Vegetation between the parking lot and the building had bloomed then died, curling into itself as winter raged on.

We reached the end of the lot. The larger town beyond came into view, just as dilapidated as the mall. Most buildings were looted and vandalized, but still intact. Sid pulled the truck out of the parking lot and onto a weathered road, which led to an intersection.

Trees covered the next road we took, easing my panic a bit. I hadn't realized how much space there was between the shopping mall and the security borders, but I was glad for it.

"I'll stay with you the entire time," Sid said. "That's the deal. I won't let them take you anywhere I can't see you."

"Okay."

We passed a row of narrow, boarded-up brick homes. Weeds climbed the iron gates erected around the properties. The row of buildings ended in a cul-de-sac. A dirt path at the end of the street led to a tired, old playground, with rust-covered equipment. Four of our armed guards stood around the area, and two figures sat on a bench in the middle.

Sid pulled to the side as we reached the dead end, then picked up the radio he'd discarded in the cupholder.

"Target arrived. Are we clear?" He cut the engine.

"South is clear," came Nadia's voice.

"Clear in the east," said another, lower voice I didn't recognize.

"West, clear." A crackle.

"North, good and clear," came a moment later.

"Confirmed," said Sid. He tucked the radio in his chest pocket, turning in his seat. "You ready?"

"No." My heart raced. I had started sweating underneath the heavy vest and jacket. I was thankful I'd thought to tie my hair up that morning.

I squinted through the truck's windshield out at the figures near the playground. They were blond, as Avi had described, both tall and of similar build. Even from here, I knew it wasn't Andrew or Luke. My anxiety calmed slightly. So who were they? And what on earth did they want with me?

"Hear them out," Sid coached me, opening his door. "Like Avi said, see if you can find out how they found us and what they want. Simple. I can take it from there."

He got out of the truck and retrieved his weapon from the back. I stepped out onto broken concrete, adjusting to being in the open. The cold air chilled the sweat drying on my neck, but the sunshine on my face felt glorious. I had missed being outdoors like this.

"C'mon." Sid came around the truck and I followed at his side. His jaw tightened as we approached the cul-de-sac's curb. We walked up and over onto the weed-infested dirt path that led to the playground. One of our suited security members greeted Sid with a salute.

"All good." He nodded and followed us with his gaze, his grip tight on his gun. So many guns around us. I supposed it should've made me feel more safe, and even though I knew it was necessary, I felt apprehensive.

The dirt path expanded into a wide circle, leading into an area with dark wood chips. The playground equipment's paint had peeled away, leaving blue and green shavings scattered throughout the black, like a child had dropped their paints and forgotten to clean it up. I glanced over my shoulder. The only visible buildings were the homes we'd passed. Trees obscured the mall from view.

I felt like I had when I'd swam across the brook after the storm at the Island of Repentance. Cast out in the open, untethered, and horribly exposed. Now, I had protection. But I couldn't shake that vulnerable feeling.

We walked toward the bench where the two men sat, dressed in white shirts and blue jeans. I studied the back of their heads. Both of similar height, they each had a slim build, with slender shoulders and long necks. Their neat crew cut hairstyle was the same as every Hunter in the commune. One of them was bleeding from behind his ear. They sat straight, neither touching the back of the bench, muscles tense.

Sid led me around to face them.

Both men looked up as we came into their view, holding my gaze. They had such similar features, though one still held his boyish cheeks and the other had a sharper, more adult visage. They were undoubtedly brothers. Their blue-gray eyes were rimmed in red from exhaustion. Both had beard shadows. That meant they had been away from their command for at least a few days.

I had a glimmer of recognition. Andrew had spoken to the older one once, outside the church. Just before I'd fallen in the creek. He had been recruited to the Hunters for a reason that caused some conflict for Andrew. I had overheard him telling Abigail. And then I remembered.

These men were Luke's sons. Father's ruthless right-hand man. I froze.

"Hi Maura," the older one said, his voice deeper than I expected.

He tilted his chin as he inspected me. I must've looked like a different person than I ever had in the commune. A bulletproof vest and a black jacket with dark jeans certainly wasn't an outfit I'd be allowed to wear. My hair being slicked back would've offended Andrew. I knew my skin had lightened from not being out in the sun and I had thinned considerably, now able to feel my ribs through my nightshirt.

"You're Luke's—?"

He gave me a soft smile, revealing boyish dimples. He couldn't have been older than eighteen. "My name is Silas, and this is my younger brother, Gabriel. We are Luke's kin, yes. And no, he does not know we are here."

I laughed, unconvinced. The man named Silas leaned forward.

"My father is a cruel man. Trust me. If he knew where you were, he'd have already dragged you back to the commune. He would never be able to resist the pride that would come with hand-delivering you to the Prophet."

"Then why are you here?"

Silas sighed, absentmindedly caressing his forearm before he spoke again. "I'm here about your sister, Morgan."

16

MAURA

My knees threatened to buckle.

"Morgan?" My breath floated away in the frigid air. "How do you know my sister?"

"I—"

"Is she okay?"

"Yes," he said, sounding apologetic. "Relatively speaking."

I inspected him, afraid to pry further, but more afraid not to. "Meaning?"

"Meaning she's alive."

"Alive, and—?" I shook my head. Her being alive didn't mean she was okay.

"Let me start at the beginning," he said matter-of-factly. He glanced nervously at Sid. "Maybe you want to sit down?"

I looked at my companion. Sid shrugged. I took Silas's suggestion and sat on the mulch. Sid remained standing behind me.

Silas glanced down at his lap and Gabriel cast him a look of concern. The younger brother seemed frightened, like he might take off into the trees if there were any sudden, loud noises.

"I was with the Hunters that took down your friends," Silas said to his knees. "The group of people that lost that man to the land mine."

"Jae." I clenched my jaw.

Silas looked up.

"So that's how you found us, then? You followed them back here?"

Sid shifted his weight behind me, the mulch moving beneath his feet. Silas nodded. "Yes. Into the vicinity, at least. Near the prison, we had a spotlight on someone from your community. An Outsider recognized him as the man you were reported to be traveling with. And I knew then that I needed to come speak with you no matter the risk."

"An Outsider was with you?"

"Yes." He sighed, conflict crossing his features before he spoke again. "The Prophet had always confided in the Hunters that there might be Outsiders since the Great Plague, but they were few and far between, people he brought in to blend with the rest of us. Now he's revealed knowledge of large communities. Outsiders he's been colluding with from the very start. He used them to help capture your people."

The Coal Creek men. Were there others out there like them? Would Father really put his belief in God aside to partner up with people like them? And why would he do that? Those men had nothing to offer but alcohol, drugs, and women.

Women.

I shivered.

"After one of your men got hurt in the embankment, we stayed hidden until the rest of your team killed who remained in our squad," he continued. "Changed out of our suits into civilian clothing, and came to the borders the next day."

"But you're — you're breaking protocol." *Sinning against Father. Breaking all of his rules.*

"I know." He hung his head. His brother frowned. "We made a risky choice. One I hope will be worth it in the end. So, I'm humbly asking for your help."

"And why should I help you?"

Silas bounced his leg and glanced at his brother momentarily before he spoke again. "I met Morgan months ago, after you'd first gone missing. I was tasked with patrolling your Mother and siblings."

"Patrolling?"

"Watching them. Reporting back to my father about their whereabouts, comings and goings, if they were being devout. Mostly, if they showed any sign of knowing where you'd gone." My heart took off again. I hadn't considered this a possibility, but of course it made sense. "Your sister tended to the kids outside during the summer. When your mother was away, we'd talk. Sometimes she'd ask for my help to watch the younger ones. We got to know each other." A pink flush spread across his cheeks and up his neck.

I softened at his embarrassment. Hunters didn't blush at the mention of outcast women like my sister. They most certainly did not get to know daughters of sixth-wives. Especially the son of my father's right-hand man. The Prophet would've assigned both Silas and Gabriel daughters of other Hunters or first wives. Morgan would have been a last resort. No, this relationship was born out of something else.

"You and Morgan?"

He nodded, looking back at his lap. "Eventually I got switched to nights. It was a lonely job out in the dark, making sure nobody went anywhere they shouldn't be. Morgan began to come out after everyone was asleep to keep me company. We talked, got to know each other." A smile crept across his lips. "Morgan, she's…interesting. Smart. Beautiful. And her edge of rebellion, that bravery she has. She helped me see the harm the Prophet and my father were doing to our people." His eyes became distant. "I fell in love with her."

He cleared his throat, catching my gaze. It took some effort to keep my jaw from dropping. My doubt was thinning. I saw the longing in his gaze, the desperation behind his words. But a Hunter, seeing through Father's facade? How could that be?

"We started seeing each other secretly at night, sometimes during the day when we could. Whenever and wherever. It was risky. We both knew that, but we didn't care. It didn't matter. I'll admit, it was reckless. She talked about running. Finding you. Going to a place where we were free to be married, to make our own choices and decisions. But then I was promoted in the ranks and drafted for training.

"Part of that, of course, was being married off, which happened quite quickly." Silas shifted on the bench, brow furrowing at the memory. "Morgan was deeply upset, wouldn't talk to me when I tried to see her. They put a new recruit on your family's patrol." He glanced sideways at Gabriel. "She wouldn't talk to me, but she spoke to Gabriel. She said I messed everything up by getting married, that we should've left when we had a chance. But I couldn't just…" He shook his head. "I should've left when she asked me to. I should've been braver, but I wasn't."

I leaned back, pressing the mulch between my fingers. "She *can* be stubborn."

Silas forced a laugh. "You can say that again. I knew I messed up, but it didn't mean I loved her any less. Gabriel and I were able to keep the trouble away from your family. After the Prophet announced your death, I thought he would ease the pressure on them. But then they kidnapped that group — your group. And the Prophet found out you were alive."

My death?

My stomach dropped. I met his pained gaze, trying to find any break, any indication this wasn't the truth. Maybe this was all an intricate lie worked up between him and his brother and Luke to lure me back to the commune. But that would mean he was an excellent liar.

"He told people I died?"

Silas pressed his lips together and nodded. "After the storm at the Island of Repentance, the Prophet thought you to be dead. Whether or not he personally believed it, I think he thought there was no way for you to survive out here. He announced your death publicly and held a service in your honor. He used your death as proof that disobeying him would lead to an untimely end. It scared a lot of people. He's been using it as a tactic within the commune because things are becoming more...unstable as of late."

I raised my brows.

"After your group was taken, one of them talked. Told the Hunters the community had you and others and that your leader would probably consider an exchange. The Prophet was furious, raving mad that there was proof you were still alive. He acted rashly, which suggests what we've been thinking now for some time." He glanced back at his brother, who sighed.

"And what's that?"

"That he's losing his grip. More people are dying, including your sister wife, Joanna, I believe?" My chest tightened as I thought of the sharp-featured blonde woman and her three children. She had been pregnant when I'd left. "It was a preventable death, from what I'd heard," Silas continued, his voice softer. "I'm sorry."

I shook my head, blinking away the shock.

"Hunters are catching people trying to flee the commune almost every single day," Silas continued. "The Prophet insists on keeping it under wraps and punishing anyone who dares speak out about it. He's imposed curfews and mandatory church assemblies that he calls at all hours of the day, and if someone abandons their homes or posts, their families receive fewer rations and supplies. Some lose their jobs or children. He's pulled farmers and doctors and turned them into interrogators. He's drafting men as young as thirteen into Hunter preliminary training. It's putting a strain on the entire commune because we're losing workers left and right. All so the Prophet can continue to be *right*."

Silas's gaze remained focused on the ground. "He's getting more violent and unstable. Your sister has shown up at church with bruises and cuts. Your mother is missing. And…" He lifted his head, tears swimming in his blue eyes.

I leaned forward. "What?"

"He married Morgan."

"Married her?" I shook my head. "To who?"

"To Andrew."

My skin prickled beneath my jacket and I pulled it tighter around myself. The ground felt like it was moving. I struggled to draw a breath. Mother was missing. Morgan was married to Andrew.

Of course. I would've been foolish not to think something like this could happen. I had run away. Doing so put a target on my family. I had put a stain on Mother and my siblings. I had made Father look bad. What better way to punish them and reward Andrew than offering up my beautiful sister and forcing Mother behind closed doors? If that's where she was at all. Maybe he'd killed her. I dug my fingernails into my jeans until I felt a pop of pain.

Sid shifted behind me again, taking a step closer. His shadow blotted out the sun. I looked up at him. His mouth was set in a straight line, but I saw pity in his features. Sid knew what it meant to lose family. To love a sibling.

You okay? he mouthed.

I forced a nod, even though tears leaked from my eyes and down my cheeks. Hastily, I wiped them away.

"Do you know where the rest of my siblings are?" I whispered, unable to help the quaver in my voice. Ten of them, younger than Morgan and I, still lived within Mother's house. My oldest brother, Mark, would be eligible for work, but the rest were too young. If Mother was missing, what had Father done with them?

"The Prophet assigned them to new households."

So that was it, then. Father had split my family up, sprinkled them around the commune, leaving them orphaned and afraid. The boys might be okay, put to work, or given different responsibilities if they behaved and performed well. But the girls? Martha, the next oldest after Morgan, was only nine. But with no family to be tethered to, it opened up her chances of being wed early.

My stomach rolled. I tasted bile.

"There's more," he said, after a moment of silence. Slowly, I dragged my gaze up to meet his.

"What else could there possibly be?"

He took a deep breath. "We are part of a small but growing resistance within the Hunters. It's become quite obvious, especially to the newer recruits, that the Prophet and our father aren't—" He twisted his lips, looking for the words. "—practicing what they preach. The Hunters have only ever been violent when necessary, but making it the expectation was never something any of us signed up for. We were told to be warriors for God. Which means protecting those that need protecting, but it also means serving God faithfully.

"My father is an angry man. But our mother was a God-fearing woman who taught us about God's love. I was taught to accept everyone. To love everyone. To be kind to everyone. To protect *everyone*. And what the Prophet is making us do in the commune goes against everything I believe in. We're not protecting people. We're controlling them. And when we're out here?" Silas leaned against the backrest, running his long fingers through his hair. "We are ordered to capture all children and young adults, up to the age of twenty-six. Everyone else, unless providing key information or resources, is to be eliminated on the spot."

"It's ludicrous." Gabriel spoke for the first time. I shifted my gaze to him, watching his nostrils flare. "People are dying. People are trying to leave. They're unhappy and afraid. His answer is to kill, kidnap, or silence everyone. It doesn't make any sense. All this will do is frighten people."

"It's a foolish strategy," Silas said, nodding his head in agreement. "But not everyone thinks this way. In fact, I believe more Hunters than not believe this is a poor path forward. But until someone stands up and tries to change it, nothing will be done. So here we are. Trying to do something." He brought his gaze back to me. "The Prophet needs to be subdued. Violence will end us. It goes against God's will."

The gravity of Silas's proclamation was not lost on me. Everything this man said to me and in front of his brother was blasphemy. Of course, I could not go back and reveal his treachery to Father. But it was still dangerous territory to toe, even more so for a Hunter. But he was risking it all. Because he loved my sister and believed in a better world.

"So what's your plan, then?" Sid asked. "You're here for what? To tell Maura all of these things she has no way to change?"

Silas looked up at him. "On the contrary," he said. "She does have the power to change things. But it's a big ask to make." He switched his gaze to me. "Maura, you are the only person who can take power from him."

I laughed dryly. "And how, pray tell, do you suggest I do that?"

"You need to come back."

"What?"

"Uh, no." Sid's tone was final. "She'll be dead the minute she sets foot in that commune."

"Not if enough people see her before the Prophet does." Silas's gaze flickered between Sid and me. "Think about it. He's told everyone she's dead. That he *knows* her to be dead. God told him that she died as a sacrifice to show others what happens when you disobey the Prophet. He spread this knowledge to every person still existing within those borders. What do you think will happen if she shows up alive?"

My eyes widened and my heart began to race. "It proves him wrong." Like it had when I first found Eli after he'd pulled me from the creek. Only, nobody had been around to see it.

"Exactly." A smile crept onto Silas's lips. "It proves he's capable of lying. It proves he's not infallible. It takes away the credibility he's already starting to lose. And not just that, but Maura becomes a living martyr. She would become the antithesis to everything the Prophet is trying to do. And there would be no way to stop that once people saw her return."

"How would you even manage that?" Sid asked skeptically. "There are Hunters crawling all over that commune. What if they shoot her before she even gets in there?"

"I won't let that happen." His eyes narrowed. "I can promise that."

Sid tilted his head skeptically. "Okay, and once she's in, then what? Everyone in that commune is widely spread out, aren't they? You can't gather everyone in one place."

"Perhaps not. But the New Year celebration is in a few days. It's a full day of worship and showmanship to articulate all the commune has accomplished in the past year. It's covered by our media hub from sun up to midnight. All we need is to get Maura's image out broadly on that day to prove she's alive. The rest will happen naturally. Word spreads like wildfire in the commune. The Prophet won't be able to explain it away because people will have already seen Maura. We'll have power in our hands and then we might be able to convince more people that what the Prophet is doing is wrong."

A thrill crept up my spine as I considered Silas's idea. Telling Father about the Outsiders hadn't worked. He no longer seemed to care about right or wrong, so much as he cared about maintaining power. The power worked because of the people who believed him. If we took that away, it would hurt him where it mattered most. It would knock him off his throne. It would show people the thing I knew to be true. That Father was no Prophet. He was simply a man. A lying one, at that.

"But then, what?" I asked. "*If* people begin to see through his lies, we'd still have to keep them safe from his wrath. From the Hunter's wrath. How could we possibly do that?"

Silas offered a grin. "Like I said, we're part of a small but growing group of Hunters who are ready for change. I know we can get more support. If we're strategic about this, we can target the key parts of the commune to cut down the Prophet's power."

"Key parts?"

"We have rebel contacts who work closely with Abraham Coutts, who runs Media. Two work with Caleb in Agriculture. I work with my father and Andrew, of course, in Security. Sciences and Innovations will be a little harder to infiltrate, but from what I hear and see, the doctors and scientists are overworked and unhappy, too. That's four of the major departments. If we can coordinate efforts, we can form a larger resistance group, spread the word—"

"That's a big *what if*," Sid said grimly. I looked back up at him and he gave me a worried gaze.

"If the Prophet is distracted and focused on other things, like keeping people controlled, and having to fix his follower's perception of him, it will help. The more doubt we cast, the more people we can convince. We can open people's eyes. We can shed light on the wicked acts he's committing. Expose him so people see who he truly is."

Silas's face reddened as he spoke, his shoulders trembling with anger. His brother placed his hand on his shoulder and Silas let the tension in his upper body ease slightly. He was angry and horrified. All the things I felt when I had told Father about the Outsiders months ago. And he had made me feel like that was my burden to bear, alone.

He'd been wrong. He'd lied. Of course he had. Of course there were others like me in the commune. People who saw through him. He'd just made me feel foolish and small, to convince me my concerns had no merit. That I'd made it all up and couldn't trust myself.

But there was power in numbers. If there were other

people brave enough to speak out against Father, there would be even more who had these thoughts in silence. They just needed the catalyst. It could spark the very thing that was necessary to push Father from his place of power. Not just that, but I could give my family a better life. A good life. One where Morgan could be with Silas, one where I could let my two worlds intertwine without fear of retribution.

For the first time in months, I felt light, like I could rise up from the very ground and ascend to the heavens. The world seemed brighter. I looked up at Silas and Gabriel, marveling at what they'd just done. This was it. The way forward.

"It would work," I whispered, heart pounding.

"Maura…" Sid's voice held a warning tone. He squatted down to where I sat and leaned his head forward, close enough that our noses could touch. "With all due respect, what the absolute fuck do you think you're doing?"

His eyes were wide and wild, the afternoon sun making them look honey. He studied my face. I let my lips lift into a smile.

"I'm going to save my family. I'm going to save those kidnapped people. And I'm going to show the world exactly who my father really is."

17

MAURA

Sid and Nadia spoke at the edge of the playground. The tall woman's eyebrows moved up and down, her usual smile fading from her lips as she listened. Her eyes flicked to us, then back to Sid before they widened in surprise. Sid put his hands on his hips, then up in the air. Nadia nodded, pulling the radio to her mouth.

Was she angry? Surprised? Afraid? I couldn't tell. My head throbbed. There was so much to weave through, so much to untangle. I wished I could take my brain out and wash it in the laundry. First, we needed to speak with Avi. Then, if he agreed, we needed to make a plan to infiltrate the commune and figure out how to start getting people back to the Centre. The kidnapped group. My family. Judging by what Silas said, there were plenty of others. Once they were safe, I could focus on Silas's suggestion. Taking down Father.

My fingers roamed over the top of the mulch. I also needed to tell Eli what was happening, and fast. If I didn't like him going out on the scavenging mission, he *certainly* was not going to like Silas's plan. But I knew he would see reason better than I had. If we were going to keep the community safe and have any chance at living the rest of our lives free from Father's influence, we needed to try and do something. This was that chance. I knew it. Sid knew it. Silas and Gabriel knew it. And Eli would know it, too. Even if he didn't like it.

Sid ambled back to where the three of us sat, thumbs hooked in the gun holster belt around his waist. I looked up.

"What did Nadia say?"

He chewed his lip before answering. "She's talking to Avi now." He eyed the two boys. "You know, if you come with us into our community, you'll be in a locked area."

Silas squinted up at him. "Understood."

Sid raised his brows and looked at me. In the distance, Nadia made large strides across the grassy lawn toward us. She fixed her gaze on Silas and Gabriel, features neutral, no sign of stress or worry. She looked tired, but who didn't these last few days? As she approached, she secured the radio to her belt.

"Avi's ready. We'll secure them first and do intake in the garage. We'll get someone to prepare the cells." She turned her gaze to the two boys. "If we consider Maura helping you, our leader, Avi, insists on a truth in good faith," she said. "The location of our community members might be a good place to start."

Silas kept his face neutral. "Understood."

The balls of Nadia's cheeks flushed pink, a simple, unavoidable sign of her frustration. Even though the boys didn't trust Father, they still held the same fears I had when I'd fallen into the creek. Outsiders were the enemy. You couldn't trust them, even if they wanted to help you.

"Stand up," she ordered.

They did as they were told. She handed Sid a small

plastic strip and together, they secured Gabriel's and Silas's hands behind their backs. The two men kept their gazes forward without protest as they wrapped blindfolds around their eyes.

We drove back to the Centre in silence, Sid at the wheel, the two Hunters in the backseat. I kept my hand gripped on the door handle. The world felt upside down and hazy. My two worlds collided in a way I'd never anticipated.

Sid turned the truck into the deserted parking lot, slowing our speed.

"Maura," he said, turning his gaze to me. "Are you *sure* about this? You know, once we tell Avi…" He tightened his grip on the steering wheel.

"I know." Avi would like this idea, especially if it meant rescuing the prisoners and taking down Father. And that meant I'd be locked into a commitment. My heartbeat accelerated at the thought and I closed my eyes to steady my breathing.

Because it didn't just mean a commitment. It meant leaving. Again. Leaving behind this life I'd built for myself without the commune's rules or expectations. It meant leaving people I loved. I was a woman torn between two worlds. No matter where I existed, there were people on the other side I was helpless to save. I had left Mother, Morgan, and the rest of my family behind for freedom. But I'd never truly had liberation. I'd just run farther from the puppeteer. None of us would be free from Father's influence. Not unless we did something.

I leaned back in my seat and opened my eyes. The mall rose up as we approached the open garage, the sun disappearing behind us as Sid parked the truck. I blinked, adjusting to the darkness, before looking back at Gabriel and Silas. Their steel gazes fixed on me and for a moment,

I saw them as Hunters; ruthless and committed to God. Just like Andrew had been.

I'd made the mistake of trusting him. I hoped I wasn't making the same mistake now.

There was no time to reconsider. A fleet of security trucks parked, blocking us in. Two black-hooded figures appeared beside the rear doors, opening them as they helped the boys out and into the concrete garage.

Sid killed the engine. Voices echoed in the large space, bouncing off one another, increasing in volume as I got out of the car. Before I had time to ready myself, Avi came around one of the trucks, eyes wide as he drank in the scene.

"Take them to the Armory," he said to the two security team members holding onto each arm of the blond brothers. "Separate cells. Get them some food, please." He turned to us. "Good work, you two. Meet you in my office in ten."

"How about thirty?" I asked, removing the jacket and bulletproof vest Sid had given me before we'd left. I shoved them into his arms. "There's something I need to do first."

Avi inspected me before nodding. "See you in thirty."

Sid craned his neck toward me, lifting one of his perfectly manicured eyebrows.

"I'll meet you in the Armory," was all I said, before I raced to the doors leading back into the mall.

THE HALLWAYS WERE RELATIVELY empty at mid-day. Dirt and dust balls hovered in the corners I raced past, begging to be swept. I thought of Kendra and felt a fresh wave of grief. It emboldened the determination I had in each step I took, heading toward the conversation I was about to have.

When Eli had left without smoothing out our disagreement, I knew I could never let that happen again. I'd felt helpless when I heard he was hurt. He'd traveled into dangerous territory and I hadn't been able to tell him how I felt. And once it was too late, and he was gone, all I could do was be afraid. Afraid my actions were unforgivable. Afraid he would die. Afraid I hadn't made it known how important he was to me.

I'd been helpless and afraid long enough.

Weakness had gotten me nowhere. Fear built my chains, binding me to Father. To the commune. To my faith. We had a chance to do better. To make the world better. To save people and reveal Father's ugliness to the people who needed to see it most. And the only person I wanted to tell was Eli. Even if it made him angry. Even if it meant I would never see him again. I wanted him to know that this very thing was a possibility because of him. Because he was the one who made me see bravery in myself. He saw strength in me before I saw it with my own eyes. He was the only person I trusted to tell me I could do this. Because even though I knew he'd dislike this plan, I knew he'd tell me what I needed to hear.

I raced past the Armory, the bathrooms, through the Mess Hall, and into Inventory. I skidded around the curve, back toward Medical, pausing before the door to catch my breath.

Twenty minutes. That was all I had.

I entered the lobby and walked into the well-lit back room. Eli sat up, his leg still suspended from the ceiling, reading a book. He looked better than he had when I left this morning. Some color had returned to his face, and he'd trimmed his beard. He let the book fall into his lap.

"Finally," he breathed, dog-earring the page and putting it on the table beside the bed. "What the hell is going on?"

Anxiety coated his tone, his eyes darting up and over

my shoulder as though he were looking for the others. I opened my mouth, ready to let the words roll off my tongue. But they didn't come. There was so much. Too much. I didn't know where to start.

He furrowed his brow in concern. "Come here," he said, his voice gentle. "Sit down."

I came forward, sitting at the edge of his bed. I studied the freckles on my knuckles, letting my pointer finger trace the fading cut I'd gotten a week ago from the scrubbing board.

"Maura?"

Tears pricked my eyes at the softness in his voice. I looked up and felt my heart sink. There was no good way to do this. I considered how he must have felt before he left on the scavenging trip that had landed him here. Complicated emotions ran rampant in my chest. Leaving was devastating. But not trying would haunt me.

"The two Hunters at the border are called Silas and Gabriel," I started, looking back down at my hands. "They're rebels. And they want me to go back to the commune with them."

Eli's brows raised, mouth drooping. He shook his head. "No," he said with a nervous laugh. "You told them that's absolutely not happening, right?" His eyes traveled over my face, and he frowned. "Maura. Come on. They'll kill you."

"Eli." I took a shaky breath.

"No." He sat up straighter, shaking his head. "Maura, *no*. You must be joking. You can't go *back*."

"I must. I *must*. This is a chance to take down my father, maybe the only chance we'll ever have."

"They're going to fucking *kill you*," he yelled.

"Stop!" I pressed my palms to my face. "Please," I said, softly. "Please listen to me. I need you to tell me this will work. I need you to tell me I can do this. Please, Eli. This isn't something I can run away from anymore. I can make a difference. A real difference."

For a moment, it looked like he might fight me again, but he pulled back whatever words were in his mouth and pressed his lips together.

"Okay," he agreed. "Let's hear it."

Eli listened as I told him what happened from when I'd reached Avi's office to only a few moments ago. Through tears, I explained Silas's plan, what he thought was possible. What I thought was possible. That there were many unknowns, but if this worked — God, if this *worked* — how it could turn the tides of power in the commune and the rest of the country. We had a chance to live without fear. I could save my family. Show them what life looked like outside of Father's rules and expectations. I told him it was essential we do this. That I *wanted* to do this. That maybe I even believed this was something God led me toward.

And that everything about this terrified me.

I looked up, his bruised face blurry. "*This* is the way we move forward," I said. "I couldn't see it before when it was just me. But knowing there are others in the commune who feel like I do?" I shook my head. "I have to try. *We* have to try. I think I can do this. Right? I can, can't I?"

His lips parted as his dark eyes studied my face. I waited for him to fight me again. To tell me this was wrong, and I needed to stay here and we'd figure something else out. But he didn't. Instead, he reached out for me, touching the bottom of my chin. He was gentle, letting the pads of his middle three fingers brush my skin before he cupped my cheek. I leaned into his warmth, relishing in the comfort of the gesture.

"As badly as I don't want you to, I know, if there's

anyone who can do this," he said in his hoarse voice, "it's you."

My face crumpled. His fingers worked over my cheeks as he tried to wipe my new tears away. But there were too many, and this was too much. I moved, inching upward on the bed and carefully laid up against his chest. I knew it was intimate and uncharacteristic of our friendship. But he welcomed it, cradling me as I calmed in his arms.

"I don't want you to go," he finally whispered, so close I felt his breath in my hair. "I hate it. It scares me. Losing you…" I felt him shake his head. "But—"

"But?" His thumb caressed my shoulder.

"But I think you're right. I don't know if there'll be another chance like this. If there was ever a way to knock Peter out of power, then this is it. I think Avi will pull out everything we have to make sure we take full advantage of this." He sighed, and I felt his chin against my forehead. "And I think it will work."

"You do." It wasn't a question, but a statement of relief. If Eli thought it could work, then I could trust the plan.

"I do."

"I'm afraid," I admitted.

"Me too."

"But I think I'm more afraid to not try." I turned my head to look up at him, so close I could see the individual whiskers in his beard, the small bumps from where he'd trimmed too close to the skin.

He sighed, his chest rising with me on it. "In an ideal world, we could run. Go somewhere else, where nobody would find us, where we could live without fear. But the horrible truth is there's nowhere to go where we'd be free from Peter's vengeance."

"I have to do this," I whispered.

"I know you do."

I nuzzled into Eli, inhaling his scent, memorizing the earthy undertones and sour sweat that was so distinctly him.

"I have to go see Avi."

"Go. I'm not going anywhere."

I stayed there for a moment longer, wishing I could freeze time, that I could stay huddled up beside him for eternity. But reality waits for no woman. And I had work to do.

18

INSIDE THE ARMORY, three men dressed in black hovered at the far end of the room, where sun shone through small windows near the ceiling. They crossed their arms over their chests, shielding a door behind them. As I approached, it opened and Sid stuck his head out, glancing around until his gaze landed on me.

"Here," he said, waving me over.

I brushed past the guards and entered a long, narrow room lit by lanterns. Cold stone walls surrounded us, making the space feel cavernous. Nadia and Avi sat on a metal bench pressed up against the closest wall. Silas and Gabriel occupied the two cells opposite them.

Out of the sun and in the lantern light, the blond-haired brothers both looked aged. Shadows danced across their sharp features, highlighting their teenage acne scars and tired, purple bruises beneath their weary eyes. Their arms had been untied, and they now sat at the edge of two cots facing us.

Avi sat forward, his forearms resting on his legs, the bubble of his belly hanging between his thighs. Nadia leaned against the wall, her long legs crossed in front of her. Everyone looked up as Sid closed the door.

"Maura," Avi greeted me.

"Sir."

"Before we go any further, I want to make sure you agreed to this," he said, looking at the boys. "Because from what I've gathered so far, you've agreed to go back into the Coutts commune for an unspecified amount of time to try to take your father down."

I swallowed. "I did agree to that, yes."

"And you understand this is—"

"Dangerous, yes." I tried to bite back my annoyance. "I know."

Avi's shoulders relaxed. "Okay." He rubbed his chin before he spoke again. "We have confirmation on where Dale's team is being held," he said to the room. "What these young men told us matched the information Francis and his team brought back to us the other day. That honesty is what will continue moving forward. It is what will keep our partnership open. We will offer a refuge for you and anyone else from the commune who needs it. But if that honesty ends—" He narrowed his eyes. "—the partnership ends too. Understood?" Avi kept his fierce gaze on the two boys, who gave firm nods in his direction.

"There are certain groups of people that require refuge more than some," Nadia said. "Our scavenging team, for one."

"My family," I interjected. "If I can find them."

"There are plenty," Silas said. "Hundreds. If we can develop a system to smuggle the most vulnerable out of the commune back here, that would be the first order of business. The rest we'll recruit for opposition."

Avi nodded. "If we're using Maura, we must make it impossible for Peter to harm her in any way."

"That's where Media comes in," Gabriel said. "With the New Year's celebration happening in a few days, the cameras will be out in full force. They start at sunup. Near Sciences and Innovations.

"It would be best if Gabriel and I return a few days prior," continued Silas. "We can get our contacts ready for her arrival — station friendly Hunters at the border where she'll arrive, position our contact in Media to make sure the cameras are angled where she'll emerge. The cameras can't cut away and Peter will likely still be at the church and the Hunters caught off guard. There will be plenty of time to capture her entry back into the commune to prove she is well and alive on live video. If we can get her to a microphone, it would be even better."

"And what's stopping Peter from putting a bullet in her skull?" Sid asked, his tone curt.

"He won't," Silas said. "Peter is too proud for that. It would ruin everything he's built. Even though he carries out kill orders, he keeps his hands clean. He won't participate in anything messy."

"And if he orders a Hunter to do it?" Sid pressed.

"You don't think people would know that order came from him?" Silas asked. "Inside the commune, Hunters are mostly peaceful." He shook his head. "It's too risky."

"But there's always the possibility."

"*Sid*," I said, glancing at him.

"I just want to make sure we're covering all our bases." Sid crossed his arms. "For god's sake, we're sending you, unarmed, back into the mouth of a beast that wants to eat you. This is unbelievably dangerous."

"Please. I know what I'm getting into," I said, my voice strained. "I know what this means. I know how dangerous this is. I'm okay with it."

"Well I'm not," Nadia said. "Sid's right. We need to make sure we're protecting you from all angles."

"I agree," said Avi. "She won't go in alone."

"You can't very well send an army in after her," Sid said.

"She won't be alone," Silas said. "The Hunters will protect her. I'll make sure of it." He met my eyes. "Andrew, for all his faults and shortcomings, does genuinely seem to care about your wellbeing. He won't stand for violence against you. Especially if he believes you to be a martyr."

"That didn't work so well when they took me to the Island of Repentance," I said, skeptical.

"This is different," Silas argued.

"What about friendlies?" Avi suggested. "Hunters in awe of her resurgence? Could they behave genuinely surprised at her reappearance and walk with her under that assumption? They'd be armed, correct? So they could protect her under the guise of being awestruck?"

"That could work," I agreed.

Sid chewed on his lip, tilting his head back and forth as he considered Avi's suggestion.

"So Media captures Maura, then what?" Avi mused. "We need to figure out a system to start getting people out and here to safety." He turned to Silas and Gabriel. "I assume your Media people have the means to communicate outside of the commune?"

The boys nodded. "They have high-powered radios we could potentially take control of," said Gabriel. "Peter and some of the Hunters communicate regularly with other Outsiders. So we'd need to be careful of that. But yes, the capability is there."

"Good. Then that's our first order of business. Infiltrate your communications system. Get someone who oversees radios to connect with us. We'll develop a code in case we have any eavesdroppers." He glanced at Nadia. "I'll hand that over to you. Next, a smuggling system. What would be the best way to get people out?"

"The waste center," Silas said. "Trucks collect trash from all areas of the commune and dump it in the landfills. That'd be the quickest, most secure way."

"So, someone in Sanitation, then?"

Silas nodded, peering at his brother. "I think we might know someone."

"Then we'll have people placed near that area," Avi said, glancing at Nadia. "Twenty, thirty miles out. We can establish a few safe houses and make trips every few days. We'll use coordinates to establish location."

"That'll work," said Gabriel.

"It'll take some time to build up a team," Silas said. "Months, perhaps." He eyed me warily. "We'll stay in contact to report numbers and move as quickly as possible without getting caught."

"How large is the current security team?" Avi asked. "How many Hunters does he have throughout the commune?"

"Just under four thousand, if I had to guess," said Silas. "But the Prophet is recruiting younger by the day. They're spread out across each zone. There are less on the coast, more near the Peak and northern borders."

Avi hung his head, eyes shifting in the lantern light as he sorted his thoughts. "So if we were to infiltrate when the time was right, our best entry is from the oceans and the southern border."

"I'd say so, sir," answered Silas. "But we could potentially have enough friendlies on border patrol to make it easier. We'd just need time to build those numbers and solidify those posts."

"Fair enough," said Avi. "Once you've built that up on the inside, we can coordinate a better plan of attack for when the time is right. While we wait, we'll work on training up our team. It's small, but mighty."

Silas nodded.

"And our plan B?" Nadia asked the room. "If things go sideways?"

"We'll coordinate with the Hunters to get her out to safety should we detect any danger to her life. Diversions are easy enough to cause," Silas assured us.

"Plus, the Prophet will be on his best behavior because of the cameras," said Gabriel. "If things go sideways, it'll be after the events, once night has fallen. And in the dark, it's always easier to leave."

"But," Silas said, directing his full attention to me, "in order for this to work, you're going to have to act the part completely. That means your return will not be pleasant. I highly suspect you will be subject to distasteful behavior behind closed doors. And there will be nothing I can do to stop that."

I stiffened. I had known this from the minute Silas proposed his idea, but having him dangle it in front of my face was another matter entirely. If I thought Father had been furious when I'd fallen into the creek, this would drive him mad. His hands would be tied to maintain his public image, but I knew he wouldn't hesitate to throw anything he could at me in private.

"The worse he is toward me, the more scared I'll assume he is," I said, hoping I sounded brave.

"And you'd be right," said Avi.

"The story you bring with you will matter," Silas continued. "People will want to know where you were, how you survived, what you learned while you were out here. They will want to know if you were alone. What you can teach them. And you're going to have to tell them all of these things in a way that makes it impossible *not* to follow you so that they can learn to trust you. So that when you show them the atrocities the Prophet is committing, they believe you. You must maintain a level of serenity that the Prophet can not touch no matter how hard he tries, no matter how much he threatens you. I will do all I can to ease it for you, Maura, but it may be torturous."

"And what part of my life hasn't been?" I shot back, surprised at the anger in my tone. "I've been stuck in some version of this hell my entire life. Watching my sister get ostracized from our family because she tried to run? Having to listen to her cry every single night for a life she knew was out there, but she'd never have? Watching my Mother raise her children without help, under impossible rules and expectations? Being married off to my uncle? Unable to bear children and be reminded of that pain nearly every day?" I shook my head at him. "I know pain. I know sacrifice and I know what it feels like because I lived it every day of my life."

I was trembling. I focused on steadying my breath, wishing I could stop the roll of emotions flooding through me and the words pouring from my mouth. But just like with Eli, I needed them to listen. I needed them to know.

"I'm terrified. I'd be stupid not to be. But I also know I am the person to do this. This is where God has led me. The past few months have shown me my strength, what I'm capable of. The people who have surrounded me, taken me under their wings, they've emboldened me, made me see things in myself I would have never seen otherwise. I've seen the evils within Father. What he's done to this world, to our commune, to our religion. I dedicated my life to him. To the false things he's preached. I believed them. I trusted him.

"I don't want anyone else to feel like I felt. Nobody deserves this. Outside or inside the commune. People shouldn't suffer if they don't have to. There is no reason we can not live in harmony, share our resources, and love one another. That's what God tells us. That's what I've always known to be true in my heart. Someone like my father does not belong in a position of power. He deserves to be exposed for who he truly is. So if I need to endure his wrath, so be it. If that's the cost this takes, I will gladly pay it."

The tears that came were hot and angry, the culmination of my frustration, fear and anguish. A scream built in my chest, begging for release, like a ticking bomb I could never detonate. I had buried so much under the surface, saved up my rage to fuel the bravery I knew it would take for me to go back into the commune that had stripped my very soul. But I was stronger now. Wiser. I would need to hold on to that, cling to it like the buoyant branch in the river when I'd left the Island of Repentance. It was essential to my survival. To maintain my identity. Because once I stepped foot back in his borders, Father's only goal would be to make me lose myself once more.

19

ELI

Dinner's lingering smell wafted through the empty Mess Hall. The crutches Holli found for me were too short, and I hunched over as I hobbled between the tables, cursing the stupid bullet that pierced my leg. The pain was much more manageable than it had been when I'd arrived, but an ache still shot into my hip with every step. My throat was healing, too. Swallowing now felt more like dull butter knives rather than porcupine quills.

But it was all background noise to the staggering fear that hung like a weight on my chest. I wanted to know what was going on with Maura. What plans Avi had put in place for her mission. A mission that terrified me.

Every single fiber of my being wanted to dissuade her from pursuing the Hunter's plans. But she'd been clear when she came to me earlier that day — she didn't want my protection. She didn't want to hear how dangerous it was or how afraid it would make me. She just wanted me to tell her she could do it. And even though I didn't want her to, I knew she could. Maura was capable of great things. She always had been.

But internally, I felt like my guts were going to fall out of my butt.

People lingered in the darkening halls after dinner, decompressing after work, sharing stories about their days, none the wiser. As I passed, I strained to listen for mentions of the young Hunters that had arrived at our gates, but it didn't seem to be common knowledge. Not yet, anyway.

The open gate to our room revealed Holli, Sid, and Maura sitting among the lantern light, chatting. Holli sat on the loveseat beside Maura, her eyes swollen red. I had hinted Maura had big news to share, but hadn't provided her the details. She was clearly clued in now.

"Welcome home, you big brute." Sid hovered near the front of the room, patting the recliner next to him. "Are those children's crutches?"

"I'll hit you with them," I threatened, waving one in the air.

"Consider me terrified."

I limped past him and sank into the recliner.

"Ladies," I greeted. Maura smiled and Holli looked up from the tissues she clutched in her hands. "Any updates?"

Maura sighed, warily eyeing Holli. "Well, I leave in three days," she said. "Silas and Gabriel are going to leave tonight. Get back to the commune to get the radio communication settled and get things situated so nobody kills me before I can step foot inside." She forced a dry laugh.

"Don't say that," Holli whispered.

"Sorry." Maura looked at her lap. "They assigned Sid and Darius to my transport. They'll leave me as close as possible to the drop-off point we coordinated with Silas. From there, I walk south. They capture me on live camera to prove I'm alive and have returned and then..." She threw her hands in front of her lackadaisically, "...we go from there."

"I just can't believe Avi's sending you alone," Holli said.

"There's not really another choice," argued Sid.

"And I won't be alone." Maura touched her arm. "We have a plan. It will work." She glanced at me, and I gave her a small, affirmative nod.

A knock came from the front of the room and Sid stepped aside, revealing Nadia and two blond-haired boys dressed in dirty clothing. They were sharp-featured and stern-faced, gazes focused only on Maura.

"Got a minute?" Nadia rested her knuckles on the gate's frame.

"Come on in," Maura said, standing.

The three people came in, crowding around the living space. "This is Silas," Maura pointed to the older-looking boy, "and his brother, Gabriel."

"Hello," they said in unison.

"This is Eli, Holli." Maura pointed to each of us. "And you know Sid."

The boys nodded, glancing around at each of us. They were younger than I thought they'd be, the little brother no older than sixteen. These were the men Avi was trusting to keep Maura alive? I bit my tongue to curb my skepticism.

"We're heading out to the safe house," Nadia said. From the corner of my eye, I saw Maura straighten. "They'll rest there, head out in the morning. We settled on the signals for when you get there."

"Red or green marks on the trees," Silas said to Maura. "We'll cover a small radius at the coordinates so you can't miss it. Turn around and go back to the safe house if you see red or there's nothing on the bark. Green means you're free to proceed."

"Hunters won't suspect?"

"We'll make sure everyone there knows the plan."

Maura nodded. I chewed on my tongue. It was a good plan. Simple, but good.

"Friendlies will meet you at the border," said Gabriel. "And then you'll do just as we discussed."

"Got it," Maura said.

"This will work," Silas said, taking a step toward her. His lips were set in a straight line, eyes locked in on Maura's face. He looked so determined one could almost confuse it with anger. That was good. Trusting Hunters still felt like suicide, but I saw this man's resolve in his features. He was fed up. Ready to fight.

"Please protect her," Holli whispered from the couch. She sniffled, catching the gazes of the two boys. "Please protect our girl."

She'd said what I wanted to, but hadn't had the courage for. In three days' time, what happened to Maura would be out of our hands. We'd be at the mercy of the long-distance radio and two angry boys.

"We'll protect her with our lives," the older brother said. "She's the key to this plan. Without her, it cannot work."

The gravity of that statement hung in the room like a wet cloud. Nadia cleared her throat and crossed her arms over her chest.

"Alright then," she said. "Let's get a move on, boys."

We waved goodbye to the young Coutts Hunters and Maura sat back down on the loveseat beside Holli, who grabbed her by the shoulder and pulled her into her arms. Maura let her, resting her head on the older woman's collarbone. I tried not to think too much about how she'd laid on me earlier that day. It had been a show of comfort. Of caring. That was all. Still, I found my fingers absentmindedly touching the bruises at the bottom of my neck where I'd felt her warmth before.

We spent the rest of the night playing games and joking around our small coffee table until the lanterns burned low and someone shushed us from the hallway. It felt good, the moment so necessary before what was to come.

I only wished we could sit in it forever.

OVER THE NEXT FEW DAYS, Maura was in and out of the room, running frenzied from location to location. Sid coached her through weapon training, from basic jiujitsu protection maneuvers, to how to wield a knife, and how to shoot a gun. Nadia and Avi discussed the intricate details of the story she would return to the commune with. She trained two new people in Housekeeping to allow Kendra to tend to her grief and manage while she was gone. Leo and the other Coutts survivors spoke with her about how to best protect her mental state when she returned.

Meanwhile, I attempted to get back to some normalcy, scouring inventory lists that had been left in the hands of a girl who seemed more interested in catching the eye of a meal server than she did maintaining an accurate count. I cursed my injury; it made everything so much more daunting. I moved at a snail's pace and struggled shaking Jae's screams from my ears every time I remembered he was gone.

The evening before Maura's departure, Avi requested the community to convene in the Mess Hall after dinner. I sat beside Holli and Shelly, Neil and Mia at the other end of our table. The area was so crowded, people stood at the edges of the room. Chatter and tension hovered in the air. I glanced around for Kendra, but she had still not returned to the public eye. I made a mental note to check on her tomorrow.

Avi approached from the Armory, flanked by Nadia, Sid, and Maura. The room quieted as they reached the Mess Hall. Pockets of worried whispers bubbled in the crowd.

"Good evening!" Avi's low voice rumbled through the space like a shockwave.

"Evening," a few people replied.

Avi nodded, eyes scanning the crowd, before he looked back at Nadia.

"I'm aware news travels fast around the community," he began. "Some of you may have heard about the folks brought back the other evening. I'd like you all to know these two gentlemen were from the Coutts commune." Murmurs broke out between a few people. "They are two young Hunters—"

"What?" someone said loudly.

"Did he say *Hunters*?" someone beside us asked.

"—who came to our borders to ask for our help." He glanced at Maura. "We have offered to give them that help, in exchange for the safe return of our people and what we hope will, ultimately, be a takedown of Peter Coutts."

Dissenting voices in the crowd grew, questions of outrage and concern.

"You're trusting the *Hunters*?" a voice cried.

Avi turned to them. "We are. They have given us reliable information about our community members who were kidnapped and we're taking measures to bring them home safely. I am confident these men are trustworthy based on my discussions with them. They risked their lives coming to our borders to ask for our help."

"Well, that doesn't mean shit," someone to my right mumbled. I took a deep breath, holding back my nasty glare. There was so much they didn't know.

"The Coutts commune is experiencing the consequences of a ruthless dictator," Avi continued, undeterred by the grumbling. "According to our most recent intel, Peter Coutts has not only made death threats against his own people, but has been kidnapping Outsiders since the flu hit our shores. He's drafting children into his arsenal, arming them with dangerous weapons, and asking them to kill anyone who doesn't agree with him. He continues to subject children to sexual abuse and child marriage. He is indoctrinating them, denying his people access to health-care, and terrifying them into submission. And it's getting worse by the day."

"And that's not to mention us," interjected Nadia, who stood tall in black jeans and a fitted turtleneck. "Peter can't continue to hoard the basic necessities we have a right to. We've done a great job of creating a safe and thriving community. It's time we take the next step to improve our situation."

There were a few nods of agreement, murmurs of concurrence between the grumbles.

"We are working with rebels within the commune borders, men who are looking to make a better life for themselves and the innocent people still subjected to Peter's wrath. We have agreed to accept refugees from the Coutts commune," Avi continued. "And I expect you all to treat them with kindness. Once they receive medical care, they will help us with necessary projects and tasks around the Centre."

"So we're just offering up our hard-earned resources to them?" I recognized that voice. It was the woman who'd given Maura a difficult time the other week at breakfast.

"With the understanding they'll participate to create more," Avi said, narrowing his eyes at her. "More hands means more output, which means a better life for us all until we have a more stable solution."

"But isn't that dangerous?" someone else asked. "What if Hunters follow them? What if they send spies?"

"The refugees will be vetted by the folks we're working with. There seems to be more unhappiness than we've been aware of."

"Then what?" the first woman asked. "Are you taking us to war?"

Avi's face darkened, and he narrowed his gaze at her. "I'm not taking you anywhere. We've been at war for years. Wouldn't you say? We have an opportunity to change the tides. The alternative is to sit here and wait for the Coutts to find our borders. I'd rather be on the offensive than the defensive." He drew his gaze back, addressing the rest of the crowd. "If you have any issues with this, please remember this is a free and open community. And you are welcome to leave at any time. I will never ask my people to fight for something they don't believe in."

The woman slumped back in her seat, looking defeated.

"That said, let me remind you all that complacency got us here in the first place. We need not revisit the mistakes of our past. It's our responsibility to fight against injustice and help those that need it. We're in a position to do that, aren't we? If we close our doors to people who seek refuge, aren't we just as bad as Peter?"

He glanced at Maura, who gripped her elbows to her chest. Her downward gaze looked deeply uncomfortable, but she raised her chin to meet Avi's eyes.

"One final note, we are looking for people to help maintain consistent communications between the Coutts commune and the Centre. If you are interested in this position, please let me know soon. All other questions and concerns should be directed to me privately."

With that, he nodded and turned around to return to the Armory. Conversation filled the air, some tinted with fear, some with outrage, and some with courage. It was all to be expected. This was big news. It would change everything about the Centre.

We followed the natural flow of the crowd out through the Mess Hall back into the walkway. Sid and Maura walked together, entering our room ahead of me and Holli. We lit our lanterns and settled around the coffee table.

"I think that went well," Sid said, breaking the silence.

"As well as can be expected," Holli agreed. "There are going to be people who have a lot to say about it."

"Let them." There was a bite to my tone. I looked at Maura, who sat still, looking down at her knees. My stomach rolled over. I clenched both fists, letting my fingernails dig into my palm.

The people who would argue and fight against accepting refugees could never do what Maura was about to do. Embarking on a dangerous journey that would be filled with trauma and pain for a chance to take down someone who she thought of as her father, as a Prophet, was unthinkable for most of us here. And if Maura, Silas, and Gabriel managed to do it, to take down Peter Coutts, to put him where he rightfully belonged, it would change the world. Forever.

"Avi will deal with them," Sid said, leaning back in his recliner with a yawn. "It's a good thing there are so many spare rooms, still."

"I just hope we get a doctor or two," Holli said, rubbing at her weary eyes. "It'd be nice to have a day off."

"You can say that again." Sid sat forward in the chair. "We should get to bed, Maura," he said. "We'll be up well before the sun."

Maura looked up and nodded, but made no move to stand from the couch. Her eyes drifted in thought. After a moment's hesitation, Sid said goodnight, moving back to his room. After peppering Maura with hugs and encouragement, Holli followed soon after.

I sat in the recliner, studying Maura. She kept her hands between her knees, head bowed, staring at the floor. Her curly hair hung down her shoulders, so much longer now than when we'd first met. Part of me wondered if she wanted me to leave her alone, but if she'd wanted that, she'd have retreated to her room.

With one hand on a crutch, the other on the armrest, I got up and hopped over to the loveseat, replacing Holli beside her. Startled, she raised her gaze, her face solemn, tears swimming in the corners of her brown eyes. In the lantern light, they looked so dark I could barely distinguish the pupil from her iris. I lingered on her face, memorizing her details, the curve of her short nose, the freckles that dotted her skin.

"Sorry," she whispered, pressing her mouth into her shoulder.

"For what?" I tilted my head.

She squeezed her eyes closed. "I don't know."

"There's no right way to handle this, you know. If silence is what you need, if it's prayer, or screaming into your pillow, nobody's going to judge you."

Maura forced a laugh, then wiped at her eyes. "I should feel more, shouldn't I?" She shook her head, looking down at the floor again. "I should be scared, or excited. Something. Instead, I just feel—" She threw up her hands, unable to come up with the word.

"That's okay too," I reassured her. My chest felt heavy. There was more I wanted to say, but had no right to.

"Are you afraid?" she asked, bringing her full attention to me. I watched her eyes as they traveled across my face, my nose, and my cheeks. She paused on my lips for a moment.

"Yes," I heard myself whisper. "Of losing you. Of you putting yourself in danger. Of you fighting this battle for us."

"It sounds so impressive when you say it."

"Because this is no small feat, Maura," I said. "You can change the world. You know that, right?"

Her pink lips rose into a small smile. "Yeah."

She held my gaze. Awareness crept into every nerve in my body. I felt her leg beside mine, the heat radiating from her skin. My heart beat in my throat, because I finally knew how to ease the persistent knot in my stomach. I was desperate for it, though I hadn't let myself feel it until now.

Gravity pulled me toward her. I was close enough to feel her unsteady breath on my nose. Her lips parted, eyes dancing across my features. I paused, waiting for her to pull back. To pull away. But she didn't.

I pressed my lips against hers.

It was gentle; a ghost of a kiss. She inhaled sharply at the touch. Hesitation froze me. I pulled back, blinking to steady my eyes on her. Did I misread her? Cross a line she wasn't okay with? She looked up at me through her dark lashes, bewildered.

"I—"

But she didn't let me finish. Maura leaned forward and closed the gap between us.

Time stilled. Her mouth fit mine like a missing puzzle piece. She was everything and nothing like I imagined she'd feel — delicate and determined. My lips roamed hers. I wanted to savor her softness. Her taste. Let my mouth show her how I felt without speaking. She smelled of fresh air and tasted like sunshine, forever the bright spot in the darkness surrounding us.

My hands found her neck. Glided up her smooth skin and into her curls. She tilted her face, sinking into my touch. I felt her fingers, hesitant on my shoulder. Gentle on my stubbled jaw.

Need blossomed in my stomach. I shifted closer, bringing a hand to her chin. Guided her face gently with my fingers to deepen our kiss. Her hands traced my cheeks. Plunged into my hair. Her mouth opened, insistent for more. Our tongues danced until it became difficult to breathe. Difficult to think.

The world fell away. I could only focus on her silky curls beneath my fingers. Her greedy lips on mine. We were desperate in a way only two people who knew their lives were about to change could manage. Minutes passed, maybe hours. It didn't matter. Tasting her fed my desire. Obliterated my fear. Made it possible to remember there was still good in this world. Forever would not be long enough to explore her. To memorize the details of her features. The softness of her skin.

It was always her.

Perhaps I'd known it from the minute I'd pulled her out of that creek. Despite the dangers, despite the fear and hatred around the Coutts, something always drew me to Maura. Brought together by chance. Bound together by circumstance. But this? This was born of our own volition. Our desires. Our inescapable need for one another.

We came up for air. My breath felt stunted, yearning stretching the muscles in my chest. Her bruised lips curled into a sheepish smile. Lantern light made her flushed cheeks shine. I caressed her jaw, letting my fingers trail across her warm skin.

"Wow." Her breath ghosted across my lips.

"Wow?"

"*That's* what a kiss is supposed to be like?"

I laughed, kissing her nose.

"I guess so."

I pulled Maura into my arms, her head resting against my chest. The room was quiet. Still. I ran my fingers over her hair, smoothing it. She ran hers up and down my bicep. What I would give to keep her here forever, to savor this bliss, to feel the weight of her body against mine for the rest of our days. With Maura, I could forget the pain, grief, and fear this world insisted on. I could lose myself in her, forget the war raging outside, and the responsibilities we had to others.

But the world was cruel, cold, and callous. And no matter how badly I wished for it, these were only dreams. I could not protect Maura anymore. She had grown beyond me; a warrior built from perseverance and fearlessness. She would do what no one else could — travel into battle, alone. Armed only with the trust of others. Back into a world that had shattered her soul. I knew she would succeed, that she was the one who would free us. Yet all I could offer her was this. And it didn't feel like enough.

"Please come back," I whispered, lifting her chin with my fingers so she'd look at me. "I will never, ever, forgive you if you don't come back."

She chuckled through her nose.

"I will," she promised. "One way or another, I will find my way back to you."

20

MAURA

IT FELT like I'd just fallen asleep by the time Sid shook me awake. I dressed in low lantern light, sleep clouding my reflexes. Avi and Silas had been thoughtful about the outfit I'd return to the commune in. A long, white, wool-lined dress with bits of lace around the hem. White represented purity. New beginnings. Innocence.

My hair would hang loose. I stuffed my feet into the boots I'd left the Island of Repentance with. The last touch was a jacket to fend off the cold, but that I would need to leave behind before I reached the border. Who knew martyrs didn't wear jackets?

One last thing. The photograph Nadia had taken of me and Eli. I took it from the pillowcase, my belly fluttering at the memory from last night. Soft, greedy lips. Strong hands in my hair. I had *never* been touched or tended to that way. After tracing our outlines, I folded the photograph, tucking it carefully into the cup of my bra. It would be the only thing I took with me.

Sid met me in the common room, checking the supplies in his pack. He and Darius would only be gone for the night, but would carry food, water, a medical kit, and a gun. As I approached, he held his lantern up to inspect me. He grinned.

"You look like an angel."

I glanced down at the dress. "I guess that's the point."

"Here." He threw me a granola bar, and I caught it mid-air. "Breakfast. Come on."

We slipped beneath the gate and into the mall's dark walkway. The Centre was nearly silent, spare a few snores and a crying baby somewhere closer to the Armory. Our footsteps echoed against the high ceiling as we walked toward the garage. I threw the crinkled bar wrapper away before finishing the rest of it in one bite. I wasn't hungry, but I'd need all the energy I could get.

Was this the last time I'd see this place? I slowed my pace in a last ditch effort to memorize its details. The Centre had been home. It had allowed me to feel safe, to laugh and have fun without rules or restrictions. Perhaps I would never come back. Perhaps I would never again laugh at one of Sid's jokes, sink into one of Holli's hugs, or feel Eli's lips against my own.

My heart twisted at the thought. No. I couldn't think that way. It was important to remain positive, even though every piece of me wished I could stay. That I could hide away, ignore this looming responsibility, and live the rest of my life in peace. But this was a mission I was born to take. One these last few months had guided me toward. And I was determined to see it through.

We pushed through the doors and into the garage. Darius and Avi stood in the distance, near the open door and the truck. Their heads raised as we approached.

"Sid. Maura," Darius greeted us. His sharp gaze made me feel scrutinized.

Avi lifted his lantern and gave me a stern look.

"Well," he said, "you certainly look the part."

I sighed. "Let's hope so."

Sid pulled me into his side by my shoulders. "You're going to do great. This will work."

"It will," Avi agreed. "We already heard from one of Gabriel's contacts via radio earlier this evening." He smiled. "Those boys are working faster than I thought."

Warmth blossomed in my chest. That was something. Hope.

"Let's get a move on," Darius interrupted, peering out the open door and into the overcast, dark sky. He rubbed his hands over the arms of his leather jacket. "We're three hours out and we'll be cutting it close. We'll need to drop you at dawn, then retreat to the safe house. Once it's dark, we'll return to the Centre. You'll have until then to turn around and come back to us if anything goes awry." He turned back toward me, his dark eyes narrowed. "Got it?"

"I understand."

"Good. Let's go." He got into the driver's seat.

"Maura?" Avi reached out his hand and I shook it, startled at his strength. "Godspeed. You have my utmost respect and gratitude. I know this isn't easy, but your bravery and willingness to confront these atrocities will change our world. Let's put this monster where he belongs." His nostrils flared as his grip tightened around my fingers. "I will see you soon."

I squeezed back as hard as I could. "Yes, sir."

Sid and I joined Darius in the car. The breakfast bar swam in my stomach as I buckled my seatbelt. Deep breaths. In and out. But my pounding heart wouldn't quit. There was no turning back now. There was no giving up, no refusals, no regrets.

This was it.

I was returning to the commune, into the hands of

someone who wished me dead. But this time, I held all the power.

"GREEN, go ahead. Red or nothing means turn around," Darius reminded me as he slowed the truck to a stop. Night had begun to lighten at its edges. We sat in the middle of what looked like a graveyard for old cars, trucks, and buses. Something the sign in front called a *Salvage Yard*. "The friendlies at the border will point you to the entry spot. Just focus on moving south."

"Right. Green on trees is go ahead. Red or nothing, come back here," I repeated.

Rubber and dew tinted the fresh air as we climbed out of the truck. Sid shifted his weight, eyes darting across the dark landscape before landing on me. His nervous demeanor softened my anxiety. For all his strength and combativeness, I was touched he was so worried about my wellbeing. I smiled at him with reassurance to remind him I knew what I was heading into.

I fell in step with the two men as we left the truck behind and walked through the decimated automobiles, piled atop each other so high they rivaled the mall's ceiling height. As we walked, Darius pointed out a small concrete building where he and Sid would settle once they set me on my path. This was where I'd return at the sign of any danger.

We walked through the rest of the salvage yard, emerging through a large break in the wire fence on the other side. Full pine tree woods covered the space in front of us, darkening the forest floor.

It felt wonderful to be outside, but what lay ahead of me filled me with dread. Once you tasted freedom, even a little bit, it seemed impossible to exist any other way. For this to work, I'd have to become the version of myself I thought I'd left behind. I was about to slip into a past life where I would need to maintain intricate lies to survive.

We walked as a tight group for a while until the pines began to thin. Darius slowed and stopped, turning to face me and Sid.

"You have about another half an hour to go," Darius said, pointing in the same direction we'd been walking. "You'll come across the painted trees soon. But we'll have to leave you here." He shook his head. "Too much of a risk to go much further."

I nodded, frozen to the spot. Existing alone was all I wished for back in the commune. Now, I'd give anything to be back at the Centre with people who loved me.

"Your jacket." Darius held out his hand.

"Right." I shrugged the material off and gathered it in my hands, shivering in the cold morning air. Absentmindedly, I touched the corner of my breast, making sure the photograph was still tucked safely away.

Darius put the jacket beneath his arm, then gave me a curt nod. "Best of luck," he said, blandly. "And...I hope to see you soon."

It was the kindest thing I'd ever heard him say to anyone. I smiled before turning to Sid.

Sid, the protector. The fiercely loyal brother. The man who had rescued me, kept me alive, and given us all reasons to keep going. He stood at least a foot above me, peering down at me with his dark eyes, his dreads neatly tied up in a ponytail. He bit his lip in worry before he reached out and pulled me into his chest. I squeezed him, feeling the muscles in his back tighten as he pushed the air from my lungs.

"You're the strongest fucking person I know," he said,

shaking my frame. He pulled back, hands still on my shoulders, and looked at me.

"I had a pretty good teacher, I think," I said, wrinkling my nose at him as I tried to curb my tears.

"You—" He shook his head, blinking as he looked up. "Listen to me." He brought his gaze back down and sniffled. "You are more than capable of being the leader those people need. Look what you've done, how far you've come. Walk in there and claim your stake. Show them who the real boss is. Give your father something to be afraid of."

"I will."

"We'll see you soon, Maura Coutts. Go give them hell."

He pulled me in again. I squeezed my eyes closed, letting the tears roll, not caring that they soaked into his shirt or that my nose was full of snot. He was the last piece of home I could touch. I heard his chest quiver, the small, uneven intake of breath. Sid reached up, wiped at his face, then released me.

I rose to my full height, watching as he readjusted his backpack and turned to Darius.

"We'll see you on the other side," Sid said, his words carried away in the breeze.

I pressed my fingers to my lips, kissed them, and sent it back to him. He put his hand over his heart and patted. With my lips pressed together, I turned and walked away, unable to bear any more. I felt like my chest would burst, like I could explode from my grief. Tears fell hot against my cold face, making me more aware of the jacket's absence.

Never had I felt so exposed or untethered. No backpack. No weapon. Completely alone. Against my better judgment, I looked over my shoulder, back where I'd left Darius and Sid. But they were already gone. Empty forest loomed.

For a moment, I couldn't breathe. It was like someone had knocked the wind from my lungs. I wanted to run back, beg them to take me home, to hide me, protect me, and tell Silas and Gabriel the deal was off.

But Morgan, Mother, and my siblings waited. Dale's scavenging team. Silas, Gabriel, and the others. The young boys being drafted. The children being married to grown men. Their safety and happiness, the chance at a life worth living, was all up to me. It depended on this plan working. I was the martyr. My appearance at the edge of the commune this morning would mark the beginning of a battle I would have no choice but to finish.

I let my legs carry me forward. Dead leaves and stiff pine needles crunched beneath my boots, but the rhythmic cadence of my footsteps settled me. Was God listening? Did he understand my plight, my reasoning for what I was about to do, what I was about to claim? He must.

Please, God. Forgive me, absolve me of these lies I must tell to save my friends. To help the innocent. Please protect me. Please, God. Please.

Light rose in the sky, shifting its color from navy to bird's egg blue. Wispy clouds moved lazily overhead through the gaps in the trees. My dress was so long it trailed behind me, collecting dirt and debris. I let it. It would all be part of the story I knew I must tell once I got there.

Onward I walked, anxiety gathering like a ball of yarn in my chest. Had it been thirty minutes? It was hard to tell. I glanced at the trees, twice mistaking moss for the green marks, once mistaking leaves for red. But finally, I saw it, in the distance — a bright green mark painted on a peeling, white birch.

Keep coming, it beckoned me.

And I obeyed.

21

MAURA

LARGE, glass skyscrapers rose above the pine trees like giants clawing their way from the earth. I'd never been this close to the Sciences and Innovations area. No woman I knew had been allowed down in the valley. Our family duties and jobs confined us to the peak or surrounding mountains. The men came here. This was their domain.

I shivered, a cold chill deep in my bones. The tips of my fingers, nose, and toes had grown numb a while back. Somehow, the temperature felt colder even as the sun brightened the surroundings. I slowed, taking careful steps toward the buildings.

Where was the person I was supposed to meet? I feared accidentally walking into the wrong territory, stumbling across a Hunter who was not friendly. The entire plan gone amiss before it even began.

From the corner of my eye, I glimpsed a familiar shade of green.

I froze. Hunters. Guns. I winced, wrapping my arms around myself, as if that would stop a bullet from shattering my rib cage. What if the Hunters had caught on to our plan? What if they'd put the green on the trees to trick me? What if they'd overcome Silas and Gabriel and were ordered to shoot me on sight?

The person in the helmet turned.

I readied myself for the onslaught of bullets. I searched for a prayer, wondered if my feet would carry me far enough to outrun death. I waited for the gloved hand to reach for the weapon strapped across his back. My heart slowed. I took a breath.

The Hunter moved his head up and down but did not reach for his weapon. Instead, he pushed up the visor in the helmet, revealing pale skin and blue eyes. Familiar eyes. For a moment I wondered if it was Andrew, but no — just another Coutts boy who'd inherited Father's genes.

"Maura?" His voice was squeaky, on the edge of manhood. A number — 3978 — was sewn to his uniform.

It hadn't been long since I'd spoken to Sid or Darius, but using my voice this close to the commune sent a fresh wave of terror through me.

"Hi," I breathed.

"Oh, my." He folded at the waist, putting his hands up as he bowed his head. "Praise God. *Praise God*! I can't believe you're here."

The odd gesture made me take a step back. This seemed like a sign of worship. Not something I was expecting. He glanced up, his face falling as he studied mine. "No!" He straightened. "Sorry. I just didn't think…Well, it just seemed a little farfetched, what Silas was saying. We wanted to believe him, you know, but…anyway, *you're actually here*."

"Yes…"

"Well, I'm here to protect you. There's a whole group of us." He puffed his chest. "We're calling ourselves the

M&M's." He laughed, as if this was very clever. "Maura's Minders. You get it?" He grinned.

"M&M's?" The term reminded me of Mia.

"Yeah!"

"That's very nice, er—?"

"Oh," he said. "My name's Joseph. I'm supposed to lead you in." His face flushed as he looked up and around at the trees. "Uh, we're going…this way."

His uncertainty bothered me — a stark contrast to the confidence Nadia, Sid, and Avi always exuded. But I was already this far, wasn't I? I couldn't turn back now.

"Do you need anything before we move in?" he asked, turning his head over his shoulder. "Water? Food?" He patted his pockets. "Got you a bit of both."

"Thank you," I said. "That was kind of you."

"Least I could do." He handed me a small bottle of water and a squished package of beef jerky. "Silas said you'd be traveling a ways."

"Yes." I ripped the beef jerky open with my teeth and ate it between swigs of water.

"There's a code word for any sign of danger," Joseph said as we walked. "But Gabriel said the Prophet is up in his office getting ready for morning mass at the peak, so when he finds out what's going on, it'll take him some time to even get down here or give orders, so I think we'll be just fine." He rubbed his gloved hands together excitedly.

He could've been talking about the weather and it made me dizzy. Did this young man understand the scope of what was about to happen? What he was about to help unleash? My heart beat in my throat. I was about to come back from the dead. The members of the commune were about to witness my resurrection. It was both miraculous and terrifying being on the other side of the knowledge I had now.

For nearly a year, I believed there were no survivors outside of the commune. When I met Eli and realized he was an Outsider — and furthermore, part of a larger group — it challenged everything I knew to be true. But I couldn't have believed it without seeing it with my own eyes.

Today, I would bring a similar revelation to thousands of people. I would offer them proof. They would *see* my father's lies laid out before them. And they would have to grapple with the truth, same as I had.

As long as everything went to plan.

We walked through thinning trees, soft rays of early morning light filtering through the pine needles. Pockets of dead grass dotted the dirt until the ground morphed into ashy gray. Finally, the tree line broke, and we emerged in the mouth of Coutts Valley.

I had never seen the commune from this angle, and the view was breathtaking. We stood at the lowest point, staring up at Coutts Peak, framed by towering buildings. The church built into the mountainside was barely visible — a distant shadow, still dark as the sun crept up behind the mountain. White covered the tip of the peak. Father once told us it was one of the last places where snow still accumulated and did not melt. Another gift from God, he'd claimed.

The buildings that made up the Sciences and Innovations area were bathed in shades of chrome. Paved roads ran in a grid pattern between the metal structures which shimmered in the low light, reflecting outward as if the entire area was underwater. Coming from the forest and the dilapidated mall, this place looked otherworldly.

Beyond, I knew, were the large nuclear cooling towers used for energy, but I couldn't see them from this vantage point. In fact, I couldn't see anything beyond these tall buildings, and it made my insides itch with uncertainty. If Eli and Sid had taught me anything, it was to always have a good view of whatever you were walking into.

This didn't deter Joseph. He continued forward like we were on our way to church and he had not a care in the world. We reached a low wire fence, easy enough to step over. Its position cut the forest off from the man-made structures, as if someone had taken part of a city and plopped it into the valley. The contrast between the two was strange and unnatural.

We walked along the fence, passing the rear of the buildings. Stacked boxy structures whirred, powering whatever was going on inside. They were so loud, the sound likely forced the wildlife away. I could barely hear myself think as we moved past them. I decided I didn't like it down here.

At the back of the next building, Joseph stopped, holding out his hand to make me pause. Twenty feet ahead of us stood another Hunter, who lifted his visor. Joseph put his gloved hands in front of him, hooking his pointer fingers together and letting his thumbs drop. It made a crude, but distinguishable *M*. The other Hunter did the same back. *M&M's*. I smiled as we approached. Another friendly. I took a breath. This was good news, a good sign. Proof that Silas hadn't been lying through his teeth, proof that this new Hunter would not turn against us, proof that the plan was still in motion.

"Jonah, this is Maura," Joseph whispered. The new Hunter turned his gaze to me, brown eyes widening in astonishment. The number on his chest was 3801. He got to his knees, stretched his hands in front of him, and bowed his head.

"Praise God!" he cried.

I straightened. Then, for the second time that afternoon, took a step back. Praise was not something I was used to. In the commune, worship was reserved only for my father. Directing that kind of gratitude to anyone else would be considered blasphemy. But I tried to put myself in their shoes. Were they desperate to have another Prophet to escape from my father's cruelty? Or did they truly believe I had risen from the dead?

"I'm, uh—" I looked at Joseph, who gave me a reassuring smile. "Thank you?" I tried. That felt strange.

The kneeling man got to his feet.

"We are so blessed to have you back." He shook his head. "Silas said, but it was hard to believe..." He straightened. "It's an honor to be part of your mission."

"Thank you," I repeated.

"I just heard from Gabriel," Jonah said. "The cameras are set, the street is decorated, and they're focused on Dr. Kaufman."

"Who's that?" I asked.

Jonah's brows raised. "The current head of the board of medical professionals. He runs the virology department, though it's a relatively new placement." He shifted his gaze. "The old head, Dr. Sebi's been missing for weeks. They brought in Kaufman as an interim solution, but apparently he's here to stay, as of yesterday. He'll be giving updates on the Sciences and Innovations area for the next hour." He pulled up his sleeve and checked the watch around his wrist. "They should be starting any minute. The plan is to walk in on his segment."

"Is he friendly?" I asked.

Jonah and Joseph looked at each other. "We're...not exactly sure," Joseph said. "But he'll be in the middle of a speech, on live television. There's not much he can do."

"And, any security?"

"A few Hunters," Jonah said. "We believe all are friendlies. The agreement is to remain awestruck. No drawing weapons. Which shouldn't be hard." He glanced sideways at me. "It's a bit shocking to see you standing here."

The anxiety in my chest began to unravel.

"We'll flank you on your way in," Joseph said. "We know how important you are and our assignment is to protect you until the Prophet gives whatever order he decides on. After that, it'll be hard to tell what happens." His eyebrows drew together in worry.

"Don't worry about that," I said as confidently as I could manage. I looked beyond the men, toward the break between the next few buildings. "I'll be able to handle myself."

Both nodded curtly, as soldiers do, then reached up to pull the helmet visor down over their eyes. Jonah remained in front of me, Joseph following behind as we followed the fence behind one more building, stopping once it ended.

Jonah stepped over the fence, holding up his hand as he came around the side of the building. He pressed himself against the structure, peeked around and down the street, then beckoned us forward. I hiked up my dress and stepped over the low fence, taking one last look at the forest before I entered the commune's borders.

"They're about a hundred feet out," Jonah said, tilting his helmet to address me. "We're going to walk right up the road, toward the camera. We'll be on either side of you."

"Okay," I said. I sucked in the cold air and closed my eyes. This was it. Once I was seen, once I stepped foot on that road, there would be no turning back. I thought of Eli's words and clung to the belief he held in me.

I know if there's anyone who can do this, it's you.

I let my eyes open, looked up at Jonah, and smiled.

"Here we go," Joseph said behind me. The three of us straightened and walked forward.

A wide road split the buildings through the Sciences and Innovations area, disappearing around a curve leading to Coutts Peak. Sunlight rose higher behind the mountain. As my eyes adjusted to the brightness, I glimpsed the doctor. The camera in front of him. The team assembled behind it. And the little red light that signaled a live feed.

"Okay, Maura Coutts," Joseph said as we fell into a single line. "Let's bring you back from the dead."

22

MAURA

SUNSHINE CRESTED the top of Coutts Peak, flowing down its front like a golden waterfall. It brushed my face as we moved ahead and my lips curled into a smile at the effect I knew it would have. God was smiling down on me.

My father would hate it.

Everything felt like a dream. My legs propelled me forward, walking in sync with Jonah and Joseph, but my body screamed danger. Pushing through it felt like walking through fire. But I carried on. For everyone back at the Centre. For my family. For me.

I counted ten men in total — Dr. Kaufman, the camera operator, four Hunters, and four men dressed in business attire. As we neared, I heard the doctor speaking in a firm voice.

"—proud of the work we do. We are working on a new vaccine that—" The camera operator lifted his head. "—should be ready by late winter. And..."

Dr. Kaufman paused, his head turning as it followed the camera operator's line of sight. I saw the operator's hand adjust. Slowly, he turned the camera from the doctor and onto me. The world brightened. Capturing their attention filled me with energy, with a feeling of authority. I straightened, elongating my neck, gaze fixed forward on the peak ahead of me.

Here I am. Come and get me, father.

I heard mechanics whirring behind the buildings and a delicate hum from somewhere in the distance. My heart-beat thrummed in my ears. I glanced down at my mud-covered boots. Dirt stained the bottom of my otherwise pristine dress. Good. It would represent the journey it took to get here.

Voices whispered as I neared the camera.

"Is that—?"

"Who is that?"

"It looks like—"

"Maura?"

"It can't be."

One of the Hunters behind the camera stepped forward, raising his visor as he did so. Wrinkles creased the edges of his eyes as he squinted at me. His breast pocket number read 394.

"Jonah? Joseph?" The older Hunter looked bewildered. "What is this?" I had expected anger, but the man's voice shook in what I took to be shock.

I slowed, stopping beside Dr. Kaufman, who backed away from me. He was a short, thin man, with a dark, receding hairline and round, wide-rimmed glasses that slipped down his narrow nose.

"Good morning," I addressed each of them in the softest voice I could manage. Avi's suggestion. The gentler, the better. "I'm so pleased to have returned."

That did it. The cameraman dipped his head behind his equipment, holding the camera steady on me. The remaining Hunters slid up their visors. The well-dressed men looked at each other, expressions somewhere between confused and mesmerized.

"Maura. We thought—" Dr. Kaufman's eyes widened. "We thought you to be dead," he croaked.

I let a smile creep across my lips. "Dead?" I said, looking directly into the camera. "Now, what would give you that idea?"

My words hung in the air. A Hunter fell to his knees. He pulled off his helmet, shaking out his sandy-blond hair, mouth open in disbelief. He brought his hands together and pushed them against his forehead. I heard his whispered prayers.

"I'm blessed to say I'm alive and well," I continued, bringing my arms outward to each side of my body to show the camera that I was not only in one piece, but relatively healthy. "My journey was not an easy one. But God has called me back to the commune."

A door slammed somewhere to our right. Shoes pounded against pavement. I shifted my gaze. People spilled from the mouth of one of the buildings, walking hurriedly toward us. Another door, more shoes, came from the left, and voices began filling the street. I didn't have long. For all I knew, my father was already giving the order to put me in the back of a truck.

I turned back to the camera. "In my absence from the commune, God showed me many things. He revealed we are not alone in this world, that there are others out there who do not wish us harm. In fact, they long to share God's gifts with us, to partner with us to create a better world."

My words were dangerous. The hammer that would crack the edges of my father's carefully constructed lies. These admissions would overwhelm people, but they needed to be said. I didn't know when or if I'd be able to get in front of a crowd like this again.

I narrowed my eyes at the camera. "God warned me of a false Prophet. He urged me to be mindful of deviance, of things that go against our faith. The world does not need to be a brutal place. We are made in His image. To truly be godly, to truly stay close to Him, we must fight against brutality. We must put aside our fear and replace it with love and acceptance. For it is the only way we can serve him faithfully."

A small crowd had gathered, some on their knees, some whispering to one another.

"She's alive?"

"Are you certain it's her?"

"Praise God!"

"She has risen!"

"Is it *really* Maura?"

From the corner of my eye, I saw three Hunters huddled around in a half circle, one with a radio lifted to his lips. Those were my father's men. As soon as he gave them the go-ahead, they would take me.

"Let us remember Psalm 36," I cried, lifting my hands as I addressed both the camera and crowd. "For with thee is the fountain of life: in thy light shall we see light. O continue thy loving kindness unto them that know thee; and thy righteousness to the upright in heart. Let not the foot of pride come against me and let not the hand of the wicked remove me."

The Hunters shifted, fell in step with one another, shoulders squared, their helmets glinting in the sunlight. My heartbeat quickened, and the cold tightened my chest. I felt the boys beside me grow tense, but, as promised, they did not leave my side. My appreciation for them grew tenfold.

I looked at the camera, hooked my fingers together like I'd seen Jonah and Joseph do, and made an M. I raised it above my forehead, a sign of rebellion, one my father would see, dissect, and outlaw.

It's too late for that. Let them see.

I kept my face neutral, somewhat pleasant. I had learned the importance of appearance at an early age and that training served me well now. I knew how to play a part. How to pretend I was feeling something I wasn't actually feeling. I had trained for this all my life. The mask I'd need to wear until I was out of this slipped on effortlessly.

"Heed my warning," I told the camera. I wondered if Morgan could see me right now. Andrew. Mother. The rest of my siblings. I tried speaking directly to them. "God is not cruel. So neither should his vessel be."

It was vague, yet damning. Whoever was already feeling critical of Father's tactics would understand what I was trying to say. It could spark a rebellion.

But would it be enough to start a fire?

A hand gripped my arm. "Maura Coutts?"

There was disbelief even in the voice of the Hunter about to do Father's bidding. I looked away from the camera to the helmeted man standing beside Jonah. He towered over us both, leering even behind the helmet.

"Back on Dr. Kaufman, please." The Hunter's voice came out strained as he demanded the cameraman to focus on the doctor who stood to the side, still looking awestruck. He shook his head at the camera.

"I, uh — what? I'm, a little, uh —" He brought his hands together, pressed them to his lips, and took a moment to collect himself. "I'm so sorry," he laughed. "But this comes as quite a surprise."

"Back on script," the Hunter beside me hissed at one of the well-dressed men. He nodded urgently, wrote something on his clipboard, and held it up for the doctor to see.

The Hunter's grip tightened on my bicep. Carelessly, he pushed past Jonah and Joseph. The pair moved to follow as he dragged me down the street toward the peak, away from the cameras, away from the crowd.

My breath was shallow and unsteady. I curled my hands into fists, shaking with adrenaline.

Calm down.

I gulped a breath. We reached a cross in the road. The Hunter pulled me to the sidewalk and stood on the corner, peering down the side road. Jonah and Joseph hovered beside me still and, as if he'd just noticed them, the Hunter holding me swiveled his helmet.

"Go back to your posts," the man said, his voice muffled. "You are not required here."

Both boys stood still, unmoving.

"Go!" the Hunter yelled.

Joseph flinched. But neither moved.

"It's okay," I said, shifting my gaze between the two. "Truly." I hoped they understood the undertone of my words. That their job here was done. That they'd done more for me than I could ever thank them for. That this was as far as they needed to go. I hoped they would not be punished.

Jonah nodded, then turned, Joseph following. They marched away, back through the accumulating crowd, past the television cameras, toward the forest. The Hunter holding me grunted. I looked up at him, wishing I could see his face.

The crowd had followed us, leaving Dr. Kaufman to his speech, circling us on the corner like moths to a flame. Mumblings of prayer and disbelief still rang heavy in the air. More doors somewhere in the distance opened and closed, and when I looked up at the tinted windows, I saw faces pressed against the glass.

My pride swelled. The anxiety I'd felt at confessing such dangerous things to the camera began to fade. There was no denying that what we were doing was already working. Silas had been right.

The radio on the Hunter's belt crackled. He softened his hold on me and picked it up.

"Two minutes out," the person on the other side of the radio said. The voice was familiar, but difficult to place.

More people had joined the crowd. I was getting disoriented by all the sounds.

"Praise God!"

"It's a miracle!"

"Welcome home, Maura!"

I looked over my shoulder back at the camera. We still held the group's attention, the cameraman occasionally lifting his head to get a glimpse of us. I even saw Dr. Kaufman turn, standing up on his tip toes as he struggled to repeat whatever talking points he'd been given.

"Back up," barked the Hunter holding me, pulling me off the sidewalk and into the street. But like the young Hunters, the crowd could not be swayed by his simple command. They followed us into the road. I couldn't help but smile. No matter what Father did now, there was no closing this door.

A black truck barreled around the end of the street and my stomach dropped. My last trip in one of these trucks had been anything but pleasant. I'd been stuffed in the backseat, blinded by darkness and plagued with confusion. I dreaded another trip in that suffocating prison. I longed to run back to the forest. Back to the Centre. Back to my bed. Back to Eli.

The truck slowed as it approached, its shiny exterior sparkling in the sunlight. A blond-haired man was visible in the driver's seat. I squinted, trying to make out his features. He pulled up beside us and rolled the window down.

Silas.

He put his fingers up to his forehead and saluted the Hunter still holding my arm. I worked hard to keep my face neutral. Any show of recognition was dangerous to us both.

"Sir," he said.

The Hunter grunted, pulling me toward the vehicle. I waited for him to open the rear door, but instead, he opened the passenger side door and pushed me forward.

I looked back at him, brows raised in surprise, but kept my lips in a straight line. So, this was the power a public show offered.

"Clean up this mess," Silas snarled, his lips curling into a sneer as he addressed the Hunter.

"Yes, sir."

I climbed into the seat, suppressing my surprise. Silas rolled up the window as I closed the door, sealing us in the truck. I was grateful for the instant warmth. One glance in the backseat told me we were alone.

"Buckle your seatbelt," he said, his tone still curt. He stared straight ahead. "And don't say a word until we're out of the city."

I nodded once, then buckled myself in. Silas drove ahead slowly, careful to avoid the still-gathering crowd. I was surprised to see they weren't all men — women I had never seen before made up at least a fourth of the people. I had always known the commune was large, but never focused on just how big. There had never been a reason to.

This time, being here was different. I knew more. I had control of the circumstances. I knew what I was about to do, the power I held over Father and the commune. My reappearance was a miracle they were all witness to

— something they could tangibly see and experience. It outweighed any of Father's claims. It challenged his credibility.

Perhaps I should've been afraid. But as we passed the crowd, their gazes following us as we turned to leave the city, I raised my hands to my cheeks. I was smiling. This was the turning point. This was how we showed my father's true colors. This was how I rescued my family. Myself. The community that helped me get this far.

This was my legacy.

23

MAURA

Silas drove us away from the tall, shiny buildings and into Coutts Valley. Similar to the edge of the forest, the city ended abruptly, making way for hilly farmland and tightly packed greenhouses. Two nuclear cooling towers framed the sides of the valley, the concrete structures more massive than I ever imagined from Coutts Peak. How strange it was to have lived all of my life in one place and only seen things from one angle.

"You did it," Silas said once we crossed deeper into the farmlands. His eyes flitted back and forth across the windshield, his happy tone tainted by fear. He was likely afraid to morph out of the Hunter persona it was necessary for him to wear.

"*We* did it," I said. "I didn't realize I'd be getting a personal driver when I arrived."

"I made sure I was the first to respond when they called for someone to pick you up."

"It's appreciated."

He smiled. "Listen, we don't have much time—"

"I assume we are going to see my father."

His features hardened, his grip on the steering wheel tightening. "Yes," he said. "Your appearance caused quite the commotion, as expected. He's ordered Hunters out to the borders to look for anyone you arrived with." I tensed, thinking of Sid and Darius at the salvage yard. "Don't worry," he reassured me, "our friendlies will avoid the safe houses."

"Good. What else?"

"Everyone's on high alert, so we need to take communication easy for the next few days. This may be the last contact we have until someone can safely reach you again. From what I've heard so far, he's uncertain what to do with you when you arrive. Your best course of action is to be as pliable as possible and go willingly. He's going to test you, to force answers out of you. And your response must always be the same."

"God showed me the way," I recited.

"Yes. No specifics. Stick to the story. God showed you the truth and nothing can persuade you otherwise. Trust that I'll figure out where you've gone and how to get messages to you." The terrain steepened as we drove on. "We have a few rebels now in Communications. They're in contact with the Centre and working on establishing new safe houses," he shared. "Gabriel has a few friendlies ready to go in Sanitation. The group at the prison will leave tonight."

"Really? That soon?"

Silas nodded. "It will pull the Prophet's attention away from your arrival," he said. "Which will be a good thing. The goal is to keep him guessing, keep him busy, so he won't have enough time to focus on any one specific thing. We've confirmed contacts in Agriculture and Media, and we're working on Sciences and Innovations. Dr. Kaufman is a terrified little fellow. We'll need to find someone else on the board we can trust to share our message."

"Message?"

Silas straightened in his seat. "Well, if we're going to get anything done, we need to hold regular meetings. The commune is big and it'll be the only way to be effective as a group. Meetings of protest are important. We can decide on how best to undermine the Prophet and the other Hunters and continue winning over commune members. Strength in numbers."

I nodded. "Could I be there?"

He shot me a skeptical look. "It'll all depend on the security around you. The Prophet won't leave you alone with Andrew and he certainly won't allow you many freedoms. We'll need to cross that bridge when we come to it."

I slumped in my seat, disappointed, even though he was right. My father was going to be furious. The gleam of hope I held in my chest dimmed, replaced with heavy fear and uncertainty. It wasn't like I hadn't known I was going to see my father. But now it was moments away. Silas and Avi had both seemed sure he wouldn't hurt me, but they didn't know my father like I did. There was always a chance.

The road curved sharply, the terrain shifting from dead grass to rocky boulders. Gravel clicked and clattered beneath the tires. We were much higher on the mountain, most of the valley and surrounding mountains in view. Side streets broke off from the main road we traveled, leading to neighborhoods with homes similar to the one I'd grown up in, or small markets where people could trade or buy things. They looked like little clusters in the distance.

Silas wiped his hand over his face as we rounded another curve and headed up the road. "One more thing.

When and if you speak to people, you'll need to be careful to distinguish between rebel and believer. Some people will want to fight. Those are the people we want to recruit. Some will be genuine believers that your appearance is a miracle. Those are the people we'll need to protect. The Prophet will not take kindly to them."

I nodded.

"There will be others — non-believers. My Father. A group of the Hunters. Women like Abigail." He frowned. "They will either need to be convinced or subdued."

I forced a dry laugh as I thought about trying to convince Abigail to follow me anywhere.

"And no violence," I said.

"No," Silas said. "Not unless we need to defend ourselves." His knuckles whitened as his grip tightened on the steering wheel.

Another piece of the puzzle I'd known was a possibility. I hated the idea of violence. It was how my father had gotten control. Would we be any better if we used it in return? But could you fight violence with nonviolent action? I wasn't sure. Perhaps it was inevitable for rebellions. Perhaps people needed to get hurt if we wanted to succeed. I didn't have the answers. I wasn't sure Silas did, either.

Who were we but two people who longed for a better world? We weren't heroes or gods. But we'd started an avalanche we'd never be able to curb. No matter who we lost or if we survived, my father's credibility was tarnished. Whether or not everyone understood, we were all better off for it. No man deserves supreme power over any group of people. That was never what God intended.

I thought of the Centre, of my friends who had emboldened me to become more. Given me the courage to step foot back in this place. A plunging ache in my heart found no depths in my soul.

From the window, I could see the steep plunge over the side of the mountain. It would be so easy to throw myself off, succumb to my death, let things play out how they were meant to. But that was my fear talking. There was so much more to do. The truck jostled us and I clung to the seat, inhaling deeply to curb my nausea.

"And everything is okay in the Centre?" I asked, hoping my longing wasn't terribly noticeable.

"No urgent updates from the inside, but they're prepared to receive the prisoners by early morning. They'll be eager to hear of the progress we've made today. Someone will reach out tonight. They will want to know you've made it safely, and that the kidnapped group is on their way."

"Things are moving."

"Quickly," Silas said, slowing the truck. We turned a few more tight corners as we climbed an even more narrow, rock-lined road up to where I knew the church was. In the distance, I saw the tips of the building's architecture stretching toward the heavens.

"I hope you'll forgive me," Silas whispered as the terrain leveled.

I turned to him. He looked much older than he had back at the Centre, dressed in his green uniform, his jaw tight, gaze fixed ahead.

"For what?"

"I must play my part as a Hunter," he explained as he gave the steering wheel a few nervous taps. He ran his hand across his mouth before he spoke again. "I may be cruel in front of others, and I hope you know that is not my true nature. Please know that I love your sister, that I'm fully committed to this cause, and that I believe in you. Okay?"

He turned in his seat and I met his fierce eyes.

"Okay," I said.

He brought his gaze back to the road. "To play this part well, to maintain my position and be believable enough to the Prophet and my father, I may do or say things that don't align with what I'm telling you right now."

"I understand. You're playing a part," I confirmed. "I know that strategy well."

He inhaled deeply, then nodded, running his hands up and down the steering wheel. My heart squeezed. It was a horribly lonely experience living your life as someone you know you're not. Like living in a skin that never fit right. I knew now how liberating it was to live in a way that aligned with the person I felt like on the inside. The person I'd always been. Going backward was torturous, but necessary.

"You're a good man, Silas," I said, reaching over the center console and patting his arm. "I know that. And I trust you."

I pulled back and let my words linger as he drove us up the steepest curve yet. High stone guardrails framed the paved incline we traveled. As we climbed, the church's nave roof appeared against the sky, followed by the rocky mountainside it was anchored to. Sunlight illuminated the structure's delicate details as Coutts Peak's church came into view. Bile rose in my throat. I struggled to swallow it.

Our vehicle emerged in a large parking lot, spotted with Hunter's trucks and an unmarked transportation van. Across the space, concrete stairs led to the towering wooden church doors. At the base stood a muscular, blond man sporting the same haircut as his son, dressed in an identical suit without a helmet.

Luke.

He leered at us, his red face screwed up in anger as Silas drove across the lot, parking in front of the stairs.

"God bless you, Maura," Silas whispered from the corner of his mouth. "And good luck."

I wasn't ready. I'm not sure I would've ever been ready to leave the comfort of that truck, not knowing when I'd find peace or a friendly face again. It was a terrifying thought, one that froze me for a moment. But as I looked at Silas, his gaze narrowed on his father who stood outside my door, I knew there was no way forward but out of the truck, up those stairs, and into the church. I unbuckled my seatbelt.

Luke opened the passenger side door, tipping his head to look inside at Silas. Broad-shouldered and filled with rage, the older man was a tired, more hardened version of his son. He smelled like incense and body odor. I breathed through my mouth.

"Did you want to roll out the red carpet for her, too?" he sneered. "Why isn't she riding in the back?"

My blood ran cold. Had Silas made a mistake?

The young driver's nostrils flared. "Did you see the video? There were hundreds of people watching us down there. How would you have liked me to explain that to them? This woman returns from the dead and so we throw her in the back seat like animal feed?"

Luke stilled, his grip tightening on the car door he held open.

"Watch your tone with me, young man."

Silas paused, then dipped his head. "My apologies," he said through his teeth.

Luke grunted indifferently, then pulled away from the truck. "Get out."

I didn't dare look back at Silas. Following Luke's

command, I slipped out of my seat, working hard to keep my expression as neutral as possible.

Frigid air pierced through my thin dress, chilling me to my core. Luke grabbed my arm, and I shivered in his grasp, wrapping my one free arm around myself. Oh, how I longed for the jacket I'd left with Sid and Darius.

He dragged me up the stairs, not allowing me to fall in step with him. I struggled to keep up with his long gait, taking two stairs at a time as he barreled up them. The urgency was an annoyance, sure, but more of a sign that he was flustered and afraid. He wanted me out of the public space as quickly as possible.

Good.

I kept my chin high as we approached the wooden doors. *God showed me the truth and nothing can persuade me otherwise.* I straightened. Tried to exude confidence. Tried not to think about what happened the last time I was here.

The doors opened, allowing me a glimpse into the church I had once called home. Even before I saw him, I felt his presence. If I had still bought into his ideals and believed he was a man of God, I might have mistaken him for a deity. The mouthpiece of God, as I'd been told. Something ominous radiated from my father.

He pressed his sinewy body against the open door. I felt his shrewd eyes on me, inspecting every ounce of my being, studying my features, my dress, and that I was still intact after all this time. Not dead. Not rotting away, like he wished. I was alive and in the flesh.

His worst nightmare.

"Maura Coutts," my father said, my name sounding like poison on his tongue.

I raised my eyes to him, peering up at him through my lashes. He was put together as always, with a close-cropped crew cut, a clean face, and piercing blue eyes. I kept my features calm. Don't show fear. Don't show resistance. Blank.

"Father," I greeted him, my tone neither pleasant nor defiant.

"It is a miracle," he said. I didn't miss the way his lip twitched or the way he seemed to snarl the last syllable of his proclamation. My father looked up beyond my head, out at the world — the commune he'd worked so hard to create. To him, I was a blemish on his holy landscape. I had the power to destroy him, to destroy his kingdom, to reveal his true nature to the people who had known no other life than to follow him.

He brought his gaze to meet mine again.

"By all means, please come inside," he instructed, holding out his arm toward the church's interior. "After all this time, you must be so relieved to be home."

24

MAURA

LUKE CLOSED THE DOORS, entombing us in the vast church. Sunlight shone through rose-colored windows at the far end of the room, bathing the wooden pews in pale pink. My eyes took a moment to adjust to the dim lighting. The place of worship was still as beautiful and haunting as I remembered, but the awe I'd once felt was gone. It was tainted with what I now knew about my father.

Father's white, heavy robes hung to the floor, trailing behind him as he walked ahead of us down the center aisle. The similarity to my dress was almost comical. We rounded a large, ornate fountain of holy water and continued toward the altar. Luke kept my arm in his grip, though I suspected he knew he didn't need to. It was a show of power. The only one they had at the moment.

Father's jaw tightened as he led us through the entryway and into the church. He was on edge, and I worked hard to hold back my knowing smile. Never had I felt so powerful in his presence before. Being this influential was something I'd only ever dreamed of.

As we reached the altar, we all kneeled before it. I

blessed myself, touching my forehead, chest, then each shoulder. A force of habit. Something I'd never even thought about before. Now, it felt like someone was pulling my strings.

Still, I searched my exhausted brain for a prayer. *Lord, I seek Your forgiveness...* But Luke gave me no time. He pulled me upward, breaking my stream of consciousness. We walked past the pews, through a side hall before climbing three flights of stairs together. He meant to hurt me, to show me his power, but the painful grip around my arm kept me grounded, tethered to the moment.

Despite the confidence I'd built on my journey up the peak, fear rolled in my belly as we reached the top floor landing. Together, we padded along the red carpet, following Father into his office. He hadn't uttered a word since he'd greeted me and the silence was unsettling. Luke used his free hand to close the door before depositing me in the chair across from my father's desk.

I followed my father's feet as he came around the desk and sat in his leather chair, letting his fingers rest against his thin lips. Luke remained standing at the corner of the desk, arms crossed over his broad chest. The room was quiet, filled with stale air. I didn't dare meet their eyes. Instead, I carried my gaze to the tips of my boots, just visible beneath the dress's white fabric. Mud had dried on the bottom, cracking at the edges. It looked so much like blood.

"Do you have any idea what you've done?" My father's voice was low and deep, soft enough I wouldn't have heard him in a crowd. But in this silent office, his tone rang between the walls.

I was slow to bring my eyes to meet his, careful to keep my face neutral. He had aged in the short time I'd been away. Deep circles beneath each of his tired eyes suggested he hadn't slept well in weeks. But his gaze was full of fire. Full of hatred. If I'd thought he was angry with me the last time I spoke with him, it was no match to how he looked at me now.

"I'm sorry, *Father*?" I nearly bit my tongue holding back my disdain.

"Your little stunt," he said, flicking his wrist as he gestured out the circular office window. "You know *damn well* what I'm talking about."

I pressed my lips together. "I plead your forgiveness," I said, gently. "But I do not."

"Where have you been?" he seethed, placing his hands on his desk as he leaned over it toward me.

I gave him a pleasant smile. His lip curled. "I was outside the commune's borders," I said, as if it were obvious. "After the storm washed me away from the Island of Repentance, God had a mission for me. He saved me from the river, taught me how to fend for myself. Live off the land."

"He did not."

"I assure you, He did."

I felt like I was free falling. Never would I have thought of speaking to my father this way. No matter how angry I'd ever been, no matter how confused. But his lies had clouded my eyes. I believed him to be holy. Now, knowing there was no truth in those proclamations, it was possible to unsettle him.

Father's face reddened. "No. There is no way that's possible."

"No way?" I raised my eyebrows. Confidence dripped from each word. "Are you questioning God's instruction?"

Beside me, Luke flinched. I'd gone too far. He stormed to my side, fists clenched, then raised. I braced for a blow to my face, but instead, he grabbed a fistful of my hair and yanked. His grip forced me to awkwardly stand from my seat, the pain forcing a yelp from my lips. It pulled my features taut. I reached up to try to pry his fingers off, but before I could, he released me and I hit the seat with a thump.

It took me a minute to collect myself, gently patting my hair back on my sore scalp, swallowing my rage. They didn't want to hit me, so I had visible bruises to show. They wanted to hurt me in unseen places. If this was the most basic of those assaults, I worried about what might come next.

"How dare you," my father seethed as he stood from his chair. "Wicked, wicked, girl. We know you were with Outsiders. We know you were with that larger community, with others from this commune. We know you had help."

"Only from the Lord."

He had no tangible proof. These were empty threats. Otherwise, he would've called out my companions by name. He wouldn't have been able to help himself by telling me he knew exactly where I was and who I was with.

"Who were you with, Maura?" he asked again, palms flat against the desk as he narrowed his gaze.

"I was by myself."

"Maura…"

"The storm swept me away, and I ended up on a beach outside of the commune. I found shelter, and the Lord provided."

Father slammed his hands against the table, so hard the frames, pens, and coffee cup rattled on his desk.

"Tell me the *truth*!" He curled his fingers inward, crinkling the papers beneath them.

"I am telling you the truth." Despite my anxiety, my

voice somehow maintained its level. I looked at my lap. "I was swept away from the creek—"

"Were you with the group that ran away last time my men found you?"

"I don't know what you're—"

"We'll find them, Maura." He lowered his head, and I looked up, catching his gaze. His eyes darkened, his sneer deepening as he spat the next words. "We'll find them and we'll kill them. We'll find the truth and torture it out of them in ways you can't imagine. I will destroy them, and you." He raised a shaking finger at me. "You—" He struggled to find the words.

I lifted my chin. "If that's how you feel, then—"

"This is what I *know*!" he screamed, his eyes bulging. "I have power over you, over those people out there." He lifted his arm and pointed out the window with a quivering finger. "I will make it so you regret ever setting foot in here again. Nobody welcomed you back and yet you parade through my borders like some saint on a holy mission. You are *vile*! Unworthy of being a Coutts! I'll make you regret every last step you took today." Spittle flew from his mouth, visible in the bright light.

I drew in my core, making a point to remain straight and not show the inner turmoil running free in my chest and stomach. I wanted to puke. I wanted to cry. I wanted to run out of the room screaming, dart back to the Centre, and hide beneath the warm sleeping pack or curl up in Eli's arms.

I wanted to go home.

The familiar longing nearly broke me. I'd been wanting to go *home* ever since my father had married me off to Andrew. Ever since he'd stripped away any normalcy I'd ever known. Didn't he know this was all his fault? That if he would just leave us be and stop trying to dictate our lives, I wouldn't have had a reason to try to cross the creek to begin with?

Of course he didn't. His ego was so large he truly believed he was doing us a service. And now, because I'd interrupted his plans, he was angry and afraid. Defiance was one thing, but I'd made a spectacle. Something expressly forbidden. Not just that, but I'd embarrassed Father. I'd challenged his word.

Father settled back in his chair, placing his head in his hands. His eyes were wild, fingers threaded through his short hair. His gaze scanned the crumpled papers on his desk before he looked up at Luke.

"Ankle monitor," he said, pointing at me. "Get one. Set it up for location tracking. Alert Andrew. We have little choice but to send her back to her duties at his estate. I'll get in touch with Abraham. I want to make sure those people are cleared out of the Sciences and Innovations area. Get everyone back to work."

An ankle monitor. I nearly laughed in relief. That wasn't so bad. Yes, Father would know where I was at all times, but I had anticipated something like this. Plus, there was always the chance Silas and Gabriel knew whoever would follow my activity. Being sent back to Andrew was okay, too, maybe even expected. I'd have a chance to see Morgan. Get back to some type of normalcy.

Luke left the room. I remained straight-backed in the chair. Father wiped his hand across his mouth. He didn't make eye contact with me, as if he was too disgusted with my presence to cast me a glance. But ignoring me wouldn't make me go away.

He stood up, sat down, ruffled through more papers. Picked up the coffee cup, and stared at its liquids before putting it down again. Luke came back a few minutes later with a small black contraption in his hands.

"Ah," said Father, his eyes lighting up as Luke brought the thing forward. "Thank you, Luke."

Father gently turned over the monitor, holding it like it was a priceless heirloom. "This," he said, holding it up to me, "is your newest accessory." His lips curled into a smile. "With this, I'll be able to track where you are at any time. You'll be given certain boundaries. Boundaries you'll be contained to." His smile widened. "Do you want to know what happens if you decide to try to remove this or travel *outside* of those boundaries?"

I tilted my head, but did not give him the satisfaction of an answer.

"Well, this monitor has a certain, shall we say, *bite* to it," he said. With his thumb, he pressed the inside of the contraption. Sharp metal teeth appeared against the black metal material, mimicking the disdain my father held behind his smile. He tilted it to show me the curved jaw. "Uncoated plain steel. Each tooth is three-eighths of an inch thick." He sucked in a breath through his teeth as he let his finger trace the sharp edges. "Imagine how badly that would hurt someone if they didn't follow the rules. They wouldn't be able to run, let alone walk."

I narrowed my eyes at him. How could I get out of this? Refuse to put it on? By the way Luke had just manhandled me, I knew they were looking for an excuse to hurt me more. Maybe kill me. Would his followers believe him if he said my death was necessary? I swallowed hard.

"And this is something God told you I needed?" I asked, testing my luck.

Father laughed. "Oh no," he said. "This is something I've decided you need. You came back, so you shall follow my rules. Things are as they've always been, Maura. You are only fooling yourself to think otherwise."

I couldn't help my sneer. *He* was the fool. But there was

no use trying to convince him. If putting this torture device on my ankle made him feel like he had power again, then so be it.

"Luke?" He held up the contraption, releasing the inside so that the teeth retracted. The wide-shouldered man took the monitor, then knelt beside me. Cool metal slipped over my bare skin, just above my boot. He hooked it seamlessly into place so it looked like one solid piece of metal around my flesh. I twisted my ankle, testing it. I couldn't feel the teeth, but it was frightening to know they were there, waiting to sink into the bottom of my calf.

"Now, don't be doing something silly like trying to take it off," my father said, an edge of joy lifting the side of his mouth. "Only Luke or I will have that privilege. Perhaps once you've proven yourself to be trustworthy again, we can consider it."

His eyes flashed malice. I made my features as blank as possible, staring at the corner of his desk, as if uninterested. I would not give him the satisfaction of fear or frustration. It was what he wanted. And he wouldn't get it.

25

———————

MAURA

WHILE MY FATHER took a phone call from Abraham, Luke led me out of his office, down the stairs, and back through the church. Despite the bright sun, frigid air ran through my dress. The ankle monitor weighed each step I took. An invisible chain that tethered me to Father. With the sharp metal teeth as a threat, I couldn't expect to go to any of Silas's meetings, let alone the communications center to speak with the Centre. I would be confined to a small area. Silas would need to bring people to me.

The logistics made my head spin.

Luke followed behind me as I walked down the wide concrete stairs into the parking lot, bracing against the icy wind. The Sciences and Innovations area loomed behind the nuclear cooling towers and I wondered what had become of the crowd gathered near the cameras. Had the broadcasters just moved on with their scripts? What were people on the farms and in the lower neighborhoods saying?

I hadn't liked the crowd, but I would have preferred it to

being alone with Luke. We walked along the path I had walked with Andrew every day since we'd been married. It had become a ritual, a morning outing to church, back to his estate, and on to scavenging. Despite my time away, the movements felt eerily familiar, like a recurring dream. Before a few days ago, I was certain I'd never take this walk again.

A thin layer of snow settled on the sides of the sidewalk. Someone had shoveled and salted the path, making the ground gritty beneath my boots, clinging to the edges of my too-long dress. The estates came into view, the tops of the large houses visible against the bright sky. This place looked the same as I remembered it, with every edge manicured, every home perfectly maintained.

Each Coutts' brother had an estate up here with homes built for each wife and their families. Andrew's was the first on the right. My heart thudded deep in my chest, making it difficult to breathe. This was always how it felt approaching the estate. Dread flooded my belly. I had the urge to run.

I forced myself to think of Morgan. She would be on the estate, at the very least. Even if I only saw her from a distance, it'd be enough to ease the tight knot in my chest. After being surrounded by people who cared about me these past few months, I longed for the familiarity of someone I knew would stand with me until kingdom come.

It was a selfish thought. I wouldn't wish a marriage to Andrew on anyone, especially Morgan. But she was first on my list of people I'd want to sneak out to the Centre. To do that, I needed to play this part well. I needed to be convincing.

I held my chin high as we approached the tall columns that marked Andrew's estate. A familiar figure hovered there, pacing back and forth, his shadow casting across the road.

Andrew looked the same as I remembered him. Whatever stress my father felt hadn't made its way to him. His round face was pink with life, blue eyes sparkling in the sun. He was freshly shaven, dressed in a pair of pressed khakis and his heavy, black overcoat. But even in his immaculate state, I found it impossible not to think of him as the murderer I knew him to be. I had seen him raise that gun and shoot that man without a second thought. Cruel, ruthless, and good at pretending.

Two could play that game.

My husband's lips curled into a soft smile. A jolt of guilt pierced my heart as he stepped forward to greet me. Andrew was not a good man, but I had betrayed his trust. And despite knowing everything I did, for some reason, it made me feel bad.

"Maura," he said, reaching out his arms. I sank into Andrew's embrace. An obedient girl. What more could anyone want?

He squeezed me, pulling me tight to his chest. I turned my head to breathe, inhaling him — a tangy musk and cigar smoke. "Praise God."

"Praise God, I live to serve thee," I said, in greeting, as I'd been taught. My teeth bit down on my tongue. I winced at the pain and the realization. Those familiar words rolled out of my mouth as a force of habit, remnants of Abigail's teachings during adolescence.

Andrew's smile grew. Was it possible to regress this quickly?

"Very clear instructions from the Prophet," Luke said, nodding toward me. "I assume you have it all under control?"

"Don't speak to me like I'm your subordinate," Andrew

growled at Luke, slipping his heavy arm around my neck. "We'll be fine. I am blessed to have her home."

Luke snorted before rolling his eyes. "Do let us know if you have any concerns."

Andrew's arm tightened around my shoulder, forcing me to lean into him. "I will." His icy tone gave me pause. Tension hovered between the two men. But for what, I had no idea. Could it still be Silas's hiring? Or something else. Something about me. I peered up at my husband, who narrowed his eyes at Luke. Perhaps I could use it to my advantage?

The men saluted each other before Luke stormed off with no lingering looks in our direction. I found strange comfort in being rid of his presence and back with Andrew.

"Come on," my husband said, pulling me in step as he turned to face the houses on his property. The serene landscape and quiet surroundings settled my nerves. I strained my neck for Morgan, hoping to glimpse her curly hair, her bright eyes, her evasive legs. But the yards were empty, devoid of adults and children alike.

"Where is everyone?" I asked.

"Away," he said, not bothering to explain further. "I figured it would be much easier for you to settle in without distraction. You'll shower and change first," he said, glancing down at my form, which was, for lack of a better word, disgusting.

My muddy dress felt wet against my bare legs, which I hadn't shaved in months. My greasy hair was tangled, matted in places, and filled with twigs and leaves. There was film on my teeth and the sour taste of hunger rose from my belly. I was sore and bruised and reeked of sweat. I was surprised nobody tried to hose me down at the church.

"Abigail and Morgan will prepare a large meal for us tonight. I'm sure you've heard that God has called your sister Joanna home," he said, his jaw tight.

"I'm so sorry," I said. "God makes no mistakes and must have needed her for reasons we can not understand. Praise God." I spoke on autopilot, the phrases forming somewhere in the back of my brain, rolling out of my mouth like manufactured goods.

"Too right," he said. We approached Andrew's home — a six-bedroom lodge built from rustic, dark wood. Inside, it smelled of Andrew, of gunpowder, and cedar. Everything was as I remembered it, the Hunting uniform in the mudroom, the locked, standing gun safe. I caught sight of my old rain boots, slicked with new mud. I could only assume Morgan had been wearing them in my absence. In the main area, a fire crackled in the hearth, warming the interior from the frigid air outside. My stomach contorted as I inhaled the lovely scent of burning wood. It felt like home.

I winced. No. Home was at the Centre. Home was with Eli. With Holli and Sid. *Home is with Morgan*, another voice repeated. *With Mother. Father. With Andrew.* I clenched, my footsteps faltering as I squeezed my eyes closed, trying to get rid of the intrusive thoughts and feelings. This was wrong. I was stronger than this, different now. This wasn't home. This place had held me captive. It had convinced me I was worthless. That I was nothing more than a pawn to be moved by my player. By Andrew.

Then why, oh God, why did this feel so wonderfully familiar?

I WASN'T sure how long I spent in Andrew's bathroom washing up. Until the muddy water ran clear. Until I could separate my curls. Until I picked the dirt beneath my fingernails clean. I cried, just quietly enough to ensure the water pressure's roar drowned out my sobs. When I got out of the shower, my pale skin was rubbed raw.

I didn't recognize myself in the mirror. My face had thinned, my cheekbones so hollow I could see their sharp outline. My eyes seemed smaller and more sunken, dark features startling against my lightening skin. There was no scar on my cheek, as Holli had promised, but the faint lines of my wound were still there. I let my fingers linger there for a moment, my features distorted in the foggy mirror. As I leaned up against the marble countertop, fresh water available at the turn of the handle, I thought of the bathroom in the mall. The unused shower. The long list of exhausted people that deserved so much more than what they had.

Was the woman who'd given me a hard time in the breakfast line correct? Had I ever any right to infiltrate the small comforts those people had when I'd had fresh, hot water at my disposal for my entire life? Shame raged in my belly and wondered if that feeling would ever go away.

Andrew left me towels and new clothes, cream, nail clippers, and a hairbrush. I dried off my tired skin, inspecting every inch I could, every new blemish and scar, a reminder of how much life I'd lived in the past few months. I would need them.

I dressed in a simple long-sleeved cotton dress that hung to the floor. My only belonging — the photograph of me and Eli — I tucked back into the side of my bra. I tried pushing away the jolt of longing I felt as I swiped my thumb over his handsome face.

I entered Andrew's massive bedroom. Everything was

in its place. I wasn't sure what I was looking for — some sign that Morgan had been here? I knew she had, even if I hadn't seen it. A velvet green spread lay over his mattress. A mattress where Morgan had laid as Andrew's new wife, same as I had.

After checking myself in the reflection of Andrew's full-length mirror, I smoothed the dress and went into the hallway. The warm scent of charred meat wafted down the hall, luring me to the kitchen. Someone closed a cabinet. A pot clanged against something solid. My stomach leapt in my throat.

Was it Morgan, Abigail, or the children? The possibilities made me want to run back to the bathroom to get lost in the steam, to hide until someone found me. But the prospect of seeing Morgan propelled me forward, and I walked into the kitchen.

For a moment, the world stopped. Sunlight fell through one of the windows, illuminating the figure standing at the stove. Her black curls were tied tight up in a neat bun at the crown of her head. Her dark skin glistened with sweat from the oven's heat. She turned the meat in a cast iron pan slowly, charring the edges of a large roast.

"Morgan." Her name fell out of my mouth before I had a chance to make sense of anything else. My sister looked up, her dark brown eyes widening as she took me in. The meat fell from the tongs, which clattered on the counter beside the hissing pan. She wiped her hands on her apron, eyes darting wildly around the kitchen for any sign of someone else. Morgan came to me, arms outstretched, and pulled me into her.

My sobs escaped me before I caught them in my chest. I let myself sink into the warmth of my sister's breast, inhaling her, startled at how wrong my memory of her scent had been. It felt like years since we'd been this close, since I'd been allowed to hold my own family this way. Before, it had been a rule I'd obeyed. Father was adamant that once you married off, you had little business fraternizing with old family members. But now I knew it was just another control tactic. Just another silly idea he'd convinced us was God's word.

My arms came around her small frame, squeezing her, feeling her weight. Her shoulders shuddered as she caught her breath, sucked in the emotion I knew was bursting its way forth. But now was not the time. We needed to stay composed, needed Abigail and Andrew to understand there was nothing here between us, no connection and certainly no allegiance to one another. Otherwise, I could forget ever getting a moment alone with her again.

"You brat. I thought you were dead," Morgan said into my neck, before holding me at arm's length. Her brown eyes studied my every feature, lingering on the scar on my cheek, the length of my now clean hair. She scrutinized my thinning torso and the color of my faded skin.

"Alive," I croaked, studying her. Her rosy cheeks were plump, her smile genuine and wide. The sparkle she'd had since we were children remained in her eye. But there was something else there. Worry?

"No time now," she whispered, glancing over my shoulder toward the hall that led to the family room. "You'll be with Abigail tonight. Basement, I suspect. I'll come at night. We can talk more then." She released me, moving back to the stove to pick up her tongs.

Abigail? My stomach sank. It had been foolish to think I'd be given the same privileges I had before I fell in the creek, but the idea of living in Abigail's house, subject to her cruelty, made my blood run cold. Andrew had his soft spots, but he wasn't stupid. Putting me and Morgan in such close confines would've been a dangerous move. Still, I was disappointed.

Morgan instructed me to clean and cut up the broccoli for dinner.

"Abigail's on a tirade," she said under her breath as I chopped next to her. "She's furious about having to rear Joanna's kids. Thinks it should be my responsibility. She's angry you're home, doesn't think Father punished you enough. Just…be careful."

She turned the meat in the hot pan and a loud hiss interrupted her for a brief moment.

"Andrew seems genuinely thrilled you're back, so use that to your advantage. But he's been away more lately." She looked up, eyes darting for any approaching figures. "What do you think of Silas?" Her voice was high, hopeful.

"He's wonderful," I whispered, focusing on the florets. "A good man. He loves you, Morgan."

Even with the heat from the pan, I saw her flush. "I love him too," she answered. "But, Luke's son? Am I crazy for trusting him?"

I shook my head. "Not any crazier than I am." There was so much to discuss. My throat felt full of information I longed to tell Morgan. I wanted to ask about Mother, about the rest of our siblings, about how Andrew and Abigail had treated her. I wanted to ask what else Silas knew, how often he visited, how much influence he actually had over the Hunters. But there was no time.

The familiar squeak of the mudroom door announced another arrival, followed by small children's chattering and laughter. Beside me, Morgan tensed her shoulders, wiping sweat from her brow as she turned the heat down on the pan.

I looked up. Five children ran in, ignoring us at the counter, heading straight to the table. Two older girls meandered in, the eldest, no older than ten, held a baby on her hip.

My heart squeezed at the sight of the children. Bright eyed, red-cheeked, filled with life. Having children of my own was a wish I had started to let go of back in the Centre. But here, my infertility would be a constant reminder of my worth in my father's eyes.

"Simon!" Abigail bellowed from the other room. One of Joanna's small little blonde boys at the table straightened, his eyes widening in fear. "Get back here!" He picked himself up from the bench, walking sullenly back to the mud room. "What have I told you about these shoes?"

"Sorry Miss Abigail," came the little voice.

Skin hit skin. A slap. I winced, inhaled sharply, blinked up at my sister, who stared down at the roast, before briefly meeting my gaze. She pressed her lips together and shook her head. Simon re-emerged, his face beet red, eyes welling with tears. He dragged his feet as he made his way back to the table. My heart lurched.

No. This was wrong. He was a baby. Fury rose in my belly and I let the knife fall from my hands back to the counter.

"Maura…" Morgan's tone was one of warning.

I ignored her. I wouldn't let it go. Being a martyr had its benefits, and this was one of them. If I was going to change things, there was no better place to start. I approached the table and pulled out the chair for the small boy.

"Hiya, Simon." He looked up at me with his wide blue eyes. Tears ran down his cheeks and a trail of snot ran from his left nostril. "I'm Maura." I patted the back of the chair.

"Hello," he said politely as he sat down and wiped at his face.

I pushed his seat into the table, then squatted down to

his height. "I'm sorry Abigail did that to you. She shouldn't have hurt you like that."

"I forgot to take off my boots," he said with a sniffle.

"Oh," I said, nodding in understanding. "Well, sometimes we make mistakes, right?"

He shrugged.

I leaned close to his ear. "Mistakes don't make us bad, okay? You're a good boy."

He pulled his head back, bewildered. "How do you know?"

"I can just tell," I said, winking. He gave me a small, sad smile. Better than nothing, I supposed. I stood to full height and gently ruffled his hair, my gaze lifting to the figure in the doorway.

Abigail was a tall, broad woman, with graying red hair and a thick, wobbly chin. Her cold presence seemed to change the temperature in the room. In that moment, her narrowed eyes drank in my details, scrutinizing everything wrong with me. My mere presence, my *existence*, was inconvenient. But I took great pleasure in the fact that she'd likely been briefed on what I'd done this morning.

This morning.

Had it really only been hours ago?

"Well, well. The holy daughter returns. Praise God," Abigail seethed, stepping into the lit kitchen. I met her steady gaze and swallowed my fear. "Welcome home, Maura."

"I am glad to be here," I answered, tilting my head. "God has certainly blessed me." I glanced down at Simon, who clutched his little hands in his lap. Abigail followed my eyes, and the skin around her mouth tightened. I smiled at her.

"So he has," she agreed. "After such defiance, I am shocked to see you here." Her eyes flitted to the contraption around my ankle. "I am glad to see the Prophet has taken certain *precautions*. Though, one would question why someone so holy needs them?" She shook her head in mock confusion.

"That might be a question to ask of the Prophet," I answered without pausing.

"Indeed."

"Ah!" Andrew's deep voice echoed from the hallway behind Abigail, and we all turned as he entered the room. Abigail's lined face softened as she took in our husband, laying a hand on his back as he embraced her. "The roast smells delicious, Morgan."

"Thank you," my sister answered, turning off the heat. "I'll let it rest for a few moments before you carve it, Andrew."

Our husband came around the side of the counter and pressed a kiss against Morgan's head before coming over and doing the same to me. I froze. I should've been used to it by now, but the reemergence of his affection, coupled with Abigail's disdain, was all a little too much. I did my best to lean into the kiss, allowed him to caress my arms and back, and fell back into the role of obedient housewife.

I'd like to say I was playing the part, but the truth was, that evening, I craved the familiarity of it all.

26

MAURA

NIGHT SHROUDED the property in darkness. We walked along the walkway through the estate as we left Andrew's. Abigail's house, a white three-bedroom farmhouse with black trim, was the first of the wives' homes built on Coutts Peak. Beyond being the first wife of the second-eldest Coutts brother, she had also been given a position of honor as the Matriarch in the early days of the commune. She was tasked with what Father called *purpose training*. These classes taught every girl over the age of eight how to serve a husband faithfully. For many years, I had strived to live up to her expectations.

Andrew wouldn't marry Joanna until a few years later and it would be even longer until she bore a child. Her two-story modern home loomed empty as I followed Abigail and the children across the property. It felt as if Joanna's ghost watched us from the dark floor-to-ceiling windows.

The kids and I followed Abigail like hens to roost, up the stairs and across the wooden porch. We rounded to enter through a side door and a dark shadow came into view beyond Abigail's house — bones of a structure. A home being built. My blood ran cold. Homes were only built for pregnant wives. Had Morgan not told me something?

"Andrew is building us a larger home," Abigail said, answering my question as she opened the side door. The children filed in, and I brought up the rear. "With so many children, we really need more bedrooms."

I didn't answer her. At her house, in her domain, under her roof, I was expected to follow her rules. Abigail had always been that way. Obedience made her tolerable. Cruelty made her happy.

What I was now, what I represented, was sure to make her almost as furious as my father. Everything about my existence went against the rules of the commune and certainly against the rules Abigail had laid out for me the moment I was old enough to understand my place. She wouldn't like a rogue student, let alone one of her own sister wives. I needed to be careful. My father and Andrew wouldn't stand for violence between women, but there were plenty of other ways for her to be vengeful.

I moved to cross the threshold into the house, but Abigail stretched out her arm, blocking me from entering. Her hand gripped the door frame as she leered at me in the shadows. One of the kids flipped on a light and a stampede of small footsteps trampled deeper into the house.

Abigail's wrinkled arm was alabaster white, aged skin hanging loose on her bones. I tilted my head to meet her gaze. She looked weary yet furious, a permanent wedge connecting the skin between her brows.

Without warning, she slapped me, open-palmed. Sharp pain stung my eye and cheekbone. I fumbled for purchase on the house's siding, cupping one hand to my face as I fought to keep my tears at bay. So much for no violence. I supposed she didn't care. And that made her dangerous.

She took a step forward. Hatred simmered behind her dull brown eyes, searing into my soul. It was the same look my father gave me earlier today. Fury, with a splash of fear. Her nostrils flared as she spoke through her teeth.

"Andrew may be fooled by you, little girl," she seethed. "He may think this is a miracle and a sign from God. But the split between your legs clouds his judgment. I know better. You're full of sin, and the Devil is guiding you. You are nothing more than a liar. God would never use a petulant child like you as his instrument."

I sucked in the cold air and it stung the inside of my nostrils. My lip curled into a sneer.

"There are more believers than Andrew," I hissed, my breath clouding. "So think what you want, Abigail. But I know my truth. I know what God has told me. I see the wickedness in *you*."

Her face contorted, pale cheeks reddening in the dim light. I shouldn't have said that. Not while I slept beneath her roof.

Abigail's arm released from the door frame, her fingers finding my throat. She gripped my skin, dug her nails in, and brought her face so close our noses nearly touched.

"You made a mistake coming back here, Maura," she whispered. "The Prophet will make things right again. He will rid this place of sin, put you in the ground where you belong. And then you'll be nothing more than a disobedient nobody."

I inhaled sharply, shocked by the honesty in her words. She wished me dead? A woman who was supposed to be a holy servant of God? She admitted that out loud? I wanted to laugh. To ask her what God she thought she was serving with that violent mentality. This was not what our Lord preached. For most of my time in this commune, it wasn't even what my father preached. Cold fear tightened my muscles.

"Get inside," she barked, grabbing my shoulder and pushing me toward the open door.

The house smelled of earth and sage. It had been some time since I'd been inside Abigail's home. It was bright and intricately decorated, every item thoughtfully chosen and placed. Once, I had longed to have a house like this.

The warm interior soothed the sharp sting on my cheek as I walked through a narrow mudroom into a large kitchen. Abigail brushed past me, leading me down a wide hallway that led to stairs at the front of the home. To our left was a sunken, carpeted living room. All the children but one kneeled around a circular coffee table, heads bent in prayer. A stone fireplace was the focal point of the room, and that was where small Simon struggled to light the wood aflame.

"Continue your prayers," Abigail commanded from the hallway, casting a lingering glare at the little boy. I caught his eye and winked. His cheeks pinked, but he turned away before Abigail could notice. She gripped my arm, pulling me back to the kitchen.

"You don't want me to pray?" I asked. Abigail tightened her grip.

"You will pray alone."

We walked past a marble countertop and stainless steel appliances to the far end of the room, where a door made from dark wood stood out against the white walls. A silver padlock, similar to the one Eli had pried from the door in Coal Creek, was attached to its side. It gleamed under the harsh light, taunting me.

"The Prophet and Andrew made no demands about your sleeping arrangements," she told me with a note of glee. "And because of the limited space we have, you'll make do with what we have." She pulled a gold key from her pocket, turning it over in her hands, before inserting it into the padlock. The open door revealed a set of stairs that led into the dark. Even from where I stood, I felt frigid air rise.

"The basement," I said blandly.

Abigail cocked her eyebrow, the start of a smile on her thin lips. "Forgive me. Is this not adequate? I can certainly send for your father so that you can give him your complaints."

"Oh no," I answered. "This is to be expected."

Her mouth tightened. "Goodnight, Maura. I'll call for you first thing in the morning."

She held the door wide and let her gaze trail me as I stepped onto the landing. With one last look over my shoulder, I saw her lips curl into a mischievous smile before she slammed the door in my face. I waited there, my heart in my throat, as she secured the lock behind me.

Dark blinded me. I fumbled along the wooden walls with my hands, pressing my toe forward to search for the edge of the step. A cobweb brushed my knuckles, and I shook it away, cradling my arm to my chest. Slowly, my eyes adjusted to the long, narrow stairs ahead.

Carefully, I descended, finding a rickety banister to my right. It smelled of mothballs and mildew and grew colder the lower I got. At the bottom, I paused. Soft moonlight shone through three barred windows, illuminating the concrete floor and sturdy stone walls.

My new prison.

The room was cluttered with cardboard boxes and clear, plastic tubs, all meticulously labeled in Abigail's handwriting: baby clothes, Matriarch training materials, holiday decorations, and a stack of freshly taped boxes labeled *Joanna*.

Her absence hadn't hit me quite this hard yet. I was no fan of Joanna, certainly, but the idea that she'd died in what Silas had called a preventable death angered me. Even more so to see her belongings tucked away in this dusty basement like a forgotten toy.

Beside the boxes, the floor was empty, and I shivered again, horribly aware of how cold it was and how little the cotton dress protected me. I needed something to sit on or at least wrap myself in. The boxes held promise, so despite knowing how furious Abigail would be, I started peeling away tape to open Joanna's things.

The first few held nothing but paperwork and trinkets. I dug through another that held jewelry and storage containers and another with Joanna's neatly folded clothes. Finally, I found one with a woven quilt and spare pillow-cases. I used the clothing to stuff a pillowcase and set up a makeshift bed beneath the windows.

My head found rest in the hollows of the clothes-stuffed pillow, but as I turned, something crinkled beneath my ear. I propped myself up on my elbows, and dug through the clothes, my fingertips scraping against some-thing that did not belong. It was thin. Sharp at the edges.

I pulled a worn piece of paper out from a pair of rolled socks. It had been folded and re-folded many times, the creases so deep it nearly cut through the material.

My dearest J,

I dream of you often and hope you don't mind my forward-ness in passing you this letter. But I can not stop thinking about your lips, the softness of your hands, the way you feel in my arms. I long for our stolen moments, for the next time I have the privilege of being with you. Do you dream of a life where we could be together, always? I know I do.

Yours forever, C.

My heart beat in my ears. These were forbidden words, a letter Joanna never intended anyone else to see but her. Abigail must not have seen it if it was still here. I let my fingers trail over the handwriting, over the dangerous words someone who cared about Joanna had written, knowing what punishment might await them if the wrong person found them.

As much as Joanna had added misery to my life, my heart ached for her. She had lived a similar life to me. Grown up in a Coutts household, married off to Andrew at a young age. I had envied the ease with which she seemed to conceive children but never really considered if it had been what she wanted. I had always just assumed there was something wrong with me for wanting differently. For struggling to adapt.

If someone like Joanna, who was living under Andrew's roof, who had lived what, on paper, looked like a devout life, had harbored a secret of *this* magnitude, what else were people hiding? Could every single person in this commune be holding onto something similar? Afraid to express themselves, to love who they wanted, to act how they chose? Could they all want change but were too afraid to take action?

I held the answer in my hand. These thoughts and feelings and desires were human nature. I was coming to realize that God created us to be this way. Yet Father worked to suppress these things, to fill us with fear and hatred and misery. It was the opposite of God's intention. It wasn't natural to live like this. It wasn't God's will to lock me in a basement or equip me with a lethal ankle monitor. It wasn't God's will for Joanna to die without having explored a love she longed to have.

I pulled the photograph of Eli and me out from my

dress and stared at our faces, leaning back against my makeshift pillow as I relived our kiss, dreaming of the comfort I felt in his embrace. That was the life I wanted. That was the life we all deserved to have.

I vowed to make it so. And to not stop fighting unless it killed me.

———

TAP. *Tap. Tap.*

I stirred, irritated at the noise as it grew into a knocking. Glass rattled in a loose frame. My shoulder hit a pocket of cold concrete.

I shot up, wincing as I turned from side to side, my upper body freezing and aching. The heaviness of sleep lifted. The world was shades of gray, washed in blue moonlight from one of the windows. A shadow passed across the pane. I blinked, rubbing sleep from my eyes.

Someone hovered at another window, obscuring the starry night beyond. I squinted at it. Was I still dreaming? Imagining? Wishing for something that wasn't there? The shadow raised a finger and tapped the glass again.

After unraveling myself from the quilt, I stood, the cold like whiplash, forcing every muscle awake. The window was too high for me to reach, but as I came closer, I could see a shadow with curly hair, her smile wide and bright, somehow, even in the dark.

Morgan waved at me, then pointed to the latch on the inside of the glass pane. My heart beat in my throat. What did she think she was doing? Abigail was upstairs, quite possibly not yet asleep. If she caught her, it could ruin everything.

I glanced around the space before settling on a few plastic bins to create a step to reach the lock. I tested my weight on the lid and lifted myself on my tiptoes, reaching through the metal bars to unlatch it before stepping back down onto the concrete floor.

Morgan pried the window outward with a slow creak, allowing frigid air to spill into the already cold basement. I shivered, reaching for the quilt which I draped around my shoulders before I peered up at my sister.

"Are you crazy?" I whispered. "What if Abigail hears us? You shouldn't be here."

"She won't hear us," Morgan said with a laugh. "We'd be lucky if she heard a bomb drop on the peak. She's been taking sleeping pills." She wrinkled her nose. "Andrew's been taking them too."

"Sleeping pills?" The tension in my shoulders loosened.

"Silas said a lot of Hunters take them. I guess it's hard to fall asleep when you're carrying so much guilt."

"That's how you get away?"

She nodded, drawing her thick brows together. "Andrew leaves them in the bathroom cupboard, so on nights when I need to leave the house I usually crush one up into his whiskey he drinks before bed." A sly grin crossed her lips. "Ah, the joys of chemical pharmaceuticals."

"He doesn't notice?"

"Does he ever notice *anything*?"

I forced a laugh.

"Is she being alright to you?" my sister asked. I met her eyes. "Abigail?"

"You know Abigail."

Her face darkened. "I thought she might reprimand you after Simon."

"Oh, she grabbed me by the throat on the way in," I said, touching my neck. Morgan winced. "But that means she's afraid, right?"

"Maybe…" Morgan ran her hand over her curls. "I just think she's a mean old bitch."

I made a noise of protest out of habit.

"*What?*" She gave me a sly smile. "She's definitely afraid. Anyway…" She turned her body, pulling a small bag in front of the window. "I brought you some things." She rifled through. "Mostly food, a couple bottles of water. Silas suggested it in case she doesn't feed you. Just make sure you hide it well."

"I will," I said, making a mental note to stuff my bounty into the bottom of one of Joanna's boxes.

Morgan began passing me the bottles of water through the bars, followed by small baggies of snacks — beef jerky, granola, nuts, and fruit — until I had a sizable pile.

"There," she said with a satisfied sigh before zipping up the empty bag. "So, how'd it go with father?"

I frowned up at her, then pulled my dress up off my ankle. The metal monitor shone in the moonlight. "He gave me this new piece of hardware."

Morgan's eyes widened. "A tracker?"

"More than that," I grumbled, letting the dress fall. "If I go out of boundaries or disobey, I'll get a nice bear trap bite around my ankle." I exaggerated a chomp with my teeth. "I won't be able to run that way."

Her jaw dropped. "*What?*"

I nodded.

"I'll talk to Silas," she said. "Maybe he knows—"

"Father said only he and Luke would have permission to remove it." I sighed, suddenly feeling very tired and defeated. "I'm stuck. I've been back for less than a day and already they've made me a prisoner. Some rebellion leader, I am."

"Are you kidding me?" Morgan hissed. "Don't say that. What you've done so far is incredible. You *must* know that."

"How am I supposed to protect anyone with this stupid thing?" I shook my leg.

"Uh, you're not."

"I'm not?" Frustration grew in my chest.

"You're not supposed to lead a rebellion all on your own, silly," she answered. "Yes, you set it in motion, but that doesn't mean you're the only one working toward the same goal. Silas, Gabriel, me, the friendlies — you've got an entire team behind you."

An entire team. I forced out a breath. Morgan was right. Just because I was locked up didn't mean the rebellion was stalled. There were others out there who could carry the torch I'd ignited this morning.

"I saw Gabriel earlier," Morgan continued. "He said the commune is in an uproar about what happened this morning. Everyone's talking about it, even though Father tried to shift the focus. By tomorrow morning, most people will know you've returned. Gabriel said Father will have a hard time if he doesn't allow you to attend church and stuff. He thinks people will demand to see you."

My heart lifted. "Really?"

She nodded. "He's hopeful. And I have to think that's a good thing?"

"It is. Silas is smart. He knows what to do, how to rally people and get them to commit to a cause. He's a fighter. Just like you."

My sister blushed.

"Any news about Mother or the others?" I asked.

Morgan's shoulders deflated. "Nothing about Mother. Mark and Matthew have been recruited to the Hunters in the South, but Matthias and Micah are still too young."

"16 and 14 are too young, too," I argued. I couldn't stand thinking about my younger brothers holding weapons the Hunters wielded. It seemed so unnatural.

"I know. But they're probably safer there than else-where." She pressed her lips together. "I've been trying to get information about the families the younger ones went to, but I haven't spoken to anyone who knows any more than I do. Silas and Gabriel are working on it too, but I know they have a lot more to worry about. Joanna had more information when she was still here, but—" She shook her head and looked away.

"Joanna gave you information?"

Morgan looked back at me. "Sometimes. If she heard anything from Abigail. I think she felt what they did to Mother was wrong."

"Huh."

"Anyway, I should go." Morgan got to her knees. "Keep that food hidden and stay strong. Don't do anything I wouldn't do," she joked.

My heart felt weak. Selfishly, I wanted her to stay here, to feel the comfort of her presence, to be spoken to like a human. But it wasn't safe here for her, and I would never ask her to jeopardize herself like that.

"Thank you," I said. "And, I love you."

"And I, you," Morgan answered, reaching her hand through the window. I climbed the box and pressed myself against the stone wall, grasping her and squeezing, memorizing her warmth and praying. Praying for clarity, for strength, and for justice.

But mostly praying that we'd all survive this.

27

MAURA

I SPENT most of the evening evading sleep on the freezing floor. Eventually, the sky lightened the frost-covered grass outside the window and I gave up on trying to rest or warm my nose, which had been numb since last night.

Abigail's gait was slow, measured, and heavy on the floor above me as she chased after smaller footsteps, no doubt getting the kids ready for their day at school. Every so often, I heard voices from the kitchen door, but nothing discernible. I would've been happy if Abigail forgot about me for the day, but I suspected that was wishful thinking.

I sat up and stretched my aching body, rolling my neck to ease a knot in my shoulder. My fingers caught in my curls, so I did my best to smooth them over my ears. Bladder pains cramped my lower abdomen, so I kept busy by cleaning up the makeshift bed. I tucked Joanna's note around the photograph of me and Eli and secured it in my bra. I wanted to save it as a reminder of what was at stake.

More time passed. I nibbled on some granola while I looked for a place to relieve myself if necessary. I had no idea if Abigail would allow me to use the restroom if I needed it. Humiliation rose in my chest, but I pushed it away. That was what she wanted me to feel. Less than human. Like a prisoner. Like I'd done something wrong.

No. It was important to maintain the certainty that my choices had been right. Just. In accordance with God's teachings. I reminded myself, just like Leo had, that God's teachings differed from my father's. God didn't want us to suffer. There was joy in the world, and we deserved to experience it.

I studied the basement and paced the floor. The house grew silent. Abigail was likely taking the children to school. I began counting the bricks on the wall.

After some time, I settled at the bottom step of the stairs, stretching my back against the flimsy wood, when urgent footsteps sounded in the hall above, louder than before. There was the distinct clink of the latch, the turn of the handle. My heart raced. I stood up. Instinct made me smooth my dress and inspect my boots. I leaned over to brush some of the lingering mud away. It scattered in clumps across the concrete floor.

The door at the top of the stairs opened. Light from the upper hall spilled down into the basement. I squinted, looking up at Abigail's silhouetted figure.

"Get up here," she barked.

"Good morning to you, too," I mumbled under my breath.

I gripped the flimsy banister and ascended slowly so I didn't trip over my dress. The ankle monitor felt heavier than yesterday, weighing me down with each step.

Abigail smelled of fresh breakfast — syrup and bacon grease. My stomach growled audibly and from the corner of my eye, I could've sworn I saw her lips curl into a grin.

"You're to wash up," she said, pointing to the door across the hall. "And then you're to pray."

I glanced down the hallway toward where I'd seen the children last night.

"Not here," she said.

"Then where?"

Now a smile crossed her face. Sly and wicked. "Why at the church, of course. With your father."

THE SKY WAS heavy with moisture as we stepped outside and off Abigail's porch, walking the path to the church. Abigail had given me a shawl to put over my dress. It wasn't a gesture of kindness, rather one of necessity. If I was to be paraded in front of the commune's people, she'd need to make sure I was at least clothed properly.

Abigail barely looked at me as we walked, choosing to keep her arms folded over her large bosom as she walked a few feet ahead of me. Would there be people at the church? What would my father say? Would he keep me restrained or allow me to sit in the church freely? Would he reprimand me and my actions in front of the crowd? Or did he have no other choice but to play into the story I'd crafted with Avi and Silas? The idea seemed impossible. He had always been so powerful, always been one step ahead of everyone else in the game.

But he was just a man. A horrible, wicked man who lied to get his way. And yesterday we caught him off guard.

Anything is possible.

We reached the parking lot. Flurries fell from the sky, slow, like ash. I came around to the base of the stairs where Abigail waited for me. She reached for my hand. Her fingers were long, bony, and cold. I flinched at her touch.

"Hold my hand, you dumb girl," she said.

"Why?" The question left my mouth before I realized I'd

said it out loud and I immediately regretted it. Her gaze shifted. She narrowed her eyes at me, hatred filling every feature, every wrinkle, boring into my skin.

"Just hold it," she hissed.

Reluctantly, I slipped my fingers into hers, wincing at her cold flesh.

We ascended the stairs together, Abigail tugging me along with her longer and wider strides. I made careful work not to stumble on my dress, lifting it with my free hand.

"You wanted to defy God?" Abigail said with a heavy breath.

"I didn't."

"You wanted to defy your Prophet, make a fool of him. Well, that won't be so easy, will it? You are not smarter than him. That you thought so is laughable."

At the top of the stairs, the tall, wooden doors loomed, leading into the church I knew so well. A church that had once felt like home. Voices came from inside, some low, some louder, like a steady hum. There were people in there. A crowd. The realization startled me, and I froze where I stood, letting Abigail tug my reluctant feet forward.

"Come on, you wretched creature," she seethed, pulling one of the doors open wide.

Voices grew as we entered. The warm air was scented with incense; the high walls dim from the lack of sunshine. The pews were filled, and people spilled over to the side aisles and back of the church. As we took a few steps forward, the people around us silenced, their eyes wide as they looked me over.

"Come on." Abigail pulled me up to the holy water fountain. Ceremoniously, we blessed ourselves with the water. At the end of the center aisle, my father kneeled at the altar, his back to us. He was dressed in green and white robes today, complete with a mitre upon his head.

One of the altar boys cleared his throat. My father raised his head, then looked over his shoulder before rising to his full height. The crowd hushed. He stepped behind the marble table on the altar, adorned with a gold-edged Bible in a holder. Beside the altar sat a white, cushioned chair. Abigail pointed at it from where we stood.

"You wanted to be a martyr, Maura," she said. "So go be one."

She released my hand and gave me a soft push forward. I let momentum carry my weight and stumbled to the middle of the long aisle, staring down at the faces turned toward me. It felt disconcerting, having that many eyes on me. I was too aware of my limbs, of my face and hair. I didn't know what to do with my hands, or if I should smile, or where I should look.

I focused on my father, whose eyes didn't leave mine. Was he angry? Happy? It was hard to read his expression. He held his lips in a straight line as he looked down the aisle at me. Then he beckoned me forward with a swoop of his fingers. I began to walk, and he lifted his hands to the crowd.

"My children!" his voice boomed, amplified by the microphone attached to his chest, "what a glorious sight we witnessed yesterday. My daughter, who we believed was lost to the elements, arrived home. A surprise to us all."

We believed. As if he wasn't responsible for dictating what these people thought. As if there was someone else to shift the blame to.

"We praise God for showing her his mercy and for delivering her back to us."

"Amen!" the crowd cried.

But they did not turn their gazes toward my father. They kept them on me. As I passed the pews, the occupants fell to their knees. Some came out into the aisles, fully on the floor, their arms outstretched toward my feet. Others bowed with their heads, resting their arms on the pews in front of them. Ahead, hands reached for me. Awed expressions filled people's faces. The way I remember people looking at my father when I was a child.

This was worship, or at least some form of it. These people showed reverence. To me. Somewhere in my father's teachings, I was sure this was blasphemy. But would he really deny them what seemed like a miracle? Hands grasped for my ankles, statements and prayers muttered between clacking teeth.

"She's been resurrected."

"The Prophet thought her to be dead!"

"God has saved her!"

"She will rescue us and lead us to heaven!"

"Divine Maura, oh holy daughter—"

The words calmed me. I straightened, holding onto the belief that I had power in this moment. That my father truly *didn't* have a choice but to raise me up on a pedestal. The prodigal daughter returned. Not a sinner, not a jezebel, not filled with the Devil's rage. Calling me those things would only cast more doubt on him. And he knew it.

"God above, protect Maura Coutts!"

"Blessed be the Prophet's holy daughter."

"A true miracle, in the name of the father, the son—"

Fear slid away from my body. I reached the center of the aisle. Father's lips were still moving, his voice filling the large space, but I didn't listen to the words. They didn't matter.

I stopped walking. I turned to the people on their knees, and I smiled.

"Thank you," I said gently, meeting people's tear-filled gazes. "Your kind words mean so much to me. I can only assume my father brought me here to answer your many questions."

"Yes!" someone cried.

"Where have you been, Maura?" a woman at my feet asked. "After all this time, after the Island of Repentance was destroyed, the Prophet proclaimed they'd found your body. We attended your service. I do not understand." She wiped a tear from her cheek.

I pressed my lips together. My heart beat in my ears. I couldn't risk a look at my father, though I still heard his prayers echoing against the church walls as he tried to demand the crowd's attention.

"The Prophet was mistaken." My voice shook.

There was chatter and shared skeptical looks. More fingers on my feet.

"Mistaken?" a young man whispered, looking up at me.

A young girl, not much younger than me, latched onto my ankle and moved her hand up the back of my heel, fingers brushing up against the tracker that lay secure against the lower part of my leg. Her brow furrowed. She looked up at me and then at Father, who continued reading from the Bible.

"Yes," I said in response to the man, but I nodded at the girl.

Yes, you are feeling what you think. Yes, he is keeping me locked in a basement and tracking my every move. He's afraid of me because I will reveal the truth.

"But how can the Prophet be mistaken?" the girl asked, her voice so low I struggled to hear.

"He is but a man," I said, leaning down to bring my face

close to hers. "Remember to believe what you can see with your own eyes. Beware of shifting stories, the new explanations, the masking of truth. Pay attention. The time has come to make your own choices and decisions. To choose love, acceptance, and kindness. To understand that the world is bigger than this commune."

There was a struggle to maintain a balance between vagueness and specificity. If I outright defined my father as a false Prophet, the tide might turn against me. These people needed to see it for themselves. To decide for themselves. I just had to give them a push in the right direction.

"Listen to everything you hear," I urged them, letting my voice rise in volume as I turned to face the crowd behind the girl. "Don't be afraid to fight against things you don't understand. I am not able to speak any more freely than this."

I moved forward, knowing my last statement was unbelievably blasphemous. My father glared down at me from behind the marble table, reciting prayers he knew by heart. I couldn't be certain he heard me, but conflict crossed his face. He had to be troubled by the reaction his crowd gave me. He must have lost sleep over what to do with me, how to solve the problem I'd created. People were questioning him for the first time in his life.

My heart pounded as I covered the rest of the ground between my father and me. People continued falling at my feet, continued reaching out their hands to me. But as I walked further, I noticed something else — the opposite of awe. There were people standing up against the walls of the church, arms crossed, glowering at me. The opposers. The people who did not believe my words, who thought like Abigail, Luke, and my father. They were threatened by me. My presence angered them.

Let them seethe.

I reached the edge of the altar and peered up at my father. He glanced at the chair I was expected to sit in, and I obeyed, climbing two stairs to take a seat. I faced the crowd.

"Return to your seats!" Father bellowed, his voice tinged with frustration. His words commanded obedience, snapping people from their stupor. They lifted themselves from the ground and climbed back into their pews. In the back of the church, I watched Abigail slither into a seat, her anger palpable even from the front of the church.

"All rise!"

Thunderous shuffling filled the space as everyone rose in unison. I looked at my father, at the way he held himself, at his blue eyes blazing with anger and hatred. I wondered if the congregation could see it. Would they understand my words? Would they sow seeds of doubt that would continue to grow? Perhaps then our mission would take on roots, sink its hooks in the community, and there would be more power behind what the Centre and the commune's rebels were trying to do.

Enough that we could overthrow a self-made Prophet.

28

MAURA

My father spent the rest of mass preaching the importance of obedience and subservience. He thanked God for my return. But never once did he admit fault. Doing so would admit weakness.

I scanned the crowd as I sat in my designated seat. My father had gotten their attention, but most gazes remained on me. Remnants of power lingered within my body at the thought of how the congregation had fallen at my feet. The girl who'd felt the ankle monitor. The claim that my father was only a man and nothing more. God was not whispering in his ear, as he'd once claimed. He had the ability to be wrong.

My father's pride made me livid, despite the benefits it created for our cause. He didn't think people would care if I returned, so much so that he let me walk up to this altar unaccompanied. If anything, I believed arrogance would be his downfall.

At the end of mass, the congregation filtered out in silence. My father moved from the altar to stand behind my chair. A few people cast lingering glances my way, but after what I assumed was a stern look from my father, they continued out the door and into the cold air. Still, I felt the change within the church and congregation. A switch had been flipped. Not for everyone, but for some. And for now, that had to be enough.

I tried not to let my pleasure show, even though I knew this would never happen again. Father would learn from this mistake, station Hunters around me, or make it impossible for people to speak directly to me. I felt his tension in the way his fingers gripped the back of the chair at the base of my neck. Perhaps he imagined strangling me from that position. I was sure he wanted to. But I needed to maintain my image, and so did he. I was still at the mercy of God. And he? He was at my mercy, whether or not he liked it. My confidence continued to grow.

The church grew quiet as the last people filtered out. The doors closed, sealing us inside. My father released the chair.

"Get up."

I followed him through the hall and up the stairs. I was a little stiff from sitting in one place for so long, but the buzz of power lingered as we climbed to the third floor. Perhaps pain awaited me, perhaps another fear tactic. Whatever it was wouldn't stop the ball from rolling. My father had to know that. He could hurt me all he wanted. Kill me, even. But Silas, Gabriel, Morgan, and I had started a fire. One that might be impossible to tame.

We reached the top of the stairs in dead silence, the only noise our footfalls against the carpet. I walked, anticipating entering Father's office, but he stopped short, pressing on a panel embedded in the wall. For a moment, nothing happened. Had he lost his mind? Was he hallucinating?

The solid wall fell inward, revealing a hidden door.

"Ah, yes," Father said, sounding pleased. "Here you are."

Dread dropped in my belly. He should be angry. He should be *fuming*. His joy jolted me with fear. He said it as though it was something I should have anticipated. And perhaps I should have. But I did not yet know the depths of my father's cruelty. I did not yet know how deep he would reach to break my spirit.

My father held the door wide, and after a moment's hesitation, I entered the room. It was lit by a single overhead light. There were no windows. The space was barely large enough to fit the desk and chair against the far wall. Without questioning, I knew this place was a prison, just like the basement. Just like the Island of Repentance.

Luke leaned against the side wall, dressed in uniform, using a toothpick between his teeth. He lifted himself as we entered, flashing a smile. My stomach dropped. Terror filled my veins.

"Just remember, this is your fault." My father smiled at me and closed the door.

A whimper came from the other side of the room and I turned my full attention to a shivering mound in the corner. The figure was so malnourished and dirty, it was hard to discern my mother's features at first. But when she lifted her head, there was no mistaking her familiar, faded brown eyes.

A gasp escaped me. She wore a dress stained with old blood and dirt. Her tawny-colored legs and feet were bare and bruised, bloated with red scabs. Her sunken eye socket made her once beautiful face look lopsided, though it was hard now to imagine what she'd once looked like. Gradients of purple and yellow covered her cheeks, neck, and arms, forming unnatural lumps, like small tumors.

My legs moved on their own, hurrying to where she lay, curled up in the fetal position. But before I could reach her, hold her, yell for help, Luke grabbed my hair and yanked me back.

I screamed at the pain consuming the nerves on my scalp, feeling my hair tear from its roots into his beefy hand. With a growl, I kicked my legs, bringing my hands up to claw at his grip. But it was useless. Though I drew blood, dug my nails into his knuckles, he didn't let go until he'd dragged me to the other side of the room. I slammed against the wall, head hitting wood so hard I struggled to open my eyes again.

Mother cried, lashing out a hand. Luke was quick to slap her wrist, and she pulled the limb inward to cradle at her chest. Terror coated me from head to toe. I'd known what was at risk when I bought into Silas's plan. We had talked about Mother, getting her and Morgan and the rest of my siblings to safety. But I knew now we were already too late.

I couldn't breathe. My body trembled, hands shaking as I used them to get to my knees. Tears and snot coated my cheeks, and I tasted them, but couldn't move to wipe them away. Luke leered at my mother, shifting his gaze back to me with a maniacal smile. How Silas or Gabriel were born from this man went beyond my level of comprehension. Luke was evil reincarnated. He did all the things I knew my father wished he could do. And God would never forgive either of them.

"Please," I heard myself beg, my voice small and weak. "Please don't hurt her anymore."

"Unfortunately for you, you've secured her fate, Maura. God agrees."

"God agrees?" I cried, scraping my knees against the taut, rough carpet as I crawled back toward my mother. "God agrees with this?" My voice rose, chest heavy with rage. "God doesn't agree with you! How dare you say that? How can you look at her and think that?"

His nostrils flared. He stormed over to me and raised his foot to my face, the bottom of his boot at the tip of my nose. I recoiled, falling back to the floor, wincing. Waiting.

Hit me.

But he didn't. He couldn't. The obedient servant knew better than to mar my face. He growled, putting both feet back on the ground and covered the space between me and my mother. He kicked her face. Something cracked, like a twig snapping. She moaned, bringing up a shaking arm to shield her head.

"NO!" I cried, struggling to get to my feet. I lunged at him, latching on to his arm. Blind with fury, I dug my nails into his skin, grabbed at his hair, his ears, nose, and eyes. But he was too strong and with one forceful push, he sent me sprawling backward onto the floor.

My back and shoulder erupted in pain. I rolled on the ground, helpless. He grabbed me again by my hair and pulled me up, dragging me toward the desk. The wooden chair behind it had restraints secured to the armrests. Effortlessly, he plopped me in the seat.

The room spun. I kept my focus on the small, shivering body that was my mother, hoping she would get up and run, that someone would come and save her. I wanted to call for Silas, for Gabriel, for *Andrew*, for anyone. But who would come? We were alone all the way at the top of the church. Nobody could hear us up here. And that was by design.

Luke secured my wrists with the leather straps, then took a piece of fabric from the desk and shoved it into my mouth. My eyes bulged. It tasted like mildew and mold and I coughed, spluttering, trying to blink away the tears that wouldn't stop building in my eyes. Luke opened a drawer, pulled out black duct tape, and ripped a piece off with his teeth. He pressed it over the fabric, over my mouth, the glue sticking to my hair.

I tried to scream at him, but my words were muffled and confused. My face leaked from panic and fear and terror, but he didn't care. He kneeled in front of me, securing the straps around my ankles. I smelled him — the scent of rage, of sweat, of blood. He lifted his head, met my eyes, then moved his gloved hand from my ankle up my leg.

I squirmed as his palm slowly trailed up my knee, letting my dress bunch up as he came closer to my groin. He took his time, staring at my bare flesh before he gripped my thigh tightly. More pain. I hunched forward, screaming into the fabric, unable to move much because of my restraints. He grinned.

"They say you're barren," he said, placing his free hand gently on my belly. "That's why Peter gave you to Andrew and not me." He tutted. "What a shame it is. You know I used to *long* for you." He laughed in disbelief. "That pretty face could've been useful for all kinds of things. You were so obedient, so pious. But now?"

He rose to his full height, hovering over me. With a tilt of his head, he caught my eyes, lowering his chin and lips until his face was level with mine. I pressed my back against the chair, desperate to move away from him. He leaned in. I sucked in a breath, wincing as I heard him gather saliva in his mouth.

He spit. It landed on the duct tape and I gagged, afraid I would vomit into the cloth. My stomach roiled. Anger flared. Tears I couldn't stop streamed down my cheeks. I dug my fingernails into the side of the chair so hard splinters pinched the skin beneath my nail beds, adrenaline firing but unable to emerge.

But Luke didn't care about my anger. He turned his attention back on my mother, who had come to, her eyes staring blankly at the ceiling. I thrashed in the seat, slamming the feet against the carpeted floor. Maybe, by the grace of God, someone else was still in the church. Maybe they would hear these noises, know something was wrong. I tried screaming again, but my voice was hoarse and muffled by the cloth.

Luke pulled up my mother by the front of her outfit. She came with him effortlessly, sliding up the wall like a rag doll, her head limp on its side, face devoid of any fight. It was the first time I saw her fully. She was so thin and frail, she barely looked human. They had withered her to bones.

"Maura," he taunted without looking at me. "Ask your Mother for forgiveness."

I screamed. I screamed so hard it felt like my throat was bruising. Mother turned her head. Caught my eyes. A sob stuck in my throat and I gagged, using my full strength to propel the chair forward. I heard blood in my ears.

Luke pulled my mother up toward his chest, then slammed her back against the wall and, God forgive me, I closed my eyes. He slammed her into the wall over and over and over again until I heard her bones crack and give way. But there was no noise of protest, no fight left in her battered body. Only me, wailing into the fabric in my mouth.

The room quieted.

Her body fell with a thump, but I was too afraid to open my eyes. I knew she was gone. I knew there was no coming back from the damage he'd dealt her. That was the point.

I gasped, moaning with grief, unable to stop the sounds leaving my body. I released my tension, let the restraints go slack against my wrists and legs, and slowly opened my eyes.

Luke stood beside me, untying me from the chair. He ripped the tape from my mouth, tearing it away from my skin, ripping some of my hairs out. My mouth and cheeks stung. I spit out the gag.

He hoisted me upward, to my feet, but I wasn't sure I could hold my weight. I tried to avoid my mother's body, the bright red blood that smeared on the wall from her impact, but couldn't. Luke wanted me to see. He carried me over, stopping in front of her huddled form. I saw her chocolate brown hair, tangled, lying on the floor like a discarded party streamer. Her hand, bruised and bloodied, nails chewed down to the beds.

"You did this," said Luke.

I remained silent, staring at my mother's fingers. Her wrinkled knuckles looked like the knots I'd seen in the trees on my journey here.

"You did this," he repeated, his breath hot on my neck. "You. You're responsible for this. Say it."

No.

"Say it!" he yelled, shaking me. "You did this. SAY IT!"

I felt more tears, which surprised me. I felt so empty. So numb. How could there be any left?

He shifted his grip from my arm to my hair. I winced, waiting for him to pull.

"SAY. IT."

I hesitated. Tried to bite my tongue. His grip tightened.

"I did this," I heard myself say. "I did this."

29

MAURA

I USED soap to wash my hands in Andrew's shower. Mother's blood was on my hands and I needed to get it off. I couldn't let Morgan see. I couldn't live with proof of her murder.

The water ran pink. I scrubbed harder. My knuckles hissed with pain beneath the water. I pulled my hand away, confused by the blood on my knuckles, blood on the soap. I touched my skin, startled at the jolt of discomfort. A trickle of red ran down the back of my hand.

Oh.

I moved on to other areas of my body. I still felt Luke's spit. I still smelled my mother's blood, so much so I could've sworn I was drenched in it, though somewhere in my rational mind I knew that wasn't true. The sharp iron scent mixed with pungent lavender. A smell I remembered from childhood baths. My mother rubbing soft, soapy circles on my back. Spinning my drying curls around her fingers.

My heart ached.

My fault. My fault. My fault.

The thoughts were irrational. I knew they were. But there was no one here to reassure me, no one to bounce my doubt off of. So I clung to it. This was what it meant to be disobedient. That was what my father wanted me to understand. If he could do this to his own wives, he wouldn't hesitate to do it to anyone else. That put everyone's life at risk — Morgan, Silas, Gabriel, the rest of my siblings, everyone at the Centre, and any Hunter we colluded with. He might not touch me, but the more I rebelled, the more I spoke up, the more he'd find new ways to break me.

There were no more tears. My well was dry. I held my bloodied hands against the tiled shower and let the water run down my back. The pit in my stomach widened as I thought of telling Morgan, of how it would devastate her. Would she hate me? Would she dismiss me, refuse to speak with me?

Or worse, would this act embolden her? Put her even more at risk?

I wasn't even sure how to deliver this news to her. But I wanted to be the one to tell her. What kind of coward would I be if I let her find out from Silas, or Andrew, or our father? But I didn't know how to admit I had sat there and watched. That I did nothing. That I couldn't stop Luke, no matter how hard I tried. I wished for Holli's wisdom, for Sid's strength, for Eli's guidance. He'd once had to tell Sid the same news, and it nearly ruined them.

I turned the shower off, reaching for the towel that hung on a hook outside the curtain. In the mirror, I looked even less like myself. I saw my mother's features in my face and studied them, trying to remember what she looked like before they'd beaten her beyond recognition. My stomach turned at the memory. I sat on the edge of the tub, body shivering. I clung to the porcelain lip, willing the room to stop spinning.

Abigail knew she was walking me to witness my mother's death. She had to. And now I had to sit around a dinner table with her and pretend everything was fine? That I didn't just witness something atrocious, something evil? All while knowing she would later taunt me about it before locking me up in her basement like a prisoner.

My body trembled in anger at the thought.

What were my options? Fight back and await Morgan's death? Or my younger siblings? Or play my part until Silas and Gabriel had the numbers to go up against my father? But what did that mean? What did that even look like? And how many more people had to die in order for us to get there? I had told Avi and Silas that I knew what following this plan meant. I thought I'd been through enough pain to endure my father's wrath. But I had been a fool.

I dressed slowly and ran a wide-toothed comb through my curls. My limbs felt weak, my mind numb. My knuckles burned and as I inspected them on the bathroom counter, I saw that I'd peeled away an entire layer of skin. I pressed my finger into my wounded flesh, the pain igniting my brain. It felt good for just a moment. The sweet bliss of nothing besides a deep ache.

Two days and my father had already broken me. Why did I think I could do this?

An urgent knock came at the door. I glanced down at myself, then back up to the foggy mirror. I tried to brighten my weary expression, but it was useless. My face was still swollen with tears.

"Come in," I called.

Morgan pushed the door wide, then closed it quickly.

She leaned up against it, her hands clenched behind her back, face etched in grief, or worry. It was hard to tell. I waited for her to ask the question. Someone must have told her before I'd had time to.

"Maura." Her voice came out in a whisper. She tilted her head, eyes wide and terrified.

No. She didn't know. This was something different.

"What's wrong?"

She met my eyes. I saw our mother in her, in us. Her legacies. Ones she would never see again. Tears brimmed in my younger sister's eyes. Her bottom lip wobbled. She trembled so hard she shook the door in its frame.

Instinctively, I stepped forward, reached out my arms for her, and she fell into them with a heavy sob. Her weight pushed me backward and carefully, I got to the floor, cradling her like we'd done as girls, like our mother had once done when we were children.

I knew I couldn't tell her about Mother now. She was in a delicate state, worried about something else. It would need to wait until later this evening, maybe even tomorrow. I felt shame at the relief that came with my thoughts.

"What's wrong?" I repeated, running my fingers over her soft curls. She wiped at her face and peered up at me through her wet lashes.

"Maura," she moaned. "I'm pregnant."

It came out as a whisper, like she was afraid someone would hear her admission. She turned away, devolving into tears in my lap. The walls spun and suddenly the room was too hot and too small. I steadied myself against the tile floor.

"You're *what?*"

Questions erupted like fireworks on my tongue, my brain firing in several directions, struggling to grapple with multiple emotions. Morgan sat up, hugging her knees to her chest, her back to the cabinetry beneath the sink. "I'm pregnant," she repeated.

"Oh my God," I said, unable to help my moment of happiness. "Oh my God!" I got to my knees, grasped Morgan by the shoulders, and hugged her. A baby! She was going to have a baby!

But the joy was all wrong. I felt it coming apart at the edges, stomped out by fear, by the fresh memory of Mother and what Luke had done to her. By the time I pulled away from her, the happiness was gone.

It wasn't sadness that replaced it, though. It was something between determination and fear.

"Are you absolutely certain?"

She nodded. "Silas got a pregnancy test from one of the medical teams. I told him I was late, feeling a little off. I took it earlier today, then buried it out in the garden. Oh Maura—" She sniffled.

"Do you think it's Silas's?"

She smiled.

"Andrew can't *perform*, especially since he's been taking those sleeping pills. The timing just wouldn't be possible," she said, taking a shaky breath. "I love Silas. I want this baby. I want to have a family with him. But Maura, what if people find out? What if Father finds out? Or Abigail?" She put her head in her hands. "What if they take the baby away? Oh my God! What am I going to do?"

"Hey, hey," I slipped my arms around her shoulders and pulled her into my side. "One thing at a time, okay? Don't worry about any of that yet. Have you told anyone besides Silas and me?"

She shook her head.

"Good." I thought for a moment. "Is Andrew having you take regular pregnancy tests?"

She nodded.

"Then we need to move quickly."

Emboldened by the news, I pushed away the fog grief had created. There was a problem that needed fixing. Morgan needed my help.

Her baby was a blessing, but it was terrifying to think what kind of world they'd come into, especially within the commune's confines. This place demanded obedience. It coerced and convinced and tricked, it manipulated and lied, made you afraid of things that didn't exist. It killed people simply because they were related to someone who did something the Prophet didn't like.

This was no place for an innocent life. This baby was a reminder of what was at stake. They were why I was doing this. I wanted a better world for myself and my family and friends, but for all who came after us, too.

I got to my feet and helped Morgan to hers. Our reflections appeared in the mirror, all curls and worried features. I would wait to tell her about Mother. I needed to. It would be the convincing factor I needed to smuggle Morgan out to the Centre. She wouldn't want to go, wouldn't want to leave me or Silas. But I knew neither of us would allow her to stay here. Not now. Not when everything was about to get incredibly dangerous. No. She needed to be at the Centre, under Avi's guard. Our priority would be to get her out.

A plan began to form in my head. Clarity found me for the first time in days. Adrenaline fired on all cylinders. Grief hovered, but didn't intervene. I'd like to think our mother took that pain away momentarily while we dug through all the possibilities and developed a path forward together. Because when I thought about it later, it seemed impossible that I could've been reasonable after the horrors I'd witnessed that day.

Later, Morgan and I cooked chicken. We ate dinner with Andrew, Abigail, and the children. We prayed, holding hands around the wooden table, speaking in pleasantries as we passed the food counterclockwise. Abigail kept her eyes focused on me, but I didn't spare her a look. Morgan's news had emboldened *me*. It had given me purpose after my father and Luke tried to take it away.

That night, when Abigail sent me down the basement stairs, her cheeks beet red from frustration, she called after me.

"Now you see what happens when you try to fight the Almighty Prophet?" she snarled in a satisfied sort of way, her breath heavy as she waited for me to scream at her.

I looked up the dark stairwell, squinting against the kitchen light.

"Of course I do," I answered calmly.

She scoffed, slamming the door closed and drenching me in darkness.

"But that doesn't mean I'm going to stop," I muttered to myself as her footsteps faded.

I would do everything I could to keep Morgan and her unborn child safe. I would endure my father's and Abigail's wrath. I would smile in the face of fear. I would continue playing my part to ensure their protection.

My mother's death would not be in vain. We owed this rebellion to her, to Joanna, to the countless others who had been killed by the Hunters at my father's command. We would ensure there was justice, and that people who had committed atrocities would face the consequences of their actions.

What my father didn't understand was that he could only push so far. Once people had nothing left to lose, their loyalties and priorities changed. Spark them with a bit of hope and rage, they might become troublesome. Manage-able enough if it's an individual or two. But when you assemble them and point at the common enemy, they become downright dangerous.

We were on the precipice of change, and for the first time since I'd said yes to Silas, I was certain we could win.

30

ELI

THE CENTRE WAS empty without Maura. I was plagued with dreams of her death and struggled to stay focused throughout the day. Each night since she'd been away, I relived our kiss, longing for the moment I could hold her again. Working Inventory was a constant reminder of Jae's absence. I had started eating lunch with Kendra, who told me stories of their time before the world had crumbled.

It was early morning when the first truck arrived. Light spilled in from the side entrance down to the walkway, urgent voices bouncing off the ceiling and walls. I hobbled over on my crutches, watching as Mick, Shelly, Holli, Avi, and Nadia helped the survivors down to the medical center.

A man named Jin was in the worst shape, needing the stretcher. Shelly worked on getting an IV in him as Mick pushed the bed around the corner, through the Mess Hall, and back into Inventory. Avi followed, carrying a frail woman in his arms, while two younger men leaned on Nadia and Holli as they limped back into the medical area.

Dale, the man who had survived and made it back from

the kidnapping, darted down the hallway, eyes searching frantically for his companions. They landed on the two men and he erupted into a fit of tears. Relief, joy, guilt, likely all rolled into one. We'd all felt that way at some point, I imagined.

I left the chaotic medical scene and headed back toward the garage, hoping to catch Darius or Sid. Had they gotten a chance to talk to Silas or Gabriel? Did they have any new information about Maura?

The community buzzed with excitement at the return of the prisoners. People pressed their faces to the gates and windows of their rooms, sticking their heads out into the hallway, or sitting on chairs hoping to glimpse the commotion.

Sid burst out at the end of the hallway that led to the garage, eyes searching before they landed on me. He grinned, then waved me forward. I hurried my pace and met him where he stood.

"How was it?" I asked, eager for the details of his trip to the safe house.

"Easier than we thought," he said with a shrug. "But—"

"But?"

"Come see for yourself."

He led me back through the walkway he'd emerged from. It smelled of gasoline and buzzed with noise and as we walked through the double doors and into the dark garage, I knew why. They were voices. Of dozens of people.

Women and children were scattered across the concrete, huddled together, looking around at the space fearfully. Some were dressed in normal clothes, others in more conservative attire. But it was clear they were not our people. They were from the Coutts commune. Survivors.

"We should call Leo," I suggested.

"Already done."

"Then what do you need me here for?"

Sid looked at me sideways, raising his eyes in surprise. "Because you were the first person to be compassionate to a Coutts who came into our midst. Because you know Maura better than any of us, and these people will trust you because of that."

"Me?"

"Uh, yeah." He rolled his eyes. "You act as if Maura didn't request you be part of the team to welcome people into the Centre."

"Well, that's news to me."

"Maybe because you were too busy making out with her." My eyes went wide, but Sid just laughed as he clapped me on the back. "About time, you absolute idiot."

"I—"

"Never mind all that. Introduce yourself and get them informed about how this place works. Leo said he'd bring some food and water. We'll work on room assignments in the meantime."

My heart lifted. There was a great deal of trust that went into this, and I felt pride that Maura and Avi assigned me and Leo as the ones to welcome her people to the Centre.

"Oh," Sid said. "There's one more thing." He pulled a piece of paper from the breast pocket of his vest, smoothed it out, then handed it to me. "Silas passed it along to one of the ladies we transported. Insisted I get it to you."

I glanced at it, scanning the words, and though I'd never seen her handwriting before, I knew who it was from. My heart lifted. Butterflies rattled my stomach. With a grin, I tucked it into my back pocket before approaching the newcomers.

The group shared nervous looks, children hiding behind their mother's backs or clutching their hands for dear life. A few looked around the wide space with their mouths hung open, murmuring to themselves in disbelief. I remembered what it felt like coming here for the first time. We'd been disoriented and terrified. It was hard to learn how to trust new people.

I approached with my head down, hands tucked in my pockets as I scanned the adults. Bewilderment and terror crossed their features as I stopped in front of them.

"Hello," I said, my voice echoing against the high ceilings. "Welcome to the Centre. My name is Eli, and if you're willing, I'd like to show you around what I hope you'll think of as your new home."

A few of their faces perked up and brightened, while others eyed me critically. That was okay. From what Maura had told me, they had every right not to trust men. It would take hard work to build their confidence in me.

A woman with blonde hair tied back in a long braid stepped forward. "Do you know Maura Coutts?" she whispered.

"I do," I said with a smile. "I'm proud to call her my dear friend."

Later, after settling our new arrivals into rooms, giving them a tour, clean clothes, and a whole lot of reassurance that our borders were secure, I lay in my bed. The lantern spread soft light across my pillow and I fished out the piece of paper Sid had given to me earlier.

E,

I can't say too much in case this letter is intercepted. I hope you don't mind me saying that I miss you, because I really do. I hope the groups arrive without incident and you don't mind that I volunteered you to greet them. They deserve to meet a kind soul on what is sure to be a very frightening day. I know you will treat them with the compassion you treated me with, and for that, I can not thank you enough.

Things here are as to be expected, but we are keeping strong. Please don't worry. This is a fight worth fighting — for a world where we can all be happy and free to make choices without restrictions. And I believe that day will come soon.

Please know I think of you always.

All my love,

M.

TO BE CONTINUED

ALSO BY CAITLIN MAZUR

<u>The Forgive Me Father Series</u>

Book 1: Forgive Our Ignorance

Book 2: Forgive Our Sins

Book 3: Forgive Our Survival

Book 4: Forgive Our Fight

Follow me on social media or Substack for updates!

caitlinwritesstuff.substack.com

ACKNOWLEDGMENTS

Writing a book is not possible to do alone, especially one that carries such heavy themes and narratives. I have such a wonderful group of people who surround me and have helped me get through this book in (relatively) one piece. Thank you to:

My Hell's Belles critique group — Liesl, Laura, and Laura — I could not have written this story without you three. Your constant support, encouragement, and critique make me a better woman and writer every single day. I love you three.

My beta readers, Debbie and Jen. Thank you for reading everything I put in front of you and thank you for being incredible women. I am so lucky for your friendship and feedback.

My Advanced Reader Team — a group of absolute angels who read this manuscript early. Thank you for your support, love, and kind comments. It really helps silence that inevitable imposter syndrome that plagues me before every release.

Michelle, Monica, and Deanna, three of my most extraordinary writing friends. I am so unbelievably grateful for your friendship. Thank you for making me laugh, keeping me sane, and all of your support and love.

My incredible children, who I always hope to make proud. I love you more than words can express. Thank you for being wonderful humans. The world needs more of you. I love you two more than words can express.

And of course to my husband, Matt. The Eli to my Maura. Thank you for supporting my dreams, talking me off the edge, and always doing what is right. I love you always.

THANK YOU!

Thank you so much for reading **Forgive Our Survival.** If you enjoyed this book, please consider leaving it a review on your platform of choice. Reviews significantly help indie authors like me increase visibility and boost credibility for future readers.

Leave a review:

ABOUT THE AUTHOR

Caitlin Mazur is a multi-genre author whose works span science fiction, speculative fiction, horror, and supernatural genres. As a transracial adoptee, Caitlin's work often touches on themes of found family and self-discovery.

Caitlin co-founded the Writing, Prompts & Critiques (WPC) Facebook community with over 11k members, named one of Reedsy's 50 Best Places to Find a Critique Circle. She helped develop WPC Press, a spin-off independent publisher that publishes anthologies with stories from WPC group members. When she's not writing fiction, Caitlin is a freelance writer, wife to an incredibly supportive husband, and mom to two amazing kids. Caitlin holds a degree in English Communications with a minor in Marketing from Saint Joseph's University in Philadelphia, PA, and is now living her best life in Central Maine.

Follow Caitlin: https://linktr.ee/caitwritesstuff

facebook.com/caitlinwritesstuff
instagram.com/caitwritesstuff
tiktok.com/@caitlinwritesstuff